I'M ONLY ALLOWED TO
BLEED FOR HIM...

FEAR ME, *love me*

LILITH VINCENT

Copyright © 2023 Lilith Vincent

| All Rights Reserved |

Cover Design by Soren Creation
Editing by Fox Proof Editing
Proofreading by Rumi Khan
Formatting by Book Obsessed Formatting

No part of this book may be used or reproduced in any manner whatsoever without written permission from the publisher, except brief quotations for reviews. Thank you for respecting the author's work.

This book is a work of fiction. All characters, places, incidents, and dialogue are drawn from the author's imagination and are not to be construed as real. Any similarities between persons living or dead are purely coincidental.

FEAR ME, *love me*
(An Age Gap Mafia Romance)

Lilith Vincent

Tyrant Mercer doesn't grant wishes. He collects debts, and he's here to claim me.

All I wanted was my baby brother back from the man who stole him away. My family is in Tyrant's debt, a man they hate, and they disown me when the devil's eyes stray to me. Now there's nothing and no one to protect me from the cruel man who runs this city from the shadows.

But Tyrant's not going to drag me away by my hair just yet. He's going to torment me first.

Tyrant demands that I play his twisted games. He thinks I'll crumble for his amusement, but I'm carrying a secret that's bigger than both of us. A secret that's now in the hands of the worst man possible.

All he craves is me. All he demands is everything. Tyrant will give me everything I've ever wanted—all I have to say is *I wish…*

But a wish is a curse when it's granted by the devil himself.

Playlist

HEARTBEAT – Isabel LaRosa
A GOOD DAY TO D13 – Arankai
skins – The Haunting
Little Dark Age – MGMT
The Unknown – peach tinted
BABYDOLL (Speed) – Ari Abdul
Without You – Lana Del Rey
The Summoning – Sleep Token
War of Hearts – Ruelle
Locked Out of Heaven – Bruno Mars
Keeper – Reignwolf
Make Me Feel – Elvis Drew

Search "Fear Me, Love Me by Lilith Vincent" on Spotify

A Note to Readers

Dear readers, I am utterly thrilled to bring you yet another walking bouquet of red flags in a sexy suit with a big damn dick. What are we even doing here? Why are we like this? When is he coming over? Like me, you've probably browsed your fictional crush history and noted an alarming number of gorgeous disasters. I'm guessing they date back to the first time you sat bolt upright on the sofa in front of the TV or your book and thought about someone who just committed a felony, "Him. I am obsessed with *him*."

If they didn't want us to crush on the villains, why did they make them so glorious? Jafar. Captain Hook. Kylo Ren. Lucius and Draco Malfoy. Scar. The Opera Ghost. Sesshomaru. Then there's my personal favorite and first ever crush: Jareth the Goblin King.

Jareth. *Jareth*. His outfits are stunning. His smirks are diabolical. His hair is full of secrets and his dick is *out*. The man knows how to turn a kidnapping into an event. I wasn't ready for "mafia romance but give it *Labyrinth* vibes" to slap me across the face, but as soon as it did, I scrambled for my laptop and started typing.

Fear Me, Love Me is a love letter to everyone who's ever wanted the villain to get the girl. There's no cheating or sharing. Tyrant is a one-woman man, and he's murderously obsessed with Vivienne. There are dark themes, violence, breeding, dubcon, smut, somnophilia, blood play, period play, ropes, gags, and knife play.

Please be aware that this book contains references to and depictions of cutting and self-harm and memories of attempted sexual assault.

If all that sounds like your idea of a good time, turn the page, close your eyes, make a wish, and Tyrant Mercer will come and take you away, right now.

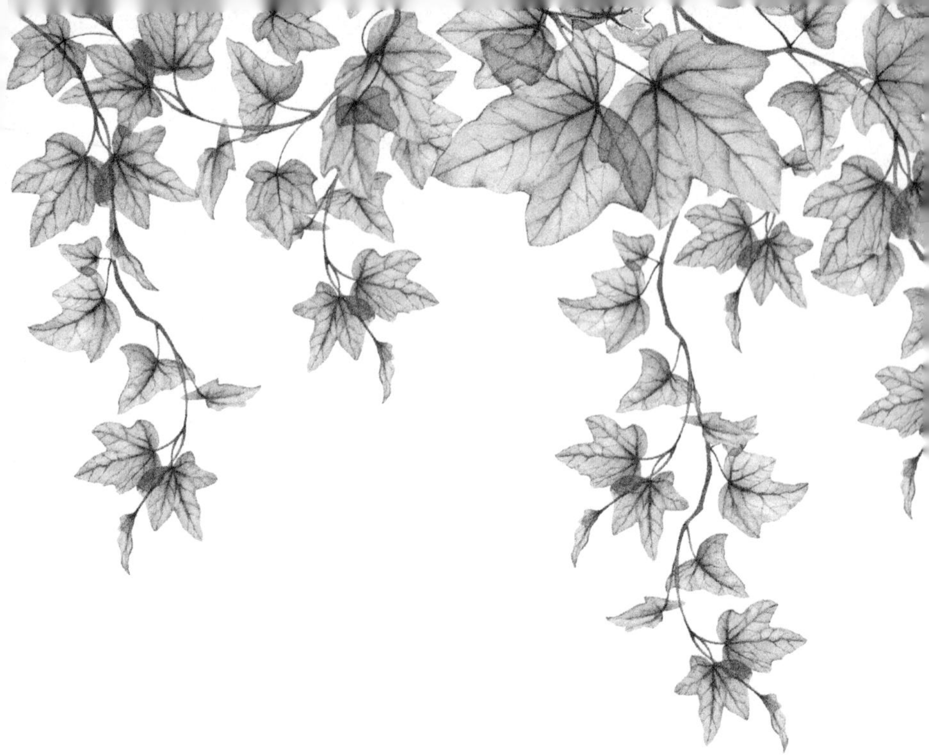

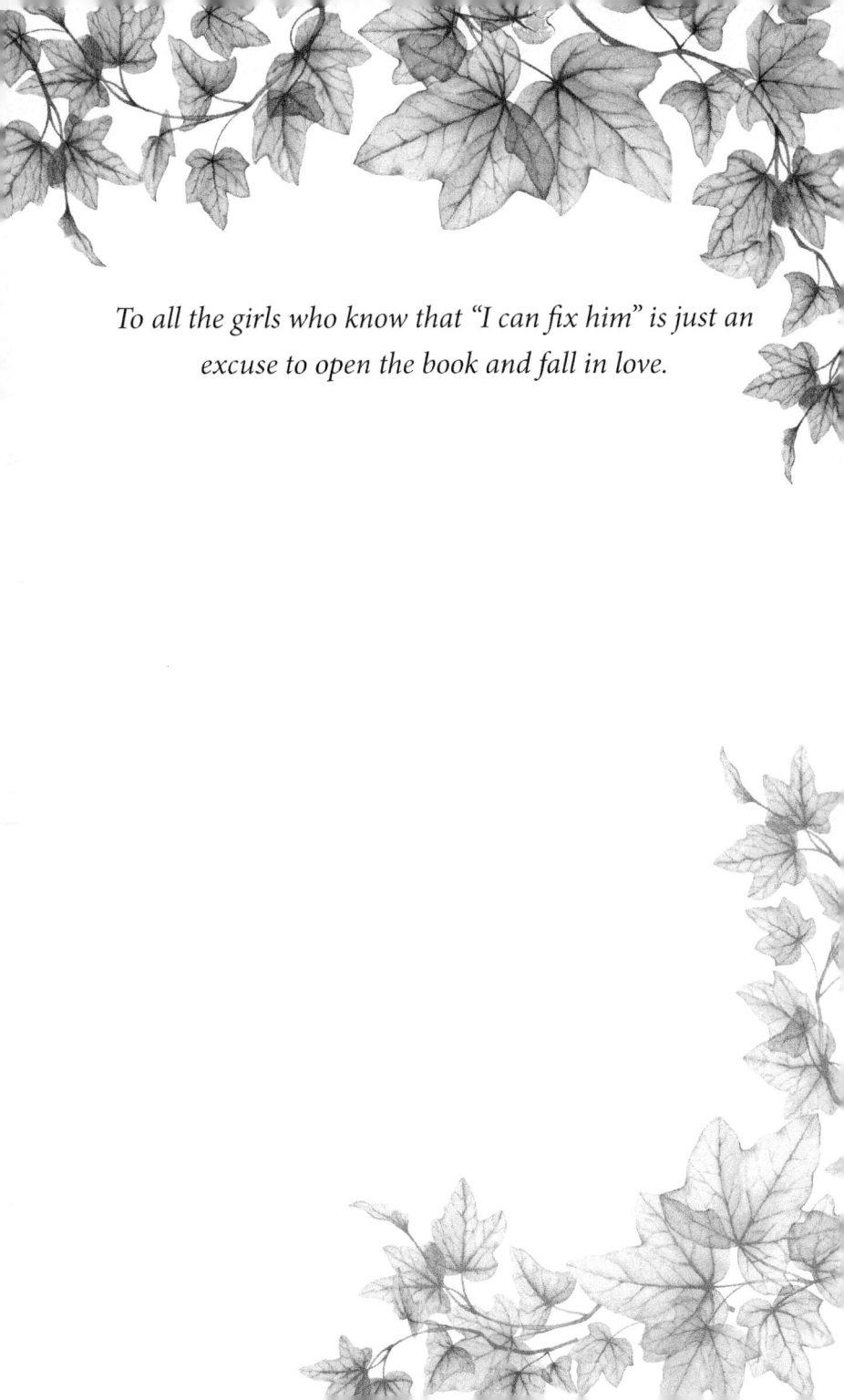

To all the girls who know that "I can fix him" is just an excuse to open the book and fall in love.

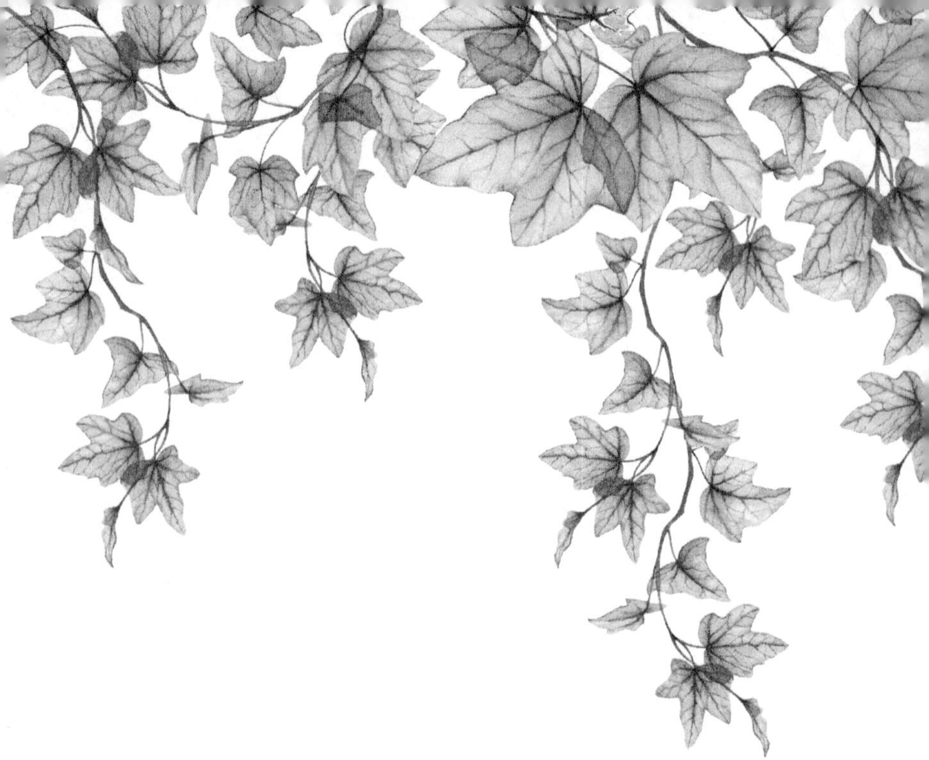

PART I:
NOW

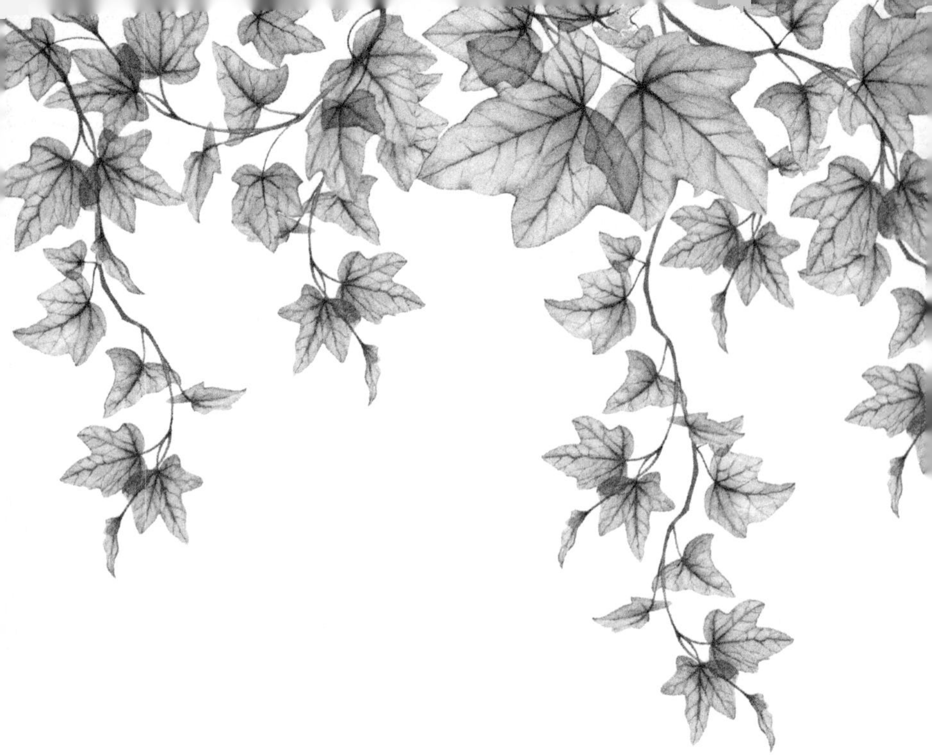

CHAPTER ONE

Vivienne

"Who's my best boy? Who's the loveliest little man in the world?" I bounce Barlow on my hip, and he laughs in the joyous way of a sixteen-month-old without a care in the world. I smile along with him and rub the tip of my nose against his while asking him silly baby talk questions. His fingers find the fine gold chain around my neck, and he plays with it while I pepper his chubby hands with kisses.

Samantha, my stepmom, is glancing between me and the clock on the kitchen wall like she's measuring the seconds I'm spending with my half-brother and begrudging every single one of them. For the moment, Samantha is busy cooking dinner, so I soak up as many toddler cuddles as I can.

"Where are the measuring spoons?" Samantha sighs in

exasperation, opening and closing drawers and cabinet doors.

I turn around and open a drawer. "They're right…oh." What used to be the baking utensil drawer is now full of placemats.

"I moved everything around months ago," my stepmother says peevishly, her tone telling me that I'm annoying her for trying to help. She fishes inside a cabinet and comes out with a set of plastic spoons on a ring. "Here they are."

This is the house I grew up in, but since I moved out to attend Henson University last year, it's turned against me. Things are never where I expect them to be, the walls are painted different colors, and my bedroom has become a storage area for Samantha's photography equipment and Dad's golf gear. Sometimes I sleep in there on the holidays, but getting to my bed feels like running an obstacle course. When I'm lying in the dark, all Dad's and Samantha's things loom over me, resenting and judging my presence. Samantha tries to pretend I'm still welcome. Dad rarely bothers.

As if thinking about him has summoned him home, the front door opens and there are footsteps in the hall.

"It's me," Dad calls in a cheery voice.

Samantha hurries forward and takes Barlow from me. Her smile is strained and her little laugh is forced as she says, "Quickly, give him to me. You'll wind him up too much before bedtime."

I glance at the clock on the wall. It's not even four o'clock, and I know that Barlow isn't put to bed until six. I'm left with an empty ache in my arms where my half-brother used to be, and I watch wistfully as Samantha places him into his high chair and turns away to greet Dad. The temperature of the room drops, and it's not only because I'm no longer cuddling Barlow. I like Samantha, and she used to like me. Emphasis on the *used to*. After what happened last year, I'm rarely allowed to spend time with Barlow, and I'm never asked to babysit anymore.

Dad comes into the kitchen carrying bags from the local hardware store, and rage erupts in his face when he sees me standing there. "What are you doing here?"

I gesture helplessly at Barlow. "I was just…"

Dad glances at Samantha and his jaw flexes. With exaggerated patience, he places the shopping bags on the kitchen table as he turns to his son with genuine affection. "Hello, buddy. Did you have a good afternoon? Were you good for Mom?" He smiles and kisses the boy, tickling his cheek.

I swallow around a lump in my throat. Of course Barlow deserves it, but what I wouldn't give for one-tenth of the same affection.

Dad and Samantha talk about the errand he just ran, and then he can't ignore his daughter any longer. "I'd ask if you've been behaving yourself at that school of yours, but I know better than to expect anything but lies from you."

The pain of his words flays my ribs. I nearly reach up with both hands to hold on to my secret and make the aching stop. Instead, I breathe through the pain.

I'm not a liar.

I'm *not*.

"It's going fine," I whisper, fiddling with the lace cuffs of my shirt. It's one I made myself from vintage lace I found in a thrift shop, adorned with flowers bursting with petals. The day I was happily showing it off for the first time, Dad laughed in a nasty way and said, "Who wants to go around wearing an old curtain?"

Me. I do. This lace probably once hung in some frail old lady's living room, and when she died her daughter or granddaughter washed it, folded it, and donated it to charity. Long before that, the old woman was a young woman, and she was in love with someone; she must have been to buy such romantic lace. She thought of the person she loved while she sewed the curtains and peeked hopefully through them, waiting for her beloved to call on her. She admired the lace flowers against Henson's gloomy sky. I'm dressed in her happiness and her heartbreak. I'm dressed in her hope. There's so little of it around lately that I'm desperate for every scrap I can get my hands on.

Dad and I stare at each other. There's so much that he wants to say, but I can feel him holding the words in. I don't know if he's not saying them because he doesn't want to, or if he's waiting for the right moment. Once he crosses that line there's no going back.

He abruptly turns away from me, and I quietly let out the breath that was burning in my lungs. I'm desperate to keep the peace so that he will allow me to spend a few minutes a week with Barlow. Being around my brother is all I want. There's nothing so important as family, and Barlow is the only one left who truly loves me. How much longer that's going to continue while he's being raised by two people who hate my guts, I don't know.

Dad slams around the kitchen, opening and closing the cupboard and refrigerator as he gets a glass of water and drinks it. Then he puts the glass down so hard it nearly shatters.

"You must have so much work to do, Vivienne." Samantha glances desperately at my satchel laying on the counter. She thinks she's being subtle, but I understand what she wants as clearly as if she were yelling, *Get out of my house*, through a megaphone.

"Yes, lots," I say, reluctantly picking up my bag. "Tonight I think I'm going to sketch the stone angels in the grave—"

Samantha gives me a brief smile and immediately turns away. "Well, won't that be nice. Owen, tonight after dinner, we must go over the credit card statements…"

I give Barlow a kiss on the top of his head, inhale his sweet baby scent, and make my way to the front door.

Dad's angry voice breaks over me just as I get the door open. "Why do you keep letting her in here? She was holding Barlow, wasn't she? I told you she can't be trusted."

He's not even trying to keep his voice down so I don't hear him. In a softer tone, I can hear Samantha pleading with him.

Humiliation washes over me. I close the door behind me and disappear out of all their lives for another week. If I cross their minds in the meantime, the thoughts won't be happy ones. Right now, Samantha will be pointing out to Dad that if he doesn't want me to come over, he has to tell me himself. Dad will slam things and shout, but he's a coward, and he doesn't want to say it to my face. He wants me just to stop coming so he can pretend he's not the bad guy. I'm pretending not to notice what he wants so I can keep seeing my brother.

I will just have to hope that, in time, what happened last year will begin to fade into nothing, at least for them, anyway. I can go back to being an afterthought instead of a liability. Just like how it was four years ago when I was fifteen.

I touch my ribs briefly as a spasm of pain goes through me.

It used to hurt being a postscript in Dad's and Samantha's lives, but now I look back on those first months in this house with longing.

Chilly fall wind whips the leaves along the street, and there's the sharp scent of a coming frost in the air. Summer is definitely over. I pull a cape coat around my shoulders to keep warm, and my brown leather satchel bounces gently against my thigh as I walk. Henson is often gloomy and it frequently rains, but for now, the sky is clear and the sidewalks are dry.

A few minutes later, I arrive at a stone arch and a wrought iron gate with lettering that reads East Henson Cemetery. As I walk through the open gate, I see that there aren't many people around on this cold Sunday afternoon. There are glossy, modern graves and showy rose beds with colorful, fragrant blossoms at the front of the cemetery. Farther back and closer to the church are the older burials. I love it there among the faded, mossy headstones where wildflowers grow between the graves.

I sit cross-legged in the long grass, take out my sketchbook, and contemplate the stone angel in front of me. She's a hundred and forty years old and is lying over a casket with her head on her arms as if she's weeping with her long dress spread out around her. The fabric is intricately folded as if it's been woven from silk rather than carved from stone. Her spread wings are bleached white and crumbling at the tips, but I can still make out many of the painstakingly carved feathers.

My fingertips tingle as I pick up my pencil and start to draw, and I'm flushed with excitement and happiness for the first time today.

I'm studying costume design and art history at Henson University, and I draw whenever I'm not sewing. I got in on a scholarship. There's no way Dad could afford to send me to college, and certainly not one as prestigious and expensive as Henson, and even if he could have afforded it, he never would have spent that much on me. Mom never set up a college fund for me either. I lived with her in Los Angeles for the first fourteen years of my life, and she was too addled by alcohol and drugs to remember to put food in the fridge, let alone consider my future. When Mom overdosed and died, Dad collected me from Child Protective Services and brought me up here to Washington to live with him and his new wife.

I remember how shocked he was that I'd grown up while he wasn't looking. He kept saying things like, "Vivienne, wow. You're so tall. I remember when you were up to my knees," and "You're really in the ninth grade already?" On and on like I was tricking him somehow, or I'd grown up behind his back just to startle him. He could have come to visit once or twice. It's not like he didn't know where Mom and I lived.

In Henson, Dad was awkward but welcoming, and Samantha was pleasant and kind. They didn't tell me they loved me or fall over themselves to take an interest in the small, serious, dark-haired girl who was suddenly in their midst. I didn't mind, as I could listen to them talk to each other about their days while we sat together at the dinner table. Other people filled the house with noise, turned the television on, and left their shoes by the front door. There was a shopping list stuck to the fridge, and the things written on it would appear inside a day or two later. I had never been part of a *we* before.

An *us*. A family. No one called us a family out loud, but I sidled up to the idea like a mistreated stray cat and hoped we were one.

I was almost happy for a time. Almost.

Then when I was fifteen, everything went wrong. Things grew dark inside my head after that, but I found ways to let the darkness out quietly so that it never bothered anyone else. I must *never* bother anyone else. I must be grateful for what I have because I know that things could be much, much worse.

It took me a long time to get used to the cold and the wet in Henson. The quiet roads and the noisy home. I was used to things being the other way around. Highways roaring with noise while the house or apartment Mom and I lived in was sad and silent. Mom tried her best for me, declaring again and again that she would get clean, but the siren call of drugs and alcohol always pulled her back, and she consumed whichever substance was easiest and cheapest to get her hands on. That's how Mom and Dad met, all those years ago. A match made in addiction. Dad cleaned up his act a few years later but Mom never did, and in the end, it killed her.

These days, Dad's pretty reliable, until suddenly he isn't. I'm never sure what will trigger one of his binges and neither is Samantha. It's probably work stress, or a yearning for the good old bad days, or both. One day he's a good husband and an interested father to Barlow, and the next, he disappears and comes home three days later with bloodshot eyes, reeking of stale whisky or vodka. Never out of his mind on drugs, but the alcohol is bad enough. Dad cries and says he's sorry and promises Samantha he'll never do it again. Samantha knows he will, but she always forgives him.

Last year, he spent most of one binge in a club on the seedy side of town, racking up an eye-watering bill, thanks to top-shelf drinks and the illegal gambling tables. Twenty-nine thousand dollars blown in three days. Dad only had six thousand in the bank, and he'd picked the wrong club to party in and then forfeit the bill.

Someone came knocking, and he wanted his money.

Someone with a steely blue glare and a ruthless edge to his temper. His fury was an out-of-control twenty-ton truck, and I stepped right into its path. My afterthought of life turned into a nightmare, but my mistake wasn't drawing all of Tyrant Mercer's merciless anger down on me to save my family.

My mistake was believing my family would thank me for my sacrifice.

The stone angel emerges on my sketchbook page, along with her dress and the ivy growing up on the casket to twine around her wrists. I find myself leaning farther and farther over the page until I realize why I'm struggling to see what I'm doing. The sun set while I was drawing. Dusk is rapidly bleeding into night, and the graves all around me are disappearing into the darkness.

With a whispered curse, I hurriedly pack up my things. The main gate will probably be locked by now, but if I run, I should be able to make it out the back gate by the church. The peace I knew while sketching the stone angel fades away, replaced by the memory of Samantha taking Barlow away from me. Sooner or later, they're going to tell me they don't want me coming around anymore. I can feel it, as inevitable as the falling night.

I'm so consumed by that sad thought that when I get to my feet and turn toward the back gate, I don't realize there's someone in front of me until I nearly bump into him. I move to one side to step around him, only to find that way blocked by someone else. A third figure presses in behind me.

I thought I was alone in the old part of the graveyard, but suddenly there are three boys surrounding me. They're all around my age, eighteen or nineteen, dressed in dark clothing. The meanest-looking one, wearing a black sweater, holds up his hand with a nasty grin and shows me what's in it.

A knife.

It's not as impressive as some knives I've held. The blade is a stubby and unremarkable shape, and the honed edge doesn't whisper like a lover or hum an enticing note when the light strikes it just so. The boy holding the knife doesn't even look like he knows how to control a weapon like that or understand what it can do.

He jerks his chin at the boy in a blue T-shirt standing to my left. "Give him your bag."

I clutch my satchel tightly against my chest and shake my head. I don't care about money because I don't have any, but my sketchbook is filled with thousands and thousands of hours of daydreams and wishes.

"I said give it to him," snarls the boy, brandishing the knife in my face.

Is this the part where I'm supposed to start feeling afraid? Blades ceased to scare me a long time ago. "I haven't got anything valuable. Just my sketchbook, and you can't have that."

The boy smiles wider, and I realize with a plummeting sensation that he doesn't care what I have. He's only interested in taking things from me.

A cold, silent wind rushes through the rapidly darkening cemetery, and I know that we're completely, utterly alone.

"Grab her arms," he orders the boy to my right, who is a copper-haired boy in a dirty white T-shirt.

White T-shirt grabs my arm, and I pull away from him, my heart beating wildly, and open my mouth to scream. Black Sweater growls in anger. He lunges for me with the knife, and fire bursts in a white-hot line along the back of my forearm.

My skin is ripped open, revealing living, pink flesh. It's always like this when you're cut quickly. The blood takes a moment to fill the wound. There's a moment where the universe stands still and the world grinds to a halt, and then the inevitable thick, ruby-red liquid wells up. I twist my arm back and forth in the deep blue glow of late dusk, enraptured by the glistening flow. Little rivers of blood run down my arm and splash onto a gravestone.

"Now you've done it," I whisper.

"What?" asks White T-shirt. He and Blue T-shirt don't seem as keen to hurt me as Black Sweater.

"You've broken the rule."

"What rule?"

I hold my arm out as if that explains everything. "I'm bleeding."

White T-shirt frowns. "So?"

"What are you? A hemo-thingy?" Blue T-shirt asks.

His friend punches his shoulder. "Dude, there's no need for slurs. Just say lesbian."

Blue T-shirt punches back harder. "Moron. *Hemo*, not homo.

That disease that means you can't stop bleeding."

"I'm not a hemophiliac," I tell them.

"She's a dead bitch if she doesn't do what she's told," Black Sweater seethes, a nasty sneer on his lips, and he slashes the air in my direction. He's keen to get this mugging or rape or whatever it is back on track.

My pulse is racing so fast it's making me feel sick, but it's not these boys I'm afraid of. How dare these idiots mock me with something so stupid as that knife. It's a shitty knife, but he doesn't deserve it.

I want it.

I snatch at the blade and Black Sweater jerks it away from me, more from shock than skill. My fingers just skim the edge of the blade and close on empty air.

His eyes go wide. "What is wrong with you, you crazy bitch?"

Hasn't he realized?

Everything.

Everything is wrong with me.

"Fuck you," I snarl, and lunge for the blade again. I nearly have it. My heart pounds with delight.

A hand seizes my wrist in the darkness, one twice the size of mine and adorned with tattoos and rings. I freeze in place and stare at it.

A deep, unforgiving voice just behind me growls, "Vivienne. You know you're not allowed to play with knives."

The three boys stare in shock as a man steps forward, his pale blue eyes narrowed, his cleanshaven jaw tighter than the grip he has on my wrist, and his nostrils flaring in fury. He looms over me in a charcoal black suit like the devil himself has risen from one of these graves.

I recognize him instantly. We all do.

He glares at my bleeding arm and then accusingly into my eyes.

I glare right back. Don't blame *me*. I didn't do this.

The rule that these boys have broken?

I'm only allowed to bleed for him.

The ruler of this town. Not the mayor. Not the chief of police. Not the rich old men who live up on Wysteria Avenue. The man who runs this city from the shadows. Everyone knows it, but no one's brave enough to say it out loud.

He lifts my wrist and licks slowly up my forearm, looking me dead in the eye. Blood collects on his tongue and he sweeps it across his teeth.

He smiles at me. A red, infernal smile.

Tyrant Mercer.

Last year, he stole my baby brother to force Dad to pay for his drinking and gambling. I couldn't let Barlow suffer for Dad's mistakes, so I went after Tyrant and Barlow and stole my brother back. Tyrant never got his money, and now I'm in his debt. I don't have any money, so Tyrant's decided he gets to play with me anytime he chooses.

I try to pull my wrist out of his grip, but Tyrant's holding me too tightly. He cups the back of my neck, drawing me toward him, his bloodstained mouth seeking mine. The rich scent of blackcurrants and cedars in wintertime clings to his clothes. I resist him and nearly overbalance, but just in time, I prevent myself from crashing into his chest. My free hand ends up clutching my skirt.

A wicked smile spreads over Tyrant's mouth, revealing his bloodstained teeth. "Afraid to touch me, angel?"

Of course I am. Touching this man is dangerously addictive. More addictive than knives. Tyrant looks like a work of art or a photographer's dream. He has a brutal face that's been carved from the finest marble, and a tall, broad, muscular body that's predatory in its beauty. Then there's the fact that the man knows how to dress. Tyrant doesn't wear clothes. He brings them to life. The suit jacket encasing his muscular shoulders looks like it formed instantaneously around his body from Italian wool and miracles.

And his *skin*. I used to think there was nothing in the world more wondrous to the touch than buttery satin, fine silk chiffon, and thick velvet that's been woven from the night sky. Now I know that nothing compares to Tyrant's warm, touchable skin, adorned with intricate tattoos that cover his body, his hands, creep up his throat, and even decorate his cheekbones and above his brows.

His smile widens and my gaze fastens on it. That mouth of his can caress and punish with kisses. His lips and tongue can drag secrets from my body and make it do things I never knew were possible. I wonder sometimes if I made Tyrant up out of scraps of fabric, desperation, and fever dreams.

Or fever nightmares, because this man is my ruin.

Tyrant keeps a tight hold of my wrist and turns to the boys. In a cold, menacing voice he asks, "Who cut her?"

We all look at the knife that Black Sweater's holding. Even he seems stunned to see it in his hand, and he hides it behind his back.

FEAR ME, *love me*

Terror is making the whites show all the way around his eyes. He brings the knife out again and opens and closes his mouth. "Um…"

"Give it to me," Tyrant orders.

The boy instantly obeys, dropping the knife into Tyrant's hand and wiping his own on the seat of his pants. He's scrambling for a way to save his life. Make some excuse. He didn't in his wildest dreams expect Tyrant Mercer to materialize in this graveyard when he was bullying an unprotected girl.

Tyrant examines drops of my blood on the blade. "That doesn't belong to you," he tells the boy, then turns to look at me as he licks the blood off the blade. "This is mine, isn't it, angel?"

It's not fair that he looks so delicious with my blood coating his teeth. I never agreed that he owns my blood, but Tyrant has decided he does, and that's all that matters to him.

"But you can have this back." Tyrant flips the knife in his hand so he's holding the tip, raises it over his shoulder, and throws. The knife flips through the air in a blur of flashing metal and buries itself in Black Sweater's throat. The boy's eyes grow impossibly wide. He scrabbles at his throat and then yanks the blade out.

Big mistake. Blood gouts down his sweater. He makes a gurgling sound, and more blood bubbles up his throat and pours over his lips. A moment later, he crumples to the ground and lies there motionless.

I should probably cover my face and scream, but instead, I'm staring down at the dead boy in surprise and interest. All that blood is such a fascinating sight.

His friends cry out in shock. Blue T-shirt grabs White T-shirt and pulls him like he's about to break into a run. Both of them are having normal reactions to a suddenly dead boy.

Tyrant pulls a gun out of his suit jacket and points it at them. "If you take one more step, after I kill you both, I will murder your families."

The boys stay where they are, whimpering and staring in horror at their dead friend.

Satisfied, Tyrant turns back to me and drags me even closer to his muscular body by my bloody wrist. An evil smirk spreads over his lips, and he murmurs, "It's been too long, Vivienne. How's my favorite girl in Henson?"

My blood is leaking between his fingers and running over his wrist. I take an unsteady breath and say, as forcefully as I can manage, "Let go of me, Tyrant."

Tyrant's smile turns cold and his eyes flash, warning me to be nice to the man who saved me. In the same purring tone, he says, "But, angel, I want to talk to you."

"I don't want to talk to you. I don't want to see you. I don't want to touch you." I try to yank my wrist from him but his grip on me is like iron.

"Is that so?" he asks, menace spreading over his features. "In that case, tell me, Vivienne. How's your baby brother?"

CHAPTER TWO

Tyrant

The second I mention Barlow, fear and hatred flash through Vivienne's eyes. She needn't worry. I lost interest in the child a long time ago when someone far more enticing came along.

But I *am* angry.

After the first time I touched her, there was a delicious smear of her blood on my flesh. All over my cock. I was very clear about the rules. She's only allowed to bleed when *I* make her bleed.

I can taste Vivienne's blood in my mouth, heavy and sweet. My girl is looking more beautiful than ever, her cheeks flushed in the moonlight and defiance sparking in her green eyes. She gave not one shiver at the sight of blood or the dying boy. Not a shriek or retch when I killed him. Vivienne Stone doesn't know it, but she has a core of pure steel.

She's exactly what I crave in a woman. She's everything I need in the mother of my children. I know her deepest, darkest secrets. Her joy and her sorrow. Her pain. Mostly, her life has been pain. She continues to let it be filled with pain, much to my fury. Vivienne won't reach out with both hands and take what she craves, so I'll have to take it for her.

Barlow is the key to her heart. All she needs to say is, *Tyrant, I want Barlow*, and I'll go get her brother for her and take them both to my mansion where we'll live happily ever fucking after.

But she has to ask me first. I will hear it from her own lips that she wants me, wants *us*. Every furious moment of my life is spent obsessing over a way to make Vivienne ask me for what she craves, and today, I think I've come up with the answer. I've been aching to be eight inches deep in her tight pussy ever since I thought of it.

I lower my mouth toward her tempting lips. She draws in a soft breath and her mouth parts, her eyes growing hazy.

There's movement behind her, and I glance up. A somber man in a dark suit is approaching us through the trees.

I let go of Vivienne and nod at my driver. "You're hurt. Go with Liam, and I'll join you in a moment."

Vivienne covers the cut on her arm with her hand. "I can take care of this back at the dorms."

My teeth grit tightly together and I bite out, "I said, go with Liam, or will you continue to test my patience?"

Vivienne glances at my driver, who holds out his arm and shows her where a black Cullinan SUV is waiting just beyond the cemetery gates. Reluctantly, she follows him.

I still have my gun pointed at the two remaining boys, and I ask them, watching Vivienne walk away and get into the back seat of my car, "Did you three happen to come walking this way tonight, or did someone tell you to hurt my woman?"

"W-we didn't know she was your woman," one of them stammers. "We're s-so sorry."

Through the wrought iron fence covered with twists of ivy, I see Liam close the door on Vivienne and stand sentry with his hands clasped in front of him.

I turn my attention to the boys. "Is that what I asked you?"

The red-haired boy scrambles to reply. "Sorry, um, sir. Mr. Mercer. We don't know anything. It was all Bryn's idea."

Bryn must be the corpse lying at our feet. I wonder if I killed the only one who could tell me something useful.

"Bryn didn't tell us anything. He just said to come with him and we were going to mess with some girl."

"Some girl. So that's what she is. Some girl." I laugh and scratch my temple with the barrel of the gun. I thought I had all the threats around Vivienne locked down but, apparently, I was wrong. The boys glance nervously at each other.

I point the gun at them again and raise it to the level of their eyes. "Turn around."

Both of them start to whimper and plead with me.

"What did I say? Turn around now, or after I shoot you, your families will die as well."

With their hands in the air, they get on their knees while sobbing and pleading with me.

"We've never even done anything like this before."

I check the bullets in my gun. "What, rape a girl in a cemetery?"

I don't know this Bryn, so either he's got a grudge against me from afar, or someone told him to get to me through Vivienne. I want to kill these two pieces of trash for thinking they can lay a finger on my girl, but perhaps they can be useful to me instead.

First I want blood. My code means they can't go unpunished.

"We weren't going to—"

I fire off four shots in quick succession. Both boys fall forward, clutching their legs and screaming in pain. Later, I might have questions for them about this Bryn. For now, they can tell everyone how Tyrant Mercer killed their friend for hurting his girl.

"Go. Crawl. If I come back and you're still here, the next bullets will be in your skulls."

Gasping their thanks, they clumsily army crawl down the path, leaving a trail of blood in their wake.

I head back to my car and put the gun in the glove box out of Vivienne's reach. There's no need to tempt my beloved into doing something foolish like aiming it at me. Then I nod to Liam to take a walk and get into the back of the Cullinan.

Vivienne is sitting on the broad back seat, her injured arm cradled against her chest. Her dark bangs are falling into her eyes, and the short jacket she was wearing has fallen from her shoulders and is pooling behind her. The ruined cream lace blouse and short pleated skirt emphasize her fragile innocence, but I know how tough my girl is. How dangerously whip-smart.

For a moment, I just take in the sight of her. Hungering for her. When the automatic light overhead goes out, I reach up and turn it on again.

"You spared them," she whispers.

I didn't spare them. I ensured that everyone on the streets of Henson will hear about this by morning and understand that Vivienne Stone is Tyrant's girl. Even looking the wrong way at her is hazardous for your health.

But she can believe I was being merciful if she likes.

I grasp the edge of her sleeve, fingering the torn lace. I recognize one of Vivienne's creations with a sigh of regret. "You made this, didn't you? It's lovely. I'm sorry. Those assholes ruined your beautiful work."

"It's just an old curtain," she mutters.

"No, it's not." I reach down beneath the driver's seat and pull out a first aid kit and set it on the seat next to me. "Give me your arm." When she doesn't move, I reach out and gently but firmly pull her arm across my lap.

There's a gash along the edge of her forearm, not deep, and it hasn't hit anything vital.

"I don't think it needs stitches."

She studies my face. "Are you a doctor now?"

"I've been around an injury or two."

Using a pair of scissors, I cut away the ripped sleeve of her blouse, and then carefully clean the wound and the blood on her arm with a cotton pad soaked in disinfectant. Vivienne hisses in pain as it stings her wound, but she lets me do it.

"I know, angel," I murmur tenderly. "I'm nearly finished."

I never get to be tender with anyone. Whenever I say the words *I'm nearly finished* it's usually because I'm torturing someone to death.

"What do you want?"

I start to wind a bandage around her arm and say with an edge to my voice, "Thank you for saving my life, Tyrant."

"You're stalking me," she accuses. "Everywhere I go, I feel like I'm being watched, and you keep showing up. If it's not you watching me, then there's a stranger across the street, hanging around campus, or in the library when I'm trying to study. You're driving me crazy."

I'm making *her* crazy? She's the one who's so lovely and exquisite, and yet she's not my wife and she's not pregnant with my baby.

Yet.

I finish tending to the gash on her arm and secure the bandage. Now she's all better, I get to hurt her some more.

Leaning closer to her with a glare that has her shrinking away from me, I seethe, "You broke my rules."

"I didn't understand back then. I wasn't thinking straight." She places her hand on the door as if she's going to open it.

"I wouldn't do that, Vivienne. Your family has never repaid your debt."

Vivienne freezes, and her chest starts lifting and falling in panic. "Leave Barlow alone."

My hand snakes around her waist, and I pull her back to me. Her hair falls to one side, exposing her slender neck. How many times have I fantasized about getting my hand around this throat and squeezing while I fuck the living daylights out of her?

"Give me one reason why I should."

Her mouth is so close to mine that I can feel her breathing. She knows what I want. I know what she wants.

Vivienne gazes at my lips. "You licked up all my blood like it was honey."

"Sweeter than honey. You always did like my tongue, angel." I slant my mouth over hers and push my tongue forcefully into her mouth. I kiss her hard until I feel her whole body melting into mine and her pulse thundering beneath my fingers. Vivienne gasps, and her hands clench my shirt.

That's right, angel. Touch me. How I've fucking missed you touching me.

When I break the kiss, she gasps for breath. "You smell like blood. You taste like blood."

"Yours. My favorite flavor. But you're only supposed to bleed for me, angel. That was the rule."

"I didn't ask for them to cut me."

She was in a cemetery at dusk, looking like a wood nymph with pouty lips and bare thighs. There are too many bad men in this city for her to go around like that without protection. Vivienne's going to be punished for acting so recklessly.

"Don't make excuses," I snarl and reach under her skirt to grasp her underwear. She grabs my wrist to stop me, but I tug her white bikini briefs down her thighs until they're twisted around her knees. "You were out at night when you know it's not safe in this town for pretty girls to be wandering around alone."

"Tyrant, please," she whimpers, wriggling in my grip.

I'll give her *Tyrant, please*.

I flip her over so she's face down on the broad leather seat and push her skirt up. I suck in a breath and my cock gets hard just looking at her plump ass. Christ, her ass is everything. I take a handful and squeeze, pulling her pussy open. She's pink and inviting and my mouth waters.

"Get your hands off—"

I lift my hand and bring it down in a sharp smack. Vivienne cries out and her ass quivers enticingly. Gathering her into my lap, I hold her down on my thighs and spank her again. And again. Vivienne squeals in outrage and tries to scramble away from me, but she's going nowhere until she's had her fix, and so have I.

Vivienne loves to hurt.

I love to make her cry.

We're a match made in hell. Her ass turns bright red and burns hot. She looks so fucking sexy like this with her rolled-up briefs twisted around her thighs and her skirt flipped up while she gets wetter and wetter by the second. My tarnished angel whose halo is slipping while she gets turned on by the devil. I scratch my nails across her red raw skin, and Vivienne moans and arches her back.

When we're both breathing hard, I pull her pussy lips open and admire the sight of her tight entrance, even wetter and pinker than before. "It's time I told everyone that you're my girl. Then they'll leave you alone. They're all terrified of me, angel."

"Don't tell anyone, please," she says, her voice muffled in the leather seat.

"Oh, you prefer being my dirty little secret?" I murmur, trailing my fingers through her wet and slippery sex, just teasing her entrance.

"There's nothing to keep secret. I don't—"

I push two fingers into her pussy, right up to the second knuckle. Vivienne cries out and braces her hands against the car door. I pump my fingers into her and groan at her grip on my fingers, which are now glistening wet. "Nothing secret? Open your knees wider for me, angel. Let me finger fuck you nice and deep."

Like the good fucking girl she is, Vivienne wriggles her legs apart for me and arches into my touch, moaning, "Please."

I twist my fingers inside her. Sopping wet and swollen. "That's my good little slut."

Vivienne moans again and clenches my fingers. "I can pretend this didn't happen tomorrow. I can pretend I didn't say that. Just like I do every time."

Didn't happen? How fucking dare she. "Is that so?" I say icily. "Then I'm going to make sure that after this time, you can't pretend."

There's a beat of fearful silence. Vivienne knows I don't make idle threats.

"What do you mean, Tyrant?" she whimpers.

I pull my fingers out of her, grasp her thigh, and flip her over onto her back. That underwear is coming off. I yank them off her legs, throw them down on the floor of the car, and then brace my hands on either side of her head. "What a sweet sight you made in the window earlier as you cuddled your baby brother."

Vivienne doesn't realize how sexy she looks doing the simplest of things. When she brushes the end of her pencil across her plush lower lip as she pauses mid-drawing to think. When she gathers all her heavy, dark hair into her hands and twists and turns it into a long braid. And especially when she cuddles her baby brother, so protective and loving, with a warm, sweet expression on her face.

"You *are* stalking me," she whispers, her eyes wide.

Of course I am. It's my business to know everything that goes on in this town, especially when it comes to Vivienne. Her schedule is packed on weekdays with classes, studying, and sewing, and she fills her Saturdays with museums, galleries, and thrift shopping. Sunday morning she does laundry, but Sunday afternoons are long and empty. Sunday afternoon is when she might do something dangerous.

"I need to see more of you." I reach for the button at the neck of her blouse.

Vivienne grips my hand with both of hers and desperately shakes her head. "No, please."

"What are you hiding from me?" I ask, an edge to my voice.

"Nothing."

"Vivienne," I growl in warning.

"Nothing…new."

"So show me."

Slowly, Vivienne lets go of me and unfastens the buttons all the way down her front. She holds the blouse closed for a moment, and then winces like she's in pain and pulls it open.

I let my gaze travel down her torso, taking in every single detail. Devouring the sight of her. She's wearing a triangle bra that I think she made herself from thin, gauzy fabric. I imagine her sewing the delicate lace and carefully fitting it to her breasts. Her nipples are standing out sharply beneath the sheer fabric. I trace my fingers down her chest and over her belly button and she trembles at my touch. Her flesh is warm. I brush my fingers over her ribs, and she gasps and tries to close her blouse, but I won't let her.

Covering her ribs are dozens and dozens of horizontal scars, all of them white and puckered. Not one of them is red and swollen and there are no bandages. Nothing fresh. The monsters haven't been howling at her and dragging her into the darkness with them lately. I'm the biggest monster in her life right now.

"Say what you said the first time," Vivienne whispers, her hands covering her face as if she's afraid of what she'll see in my eyes.

"Vivienne. Look at me."

She hesitates, and then fearfully lowers her hands. I take her chin in my hand and make her look deep into my eyes so she can feel how much I mean this. "You're the most beautiful girl I've ever seen."

Vivienne's chest heaves in a sob.

With shaking fingers, she reaches up and pulls me down to her and desperately kisses my mouth. That's my girl. That's my good fucking angel of a girl. I kiss her slowly, hungrily devouring as much of her as I can. Savoring the sweet taste of her and the desperate way she surrenders her mouth to mine.

I find the button on her pleated skirt and pop it open, and shimmy the garment down her legs. She's naked beneath me except for her sweet little bra, and I pull the cups down until her nipples pop out, tight and dusky pink.

Reaching down between us, I unfasten my belt and pants, reach inside my underwear, and drag my cock out.

"Has anyone else touched you?" I demand.

She shakes her head.

I would have known if they had, but the angry, jealous beast is roaring within me, and I need to hear it from her. That none of the boys at her college have crept into her room. Grabbed her ass in the hallways. Tried to touch what's mine. I have to know she wouldn't want anyone else to touch what's mine.

"You're only for me, angel. I killed that asshole who cut you, and if anyone else touches you, I will put a bullet in his head."

Vivienne's palms are pressed tight against my chest and her thighs are hugging my hips. The plaintive look in her eyes says that she's only ever wanted me.

"Do you believe me?"

"Yes, Tyrant," she whispers.

Blood rushes even harder to my dick.

Vivienne explores my clothing, slowly popping open every button on my shirt. She pushes it back from my shoulders along with my suit jacket. I sit up and shake the garments off while she strokes my torso, her teeth sunk into her lower lip.

"I don't even know why you like me. I'm a mess. I'm ruined." Vivienne looks down at herself and her eyes suddenly fill with tears.

I lick the tears from her cheeks. If an angel can look at a monster like me with so much softness in her heart, then that monster is going to make her believe she's beautiful.

"Like you? I don't fucking *like* you. I'm obsessed with you."

Vivienne blinks the tears from her eyes. She tentatively explores all the tattoos on my torso. The muscles of my chest and arms. The hollows between my ribs. The hard line of muscle along my hip bone.

Vivienne understands the world through her fingers, and I'm her favorite thing to touch.

"I love when you touch me," I groan, fisting my cock up and down. "After this, everyone's going to know you belong to me."

She shakes her head, her expression anguished. "My family hates you. They can't know that I've been seeing you."

Vivienne's family doesn't give a damn about her, and soon they'll care even less.

"You let me worry about your family." I grasp the thick root of my cock and play the head over Vivienne's wet inner lips until I'm coated in her slipperiness.

"I don't understand why you're here. We don't make sense together," she says desperately, enraptured by the sight of my broad head playing over her clit as I move slowly back and forth.

"We make perfect sense, angel. Don't worry about anyone else. They'll all get it through their thick skulls when my baby starts to show in your belly."

If Vivienne won't ask for Barlow to get our family started, then I'll fuck my own baby into her right now.

Vivienne's eyes fly open in alarm. "What did you just say? Tyrant, you *can't*—"

I thrust into her pussy with one swift movement.

I can, and I fucking will.

CHAPTER THREE

Vivienne

Tyrant's sudden and sharp intrusion makes me cry out. I grip his shoulders, my nails digging into his muscles, and drag a desperate breath into my lungs. He's just so thick, and I always struggle to take even a little bit of him at a time, let alone all of him at once.

His delicious, heavy body pins me to the seat, and he starts to thrust.

Shit. *Shit*. I meant to go on the pill. Buy a condom. Do something. Tyrant always appears so suddenly and rips my clothes off that I don't have time to think about anything but him.

I push my hands against his chest and try to wriggle out from beneath him, but he's too strong for me, and there's nowhere to go in the back seat of his car.

"Tyrant, stop. I said I'm not on any—"

He pulls back and slams even deeper into me, and I cry out in shock. He's so thick, and my inner channel burns as he forces it to stretch. My ass is still red raw from the spanking. Sex with him hurts, but he knows I love it when it hurts. He fucks me hard, one hand holding my thigh open and the other braced by my head.

"You're not on any birth control. I know. I want it that way. I'm going to fuck my baby into you, Vivienne. Here. Now. If you fight me, I'll hold you down and make you take it."

Tyrant has said all kinds of crazy things while we're having sex, but this is the craziest.

"You can't..." I break off and moan as the burning pain turns into pleasure. It always does with Tyrant. The sharp battering of his cock turns into a velvety glide that makes my insides heat up. We don't have a lot of room on the back seat, but he doesn't seem to need it. Tyrant has one foot braced on the floor of his car as he pumps his cock into me. He cradles the back of my head and lifts it, making me look down at myself impaled on him.

"Look at yourself being fucked," he says raggedly, moving in and out of me. "My angel always looks beautiful, but she's even prettier filled with my cock."

His filthy words send a spasm through my core, distracting me for a few seconds from his threat to put a baby in me. Tyrant's baby. A sweet little boy or girl to love and protect. He wants that with me? For real?

"I want you swollen with my baby, a ring on your finger, and living in my house where I can protect you," he says, pulling all the way out. He spreads me open with his fingers and looks at my channel, and then sinks his teeth into his lower lip with a groan before shoving himself back inside me again. "So pink and perfect for me to fuck. Who's Tyrant's good girl?"

I moan softly and close my eyes. His deep, hypnotic voice is making me lose my mind.

"Go on, tell me. Who's Tyrant's good little slut?"

"Me," I moan, wrapping my legs around his hips and giving in to him. With my hands pressed against his muscled stomach, I can feel the motion of his body as he drills his cock into me.

"Feel how stretched tight you are around me."

Obediently, I reach down between us to wrap my finger and thumb around his slippery girth as he pistons in and out of my pussy. He's so thick that my fingertips don't meet on the other side.

I drag my fingers up and over my clit, rubbing myself and gasping in delight as the pleasure doubles. Nothing else matters right now. Only Tyrant and what he's doing to me. I'm nearly sobbing again he's making me feel so good.

"I love it when you touch yourself for me. Have you been humping your pillow and moaning my name?" Tyrant gives me a wicked smile. He's just so sure that I've been masturbating over him. If I wasn't so far gone, I'd hate that he's one hundred percent right.

My orgasm starts to rush up, but I stop touching myself before it can overwhelm me.

Tyrant takes my hand and sucks on my wet fingers. "Fuck, you taste delicious. Are you going to make yourself come for me?"

His tongue feels criminally good moving against my fingers.

"I want it to last." Being here with him means my world is filled with color and light, which is ironic considering I'm being fucked by the man with the darkest heart in Henson.

"So have another orgasm. And another. Come as many times as you want, angel. I won't stop fucking you until you're a pretty wet mess."

I reach down and touch myself again, my eyes glued to Tyrant's beautiful, menacing face. He talks me through my first orgasm, watching my fingers circling my clit as his thick cock moves in and out of me.

"Angel, when I'm not with you, I'm constantly thinking about burying myself in your tight pink velvet. Will you scream if I come in through your window at night and fuck you while you sleep? You probably will. You're such a screamer, so I'll have to gag you first. If the baby doesn't take this time, I'll get you while you're out cold and can't stop me."

I gasp and take my fingers away, but I'm still going to come. I shouldn't encourage him to talk this way by coming because then he might actually do it, and I really won't be able to think about birth control if I'm unconscious.

But it's too late, and there's nothing I can do to stop what's about to happen. My pussy clenches on Tyrant's thick shaft. My back arches and my blood overheats with pleasure. He fucks me through my orgasm, and it's only just beginning to fade when another rises up and takes over me, deeper and stronger this time.

"I can feel you, angel. That's my girl. Milk my cock," he groans.

My climaxes run together until I don't know where one finishes and another one begins. The next thing I know, I'm screaming his name and clawing his shoulders, begging for more. Fuck me deeper. Pound me harder.

Tyrant braces both hands on either side of my head and hammers into me. "Jesus, *fuck*, girl. I'm going to come."

"Please, Tyrant," I moan.

A wicked grin spreads over his face, and I'm too far gone to register why he's looking at me like that.

Then I remember.

They'll all get it through their thick skulls when my baby starts to show in your belly.

"Wait. Pull out. Pull *out*."

Tyrant keeps on pounding with long strokes of his cock. His breathing is heavy and his cheeks flush red. "Do I ever pull out?"

I wasn't thinking straight those other times. I'm never thinking clearly around Tyrant. Clarity swans in hours after he's gone, bringing her best friend, Shame. Then in comes Common Sense with a heavy sigh and tells me to go get a Plan B.

"No, but—"

"Hold still while I fuck my baby into you."

I'm trying my hardest to move but he won't let me. He pushes my other thigh up to my chest and spreads my legs wider, deepening his strokes. My hands fly out to brace myself against the leather seats. He's really going to do it. The muscles of his stomach are rippling beneath his tattoos. His breathing is heavy. A lock of fair hair is falling over his forehead. He looks *magnificent*.

"Oh, fuck yes, angel," Tyrant moans, his eyes half closed. He's barely pulling back before thrusting hard and deep again. "That's. My. Good. *Girl.*" He emphasizes each word with another thrust.

He finishes with a luxurious groan and shoves himself so deep inside me that he's pressed tight against my cervix. There's a heavy, liquid feeling inside me, and I wonder if he's been saving himself up and not jerking off just for this moment.

The car windows are steamed up around us. The air smells like sex. Tyrant wraps his arms tightly around me and squeezes me. Then he half sits up and grins at me lazily. "What kind of diamond do you want on your finger?"

I glare at him.

"Pink? Yellow? How about an emerald? One that matches your eyes. You know what the hottest fucking thing is? Women in long white wedding dresses with a baby bump."

"Get off me."

Tyrant gazes at my nipples. They look like little pink invitations peeking up over my bra like that. He must think so as well because he gets down on his elbows and sucks one of them into his mouth. "Give it a minute."

"Give what a minute?"

Tyrant drags his hips back an inch and pushes his cock into me again. With my nipple still in his mouth, he says, "I want to be sure you're knocked up."

Panic and desire thrill through me.

"I'm a second-year student. I'm nineteen," I tell him.

Tyrant sucks on my nipple again. "Mm. Nice and fertile."

"And you're...wait, I don't even know how old you are."

"Thirty-four."

Jesus. Fifteen years older than me, a hardened criminal, and his cock is still lodged inside me. I'm making great life choices.

"You've probably already got a family tucked away somewhere," I accuse. "Is that right? Am I your bit on the side?"

He shakes his head and laves my breasts with his tongue. "I never wanted a family until I saw you with a baby in your arms. Fuck, that did something to me," he breathes, moving up my body to capture my mouth with his.

I soften beneath his hungry kiss, wondering if it's true. I made this dangerous man suddenly want a family? My stomach flutters at the idea.

A voice that sounds suspiciously like Common Sense snaps, *So you're just going to have his baby? Someone who's a bouquet of red flags living a life made from red flags?*

Slowly, Tyrant eases out of me, admiring the sight of his still-hard cock dripping with my wetness and his cum. He gathers all the liquid from his length with his thumb and forefinger, all the wetness that's dripping down my pussy, and slowly and carefully pushes it back inside me. I watch his face in astonishment. His expression is hard and resolute. He tucks himself back into his pants and does them up and lounges comfortably on the leather seat, still holding me down with his hand. "Stay on your back, angel. I want you filled with my cum for a few more minutes."

My cheeks heat, and I'm hyperconscious of Tyrant's eyes on my naked body. His fingers stroke idly through my hair, and he pulls my legs over his thighs and comfortably clasps both my ankles in one of his big hands.

Resigning myself to giving Tyrant what he wants for now and fixing this mess later, I let my head fall back on the leather seat. How did my life become so crazy?

Shame has wandered in after Common Sense to add her two cents. *How could a man like him want a hopeless mess like you forever? You're just a cum dumpster to him. He says he's going to blow his load into you, and you just spread your legs.*

I pull the cups of my bra up over my nipples and feel around for my torn and bloodied blouse. Holding it up, I see that it's completely ruined.

"It was special to you, wasn't it?" Tyrant asks.

I nod but feel pathetic that I'm sad about a blouse. A child who's upset that someone trod on her art project.

"I'm sorry, angel." Tyrant sounds like he really means it.

He reaches behind the seat, unzips a bag, and pulls out a black singlet of the kind ripped men usually wear to the gym. He pulls it on, and it does an excellent job showing off his muscles and the tattoos on his shoulders and biceps. Tyrant is definitely one of those ripped men.

"I'll wear this. You can wear my shirt home."

He fishes it out of his suit jacket and hands it to me. My curious fingers stroke the fabric, parsing the thread count. The materials. It feels very new and expensive. Tyrant keeps stroking my hair as I study the garment. His thumb caresses my ankle.

I love that he buys good shirts. Someone who looks as handsome as he does should wear clothes that complement his luscious appearance. I don't care about the brand or the designer, but I adore the perfect topstitching across the shoulders. The inky black buttons. The beautiful tailoring.

When I look up, there's a smile on Tyrant's lips. For a moment I think he's laughing at me, but while he's amused at me studying his shirt so closely, his eyes are gentle.

"I'm getting jealous of my shirt, angel. I wish you'd admire me half as much."

I sit up, pull the shirt on, and button it up. I admire him a thousand times as much as this shirt, which makes up ninety-nine percent of my problems. Tyrant's shirt feels as good as it looks, and it smells just like he does. A cold, sharp, and dangerous scent. Razor blades and freezing wind off a forested mountain, overlaid with dark berries. The shirt is enormous on me, and I roll the cuffs back past my wrists.

Just then, his cum starts to slip out of me. I squeak and tightly cross my legs.

A smirk crosses Tyrant's lips and he spreads his arm along the back seat behind me. "Don't worry about it leaking out. You should be pregnant by now."

"I'm worried about your car." The black leather is pristine. It's a crime to make a mess on it.

"Then let me clean you up." Tyrant opens the center console and fishes out some tissues.

I realize he means to wipe me himself, and I reach for them. "I can do it."

He holds the tissues out of my reach. "Of course you can. But I want to."

He *wants* to? No one ever wants to take care of me. They only ever do it grudgingly. I'm still gazing at him in shock when he loops an arm around my waist, pulling me atop his strong thighs with my back against his broad chest.

His lips are against my ear. "Open your legs for me."

Cautiously, I do as I'm told.

He spreads me open with his fingers and slowly dabs me with the tissues. My eyelashes flutter, and I take a heavy breath. This feels even more intimate than having sex with him.

When he draws his hand away, we both see that there's a smear of cum on his middle finger. He holds it to my lips. "Suck."

I open my mouth, and he pushes his finger inside. My lips close around him, and I taste him, musky and sweet. He's watching me with laser focus while my eyes are half closed.

"Have you thought about having my cock in your mouth, angel?" he murmurs huskily, his hot breath in my ear. "I think you'd feel wonderful with your mouth full of me. Look how relaxed you're getting just from my finger."

We sit like that for so long, my body warm and liquid in his arms while he fucks my mouth with his finger. I want to fall asleep like this. I want him to hold me close all night while his finger is in my mouth. His other hand is palming my belly, so large and warm as he holds me close. I drift off on warm, relaxed thoughts.

Eventually, I realize that I've been cuddled into him for an embarrassingly long time, and I nearly fell asleep. I pull his finger from my mouth and sit up. "Sorry. You must want to go. I'll get my things."

"I don't want to be anywhere but here."

I find my underwear and yank them up my legs, not looking at him.

"One of these days, I'll make you believe that I crave to take care of you, angel."

One of these days, my brain won't short-circuit at the sight of Tyrant Mercer. That day can't come soon enough.

Once I'm dressed with Tyrant's shirt tucked into my pleated skirt, I put my hand on the door handle. "You don't have to worry about your kink turning into something real. I'll go and fix this like I did the other times."

Tyrant's eyes narrow. "Excuse me?"

"I'm going to the pharmacy to take care of our mistake." I'll have to face the judgmental gaze of the pharmacist yet again. I think I'll go to a different place this time so I don't turn inside out from shame.

"What do you mean, like you did the other times? You took Plan B?"

"Of course I took Plan B," I tell him, confusion mounting in my chest.

Tyrant pushes his hands through his hair and curses loudly, anger blazing in his eyes.

People don't want to be tied to you after they get what they want. All the things he said and did just now were just sex talk. Weren't they?

From the outraged expression on Tyrant's face, I'm beginning to question that.

Tyrant looms closer until he has me pressed against the door. "Listen very closely, Vivienne. If you go to a doctor or a drug store, if you even look at a Plan B pill, I'll know, and I'll be very fucking angry with you."

CHAPTER FOUR

Tyrant

Vivienne's pretty, fuck-me mouth falls open. "My life is a mess. I'm a mess. Getting pregnant is the last thing I need."

It's exactly what she needs because once I have my baby in her, she'll start running to me instead of away from me. I'm the only man who can protect her and love her and give her everything that's missing.

"Then you shouldn't have let me see you with a baby in your arms." I roll down the window and shout for Liam. A moment later, he gets into the driver's seat. "Take us to Miss Stone's dormitory."

"Yes, sir."

As we drive, Vivienne turns away from me on the seat and hugs herself. It starts to rain and drops patter on the windows. All is darkness out there, occasionally lit by streetlights. The area around

Henson University is darkly gothic with the occasional coffee bar and secondhand bookshop closed for the night.

When we pull up to her dormitory, she tries to get out of the car without saying goodbye.

I grasp her good arm and pull her back to me. "Give your boyfriend a kiss good night." I growl the words like a threat.

"You're not my—"

I slam my mouth over hers. She's right, I'm not her boyfriend. I'm her lover. Her stalker. Her obsessed future husband and the father of her children. I'm the only one who gives a damn about her, but I shouldn't be the only one. How fucking dare the other people in her life neglect her so much and make her so miserable. The thought makes me so angry that I'm snarling when I break the kiss. "Get inside where it's safe. There are bad people on these streets."

Vivienne gives me a look that says she knows all about the bad people in Henson, and gets out of my car with reddened lips, a reddened ass, and her insides coated with my cum. I watch her until she's entered the door code and is safely inside her building,

"Park up ahead. I want to visit the pharmacies around here. Could you arrange for that body to be collected and disposed of while I'm gone?"

"Yes, sir. And that's already done, sir."

Liam drives up the street, and my gaze falls on the car seat. Vivienne has left a smear of her cum and mine on the leather. I smile to myself. This girl is going to be pregnant and completely protected by me in no time. No more shitty dorm rooms and scrimping to save for art supplies. Liam can drive her to class, and she can have a whole set of rooms in my house for her creativity, if that's what she wants. In between having my children. I don't want just one. I want her almost constantly pregnant for five years. That will do to start with, and then I can think about breeding her some more.

Liam pulls up by a pharmacy and, whistling to myself, I get out of the car. It's dark and the temperature has plummeted, and I don't see another soul except for the young man behind the counter.

Inside, I saunter up to the counter with my hands in my pockets, my posture relaxed. I always feel so good after fucking Vivienne. The way that girl comes on my dick? I'm addicted. Knowing she's safely tucked inside her bedroom full of my cum? Even better.

"Plan B, please," I say to the young pharmacist. Oliver—his name tag reads Oliver—has spots on his cheeks and the greenish neon lighting isn't doing his complexion any favors. He must have graduated about six minutes ago by the looks of him.

Oliver glances up at me, his gaze bored. His expression suddenly sharpens into shock and then fear as his eyes travel over my smirking face, my slicked-back hair, and my tattooed arms and chest in my gym tank top.

Oliver swallows. "Um. How—how long since you and your partner had unprotected sex?"

I glance at my watch. "About fifteen minutes ago."

The pharmacist is staring at something on my throat. I swipe at it with my fingers and see dried blood.

"Oh, this? It's not her blood. Not all of it anyway. Don't worry, I'm having things cleaned up." My smile widens. "I wouldn't want Henson to get a bad reputation."

A little joke between him and me.

The pharmacist doesn't laugh.

I kid, but without me, Henson would be in deep shit. The mayor of this town is corrupt, and so are the police. The cops are so busy taking bribes and wiping the asses of the men who are supposed to be in charge that they have no time to keep the car thieves, drug dealers, and burglars in line, or take care of the psychos, serial killers, and rapists who are drawn to Henson because they think that here they'll find easy prey.

I keep the crime in Henson organized. If it wasn't for me, things would be chaotic, but am I thanked for my service? Of course I'm not. Everyone fears me.

Which is exactly what I want from them.

The pharmacist stares hard at his keyboard. "Has your partner taken Plan B before?"

My smile widens. "She's not my partner. Yet. For some reason, this sweet little thing seems to be afraid of me. Do you have any dating tips?"

Oliver mumbles. "Sorry, I'm not good with girls. There's, um, blood on your mouth."

I run my tongue across my teeth, remembering the sweet, metallic tang of Vivienne's blood and the expression of shock in her eyes as I licked it up and swallowed it down. I meant what I told her all those weeks ago. Her blood is just for me.

"No tips? Just the Plan B, then."

Oliver places the packet on the counter in front of me, and I glare at it. Vivienne has taken this fucking pill multiple times behind my back. I pick it up and crumple it in my fist, the plastic pill tray inside popping and cracking. Destroying the pill completely and crushing it to dust.

I drop it back on the counter. "Thank you. Now give me your entire stock."

Oliver gives me a confused look. "What? Why?"

"Because I say so."

The pharmacist hesitates, but only for a fraction of a second before turning around and pulling out a box full of pill packets and placing it on the counter.

"How long will it take you to restock these?" I ask, chucking the destroyed packet into the box and putting the whole thing under my arm.

"About a week."

That will be too late for Vivienne to take a morning-after pill. Perfect. I pull out my wallet, drop a stack of bills on the counter, and turn away.

The young pharmacist can't help his professional disapproval bleeding into his voice as he calls after me, "There are safer and more effective forms of birth control if you and your partner wish to prevent pregnancy."

"Prevent pregnancy? She's not taking these. I'm burning them." I turn back and fish around in my pocket for a copy of Vivienne's university photo and place it on the counter. "If this young woman comes in here looking to buy contraception, you tell her that you have nothing to sell her. You can't help her. No contraceptive pills. No condoms. No spermicide. Unless…" I beckon the man closer, and he leans toward me. I seethe in his face, "Unless next time you'd like it to be your blood all over me?"

The pharmacist jerks back and shakes his head rapidly.

I smile at the young man. "I didn't think so."

There's a stand by the door with a series of cartoon faces from sad to happy and the question, *How Was Your Experience Today?*

I stab the green smiley face with my finger on my way out. "Excellent customer service. Have a lovely evening, Oliver."

I visit five pharmacies around the university and then call it a night. When I get back into my car, I throw half a dozen carrier bags full of Plan B pills into the trunk. I hope no young couples are making mistakes in the dorms around Henson University for the next week, or their babies are going to be courtesy of Tyrant Mercer.

As I get into the back seat, my night just keeps getting better. I can still smell the sex I had with Vivienne, and I receive a text message from one of my enforcers that I've been waiting months for.

Located Lucas Jones. Yancy Street basement.

Lucas fucking Jones, the piece of shit that I've been dying to get my hands on for months. I clench my phone in victory and then type a quick reply, telling my man that he's done a fucking wonderful job and there'll be an extra twenty thousand in his pay this month.

Liam is waiting expectantly in the driver's seat for my instructions. "Take us to the Yancy Street club."

"Yes, sir." He starts the SUV and makes a U-turn, heading toward the west side of Henson.

I can't help my malevolent grin as I settle back on the seat. "Matteo found Lucas Jones."

"That's wonderful news, sir."

Fifteen minutes later we pull up on a street with an auto-repair shop, an electrical warehouse, and a diner closed for the night. Between the diner and the warehouse is a non-descript heavy metal door, scuffed and dented from years of patrons going in and out.

The Yancy Street club was the third one I ever opened, at twenty-one years of age. It was my headquarters for years before they moved to the more upscale Larch Avenue club, but I still have a lot of affection for this place, and the basement rooms are in steady use. I don't like spilling excessive amounts of blood in the Larch Avenue club. It's a bitch to get it out of the expensive carpets. But the concrete floor here? A few buckets of water sluiced over them and it's like no one ever died.

As I approach the metal door, the bouncer within sees me through the spyhole and opens up. "Good evening, Mr. Mercer."

Music is coming from down the corridor along with the sound of people talking and laughing. Officially, this place is a legally run bar, but it's the illegal gambling rooms beyond that make money. People win and lose tens of thousands of dollars here every night. Mostly lose, as everyone knows things are weighed in the house's favor. People like Vivienne's father. It was in this club that he ruined his family, and because of that, I met my beloved.

Then I discovered all the pain she was wearing on her skin because of her family.

And a man called Lucas Jones.

Downstairs and through a locked door, the basement is dim and quiet, apart from a steady drip echoing off the concrete and the buzz and flicker of an old neon bulb. Jones is tied to a chair in the middle of the room, beaten and bloodied and dressed in a tattered T-shirt. Sandy hair is falling into his eyes. He lifts his head and he peers through it as he hears me approach through the shadows.

"Wh-who's there?" he calls in a quavering voice.

I step into the light, and his mouth drops open. He rears back in his chair, shaking his head. "No. Please. *Please.*"

We've never met. I haven't even told him why he's here. Apparently his guilty conscience is eating at him because seeing me has confirmed his worst fears.

He's going to die tonight, and it's going to be painful.

Taking my time, I remove my jacket and hang it on a hook. There's a length of heavy chain on the floor, the links almost the size of my fists. I pick it up and begin rotating a few feet of it in my right hand, faster and faster until it's whirling in a blur.

Jones is whimpering and shaking his head. "Please, Mr. Mercer. I don't—"

The first thing I want is for him to shut the fuck up. I lash the heavy chain across his face at such speed that teeth and blood explode from his mouth. Jones's head whips to one side, and blood drips into his lap as he whimpers and sobs.

Relishing the sight of him so wretched with pain, I draw the chain slowly through my fingers and spin it again. It's not one of my typical weapons, but it's so very satisfying on the right person.

The chain is heavy enough to inflict a lot of painful damage, but not so brutal that it will kill my victim in a handful of blows. I'm going to draw this out as long as possible. Make him suffer like Vivienne has suffered.

Using the chain, I break Jones's arms and ribs. Tear off an ear. Dislodge one of his eyes from its socket. He thought he could get away with the things he's done in my city. When I crack his shin bone, it's satisfying knowing he'll never walk again.

He screams every time the heavy links strike his body. Gasping in pain, he cries, "Why are you doing this?"

I don't have to explain myself to a piece of meat.

Another strike breaks his nose and lacerates his cheek, and he overbalances in the chair and topples onto his side. The pain makes him pass out for a few minutes, and he loses control of himself, urinating on the floor. When he awakens, I'm standing over him with the bloody chain in both my hands. He actually cries for his mommy. Pathetic.

With his dying, gurgling breath, he whispers, "Was one of them your daughter? Your girlfriend?"

I stand on his throat and lean in close. "She's the mother of my children. Rot in hell, you piece of shit. Pray I don't die too soon, because when I follow you down there, I'm going to rip your soul into tiny, painful little pieces while you scream in agony for the rest of eternity."

I raise the chain, whirling it again, and then slam it down on his skull.

Slowly, the light dies from his remaining good eye. I'm covered in sweat and blood spray. Watching my enemies die normally gives my mood a boost for the rest of the day, but I feel nothing but seething hatred for the corpse lying on the concrete floor.

It's not *enough*.

I can't undo what's already been done, and that's agony.

"Liam," I shout, and throw the chain aside.

Liam comes into the room with a basin of water and a towel over his arm, and I wash my hands and face. The water quickly turns red. To tell Vivienne about this, or not? Once we're together with my ring on her finger, my baby in her belly, and the rest of my plan falling into place, I will tell her. My fierce, sweet girl will put the past behind her and be ready for our future.

I smile with satisfaction when I remember that my baby could already be in her belly.

"Alan Merrick is in the club tonight, and he wishes to meet with you," Liam announces.

I shake the bloodied water from my fingers and push them through my hair. Merrick. Merrick. Oh, yes, one of the town council members. I doubt I'm interested in what he has to say, but I'm not too busy to tell him to fuck off.

Upstairs in the main bar, I take a seat at my usual table and the bartender sends over a whisky. Not three minutes later, a man in a gray suit and a cheap blue tie tries to approach, but a bouncer steps in his way. Alan Merrick gives me a hopeful smile.

I incline my head, and the bouncer lets him through. As he draws closer and catches sight of me in the dim light, his obsequious smile falters.

I glance at myself in the mirror opposite my table. I'm wearing my black gym tank. There's blood spatter on my throat and arms. Cigar smoke curls around my blood-streaked face. I smile at my reflection. It does people good to remember that I'm always ready and willing to get my hands dirty.

Merrick clears his throat. "Have I caught you at a bad time, Mr. Mercer?"

I tap my cigar on the edge of an ashtray. "I've been having a wonderful time." I gesture at a chair before me, and he sits down.

The councilor wastes no time in getting to the point. "Are you thinking about getting married, Mr. Mercer?"

My smile widens as I remember thrusting deep inside Vivienne as she climaxed on my dick.

An enormous fucking diamond. That will be her engagement ring. "Why, as a matter of fact, I am."

His expression brightens. "That's wonderful, because I have just the woman for you." He launches into singing the praises of some daughter of his, but the smile has dropped from my face and I'm already not listening.

"...and if you like the sound of her, I can arrange for you to meet. What do you think, Mr. Mercer?"

It was a mistake for him to sit down at my table and talk to me as if Vivienne Stone doesn't exist.

"Any family who wants me for a son-in-law must be crazy." I draw on my cigar and let the smoke curl around my lips. "Or desperate."

Merrick forces a dismissive chuckle. "There's no desperation, Mr. Mercer. I'm an ambitious man. I'm sure you can understand that, given how similar we are."

He and I are nothing alike. I built everything I have with my own bloodied hands. It sounds like he hopes to steal power for himself via wedding vows and his daughter's future.

"You want to be the mayor," I guess, examining my cigar.

Merrick smooths his tie with a modest smile. "My only aspirations are to serve the people of Henson."

He can't even be honest about a simple fucking question.

"And how am I supposed to help you become the mayor?" When he opens his mouth to protest, I point my cigar at him. "Don't waste my time. Be straight with me or fuck off."

Merrick clears his throat and nods. "You have legitimate businesses. I have legitimate business interests. We can help each other. We can become closer. My eldest daughter is nineteen, and very beautiful."

He holds out his phone. I don't look at the screen, though presumably it shows an image of his daughter.

"I'm not interested," I tell him stonily.

"But you must want a family, Mr. Mercer. A man of your age with no children? You won't live forever."

Until recently, I would have laughed in his face. All these years, I've never wanted a family. My own father disappeared when I was fourteen, emptying the bank accounts and leaving us destitute. It was just my struggling mother, me, and four younger siblings. Mom couldn't work because of the voices in her head, and so we lost our home and moved into a trailer park that was freezing cold and infested with rats and human scum. I found work as a delivery boy and then an enforcer with the crew that used to run the dark side of Henson. I did so well that I took over at age eighteen in a violent coup with a group of loyal men at my back. Since then, my two brothers got married. One works in construction, the other in real estate. One of my sisters is an actress and the other manages my finances. I got my hands dirty so they didn't have to.

Throughout my twenties, I never wanted a family because I'd already raised one.

All this time, I've been my own man, and a woman and children would have only slowed me down. Women are always crying and they hate the sight of blood and violence. Then I met Vivienne, a woman who grabs hold of knives by the blade and can be as ferocious as I can and yet achingly innocent at the same time. Who knew that was my kryptonite. I sure as fuck didn't.

Merrick offers me his phone again. "Just look at a picture of her. She's beautiful."

I knock it onto the table without looking at the screen. He could be showing me an orgy of Victoria's Secret models and I wouldn't be interested. Under different circumstances, I might have considered the daughter of an assassin, a murderer, or a scam artist, but I'm not getting cozy with a politician. There is a fucking line.

I jerk my head at the bouncer, a sign to get this man out of here, and he moves forward to stand behind Merrick. My companion gets to his feet with an expression of tight-lipped anger.

"My little bunny will be devastated. She had her heart set on marrying you."

His little bunny is not my problem. I don't trust anyone but myself to make decisions about my future. Even if I did trust some people, I wouldn't trust Alan fucking Merrick.

The matter of my marriage and my future is settled. I'm having Vivienne or no one.

CHAPTER FIVE

Vivienne

When I wake up in the morning, I gaze longingly at my sewing machine that's crowded into one corner of my tiny bedroom. Pieces of a poet blouse are lying over the back of a chair waiting for the moment I can sew them together. It's half past five, and Carly or Julia will hammer on the walls and tell me to knock it off if they hear the *chunk chunk chunk* of my sewing machine before seven a.m. I'm lucky that my only two friends live on either side of my room because otherwise, the dorms would feel incredibly lonely, so I do my best to keep the noise down.

Either I'm going to lie in bed and think about Tyrant Mercer and fret about being pregnant, or I'm going to get up and find a way to distract myself.

I end up sitting on the floor in silky pajama shorts and a camisole top, hand-sewing the hem of a long, cream skirt. It's my favorite type of garment. Romantic enough to feel like I'm wearing a costume, but not so outlandish that people will stare at me and wonder if I made a wrong turn from the Renaissance fair.

My whole body is sore. My forearm from the knife cut. My arms and shoulders where they were grabbed and restrained. My core from Tyrant's brutal, deep fucking. It's impossible not to think about Tyrant and the things he said, and my hand drifts over my belly. I imagine wearing this skirt over a baby bump. The fabric is cut on the bias so it has some give to it. In my mind's eye, a larger hand covers mine on the bump. A hand decorated with ink with a heavy silver ring on its pinkie. I feel a presence behind me as if the mattress I'm propped against has turned into Tyrant himself, and I imagine him pressing a hungry kiss to the nape of my neck.

I go back to sewing in such a hurry that I stab the side of my forefinger with the needle. "Ow."

Sucking on the bead of blood that's formed, trepidation swirls in my belly as I remember what Tyrant growled at me last night. *You're only allowed to bleed for me.* Here I am breaking his rules again.

He doesn't have to know, he couldn't possibly find out, and yet breaking that rule again cranks up my anxiety. Reaching for my phone, I type a message and send it. I don't expect a reply at 6 a.m. but one comes through almost immediately.

Me: *I'm bleeding.*
Tyrant: *I'm coming to the dorms.*
Me: *Wait. It was an accident. I stabbed myself with a sewing needle.*
Tyrant: *Show me.*

I take a picture of the tiny wound and send it to him. His reply comes back a moment later.

Tyrant: *Good girl for telling me.*

Tyrant: *Bad girl for going to a pharmacy last night. I'm going to punish you for that.*

My eyes widen. Tyrant knows about that? How does he know? When I went out again at half past eleven, the streets were deserted. I was sure no one was watching as I went into the late-night pharmacy. The pharmacist was no help. He claimed that they were out of stock of Plan B. Who runs out of Plan B in a university district where young people are making mistakes left and right?

Come to think of it, the pharmacist was sweating. Suddenly I realize who probably bought up all the Plan B pills.

I read Tyrant's message and feel a thrill. *I'm going to punish you for that.* He knows what I crave. A little pain to even me out. My arm was throbbing last night, but it was him putting me over his knee and spanking me that gave me the pure bliss of relief and made me brave enough to reveal my repulsive, scarred body to him. I wish there was a way to explain to my family that Tyrant is the only man who is monstrous enough to see past my ugliness. If they knew I'd even talked to him, they'd forbid me from ever seeing Barlow again. If they found out he was trying to get me pregnant…I shudder to think what Dad would do.

Pushing that horrendous thought away, I pick up my sewing once more and lean back against my mattress.

I like it here in my little room, hushed and secluded from the world. As I work, the sun creeps over the horizon and shines through the golden leaves of the enormous old tree outside my window. The cork boards fixed to my walls are covered in scraps of fabric and drawings that I hope to turn into costume projects for class or clothes for me to wear. On my bed is a quilt sewn from dozens of different fabrics. Pale golds, creams, and purples. All thrifted fabrics and old clothing that I cut up and repurposed. I never had nice things growing up, so I make them instead. I take care of them. I become lost in them as my needle dips in and out of the fabric.

I'm so absorbed in my work that I don't realize how late it's getting until I look at my phone and realize I only have fifteen minutes to get ready and make it to class. I gasp in shock and shoot to my feet.

Eleven minutes later, I fly out of the dorm while pulling a vintage knitted sweater over my head. I have an art history tutorial this morning and my tutor, Colleen, gives me a pained look as I hurry into the classroom and find my seat.

All last year she chided me for never making it to her classes on time. No doubt she's thrilled that I'm back for another, more advanced, semester.

We're focusing on post-war art for the next few weeks, and my classmates and I watch as she shows photographs of paintings by Lucian Freud, Francis Bacon, and Frida Kahlo on the large screen at the front of the room.

"What is Kahlo trying to say with this piece?" Colleen asks the class.

The room is sunk in *it's-way-too-early-for-this* apathy.

I make the mistake of meeting Colleen's eyes, and she seizes the opportunity to punish me for my late arrival. "Vivienne. What do you think?"

I don't think. I know. The painting is called *The Wounded Deer*, and it depicts a deer with Frida Kahlo's head and antlers running through a forest. The deer's chest and side are pierced with arrows.

"She's telling us what life is about."

Colleen gives me an encouraging nod. "Please go on. What's Kahlo saying about life with this piece?"

I glance at the arrows buried in the deer's flank. The blood flows into her fur, letting the pain out. Proving that she exists. "Pain is evidence we're alive."

I expect Colleen to nod or make some bland comment before moving on, but she hesitates, and her expression grows troubled. It's the same look she gave me after I wrote an essay last semester about the implicit violence in still lifes of fruit. How am I meant not to see bloodshed in pictures of gashed open plums and knives covered in red, sticky juice?

"One might argue that pain isn't evidence that we're alive. Love is," Colleen says.

Laughter bubbles up my throat and bursts out of my mouth. That's a good one. Love makes us feel alive? I've been painfully aware I'm alive my whole life, not lovingly aware. Besides, when was the last time we even mentioned love in this tutorial? Every painting we study is about tragedy, blood, violence, despair.

In other words, life.

That's the way things are, not the way we pretend they are on birthday cards or in ads for cell phones or Christmas movies. It's the reason I'm studying art history. All the despair. Hashtag relatable.

Colleen doesn't laugh with me. Neither does anyone else in class.

"Oh, you're serious." I glance left and right and realize everyone's giving me strange looks. Have I given too much away about myself by mistake? Is everyone realizing what a weirdo I am? I hug my ribs with both arms. It feels like all my carefully concealed scars are suddenly on display. My tutor looks more worried than ever.

"Kahlo painted *The Wounded Deer* toward the end of her life," intones a bored-sounding student behind me. "She'd been cheated on by her husband and was in chronic pain from a bus accident when she was younger. She was witnessing the breakdown of her aging body. The arrows represent her suffering."

Colleen hurries to praise the student for their answer, but I fail to see how it's meaningfully different from mine. Life is suffering? That's what I said.

The class moves on, but I'm still turning over what Colleen said about love being evidence that we're alive. I didn't feel very loved when my mother left me alone in a dark, empty house for hours and days on end. There's no love in the dark.

At the end of the tutorial, Colleen asks me to stay behind. She leans against the desk while I stand awkwardly in front of her, clutching my satchel.

"Is there anything troubling you, Vivienne?"

Tyrant's wicked smile flashes before my eyes. "Nothing different from usual."

She folds her arms and sighs. "I'm worried about you. Your interpretations of artistic intent are growing darker and darker."

"Are you talking about *The Wounded Deer*? It was just one answer."

"Every essay you've written for me is about pain, or how suffering is the only emotion that can be trusted."

I frown at her. "That's not true. I wrote an essay about the joy expressed in Millais's *Ophelia*."

"Vivienne," Colleen sighs, sounding exasperated. "Your thesis was that she was happy because she was about to die. If you wore black clothes and heavy eyeliner I'd presume that you were a tortured romantic or going through a nihilistic phase, but I'm worried this is something serious."

I'm not a goth girl, so she's going to interfere in my life? That seems unfair.

"Have you thought about talking to someone?"

I answer without thinking. "A therapist? But I'm fine now."

Colleen raises her eyebrows.

Shit. I said I'm fine *now*. I just narced on myself by admitting that I've had problems in the past. Heat and energy rise through my body. Colleen is trying to stir up trouble when what I want is to be left alone. I'm not about to kill myself if that's what she's afraid of. I have plenty of goals and plans for the future. I never cut so deep that there's no going back.

Outside the tutorial room, I spot Carly and Julia waving to me over Colleen's shoulder. I forgot that we're supposed to be having coffee together, but I'm instantly relieved that I have a reason to leave.

"Sorry, I've got to go." I grasp the strap of my satchel and walk out of the room. Colleen calls out my name, but I ignore her and walk quickly down the hall with my friends.

"What's going on there? Is your tutor giving you a hard time?"

Carly asks with a concerned frown.

Visions of knives are dancing in my mind. I remember how joyous I felt in the cemetery, snatching at that boy's knife. I wish I'd grabbed hold of it and sliced my palm open.

I tuck my hair behind my ear. "It's nothing. She just doesn't like my interpretation of her favorite paintings." Forcing a smile and a brighter tone, I add, "The sun's out. Let's sit on the grass while we drink our coffee."

All day, I pretend to myself that Colleen's questioning and judgmental looks don't bother me, but they cling to my body like a fog I can't shake off. She wanted to know if something was troubling me, and I could have told her about Tyrant. I could have said, *Tyrant Mercer has been forcing me into his car and fucking me raw, and I'm never sure if I said I wanted it to happen. He doesn't care if I want it to happen.* That would have made her sanctimonious eyes widen, and she would have reported him immediately to the college and the police. But Tyrant's not the problem.

I'm the problem.

Everyone knows messed-up people snap together like magnets. My mess is sad girl shit. Tyrant's mess is intestines and bullets. He's feeding on my vulnerabilities, but he didn't cause them. He's the only good thing that my damage has given me. The rest has been blood, pain, tears, and loneliness. My mess has given me a beautiful man who holds me down and fucks me hard, and I'm supposed to be a good girl and open my arms to suffering instead of to him?

The man wants a baby. Maybe I should give him one.

"Wicked child," I whisper to myself, climbing the stairs to my dorm room and shaking my head. Everyone knows you're not supposed to surrender to the bad guy even one little bit. "Wicked, wicked child."

I get out my sketchbook and sit cross-legged on the floor. In pencil, I sketch the figure of a girl who resembles me, only she has a swollen, pregnant belly and bigger breasts. She has her hand on her belly.

The drawing looks good, but it's not perfect. It's missing something I've been daydreaming about, and I add another, larger hand over the girl's. A masculine, tattooed hand.

I stare at the drawing for a few minutes, and then throw it aside and scrub my hands over my face. What would make me feel better is getting out my little box and scoring a few cuts into my flesh. As I think about the blades, I feel the ghost of a strong, tattooed hand around my throat, and it's squeezing hard. Tyrant wouldn't like finding fresh cuts on my body. The only blood I'm supposed to shed is for him. I imagine him forcing the pointed end of a knife beneath my jaw as he unzips his fly, growling at me to hold fucking still or he'll slit my throat. Wetness and heat surge between my legs. My fingers slip over my stomach and curl around my inner thigh, before slipping into my underwear. I moan and writhe against my fingers.

It doesn't take long for me to get there, but the climax feels empty and so do I. The most frustrating part is I know exactly who I'm missing, and he doesn't only leave me satisfied, he pushes me over a terrifying precipice and then holds me safe in his strong arms.

Tyrant's not here, so I crawl into bed, pull the blankets over my head, and close my eyes.

In my sleep, I'm vaguely aware of the sensation of something being forced inside me. Something thick that stretches me, and I moan softly as my dreaming brain shows me Tyrant braced above me in my mind's eye. The dangerous man who stalks me is fucking me so carefully in my dreams.

Tyrant pulls back and thrusts deeper, jolting my body. It feels so vivid. The pleasure-pain is so sharp and sweet.

This is a dream, right? I rise up through layers of sleep, my eyelashes fluttering. I'm paralyzed by my sleepy brain and the heavy heat and weight on my body.

A deep, husky voice murmurs somewhere over my head, "Shh. Go back to sleep, angel. It's just a dream."

I'm only dreaming that Tyrant's thick cock is pumping in and out of me. Filling me to stretching and then easing back again. It must be because I fell asleep masturbating to him. My eyes settle closed, and I drift off again. Dream Tyrant feels so good that my breathing grows heavy and an aching pleasure fills my body.

I move my jaw but I can't open my mouth. There's something gagging me. When I squirm a little, trying to pull the sheet or whatever it is away from my mouth, I find I can't because my hands are pinned behind my back.

There's heavy panting over my head. "Oh, fuck yes, angel. So tight. Such a good girl."

I drag my eyes open, but I can't tell if I'm still dreaming or not because it's so dark. I try to say, *Tyrant?* but it comes out as, "Mm-mm?"

"I couldn't wait until you were awake. I saw this pussy, and I had to start fucking you." Tyrant groans as he works his cock deeper, and then he gives a soft, malicious laugh. "After I pulled your clothes off. And gagged you. And tied you up. With so many people in this building, I couldn't have you screaming. Everyone might run to help you before I've finished with you."

I squirm against my bonds. Rub my cheek against the pillow to get the gag out of my mouth. It doesn't work, and I can't move. I'm pinned on my stomach with my thighs spread. Tyrant's knees are between my thighs, forcing me wider as he drives his cock into me. His hands are on either side of my head, and my body sinks deeper and deeper into the mattress with every thrust.

His breathing is getting harder, and he seethes in my ear, "You're so pretty, my helpless little slut. All tied up and taking my cock."

Pleasure shoots through me at his degrading words, and I melt into the mattress.

Use me. Make me feel like there's a point to my existence, even if it's just as a hole for you to fuck. My window is open, and a fresh wind is blowing inside. Tyrant must have climbed the tree and broken in through the window. There's CCTV everywhere around the building. The man really is crazy.

My body melts into the ropes binding me. The gag between my teeth feels like it lives there. My eyes grow heavy lidded.

Tyrant groans under his breath as he feels my body surrender. He fists his hand in my hair and holds it brutally tight. "That's it, angel. Just relax and let me breed you. I'm going to shoot my load so deep inside you and keep it there."

I forgot to try and get another Plan B pill, and Tyrant's about to come inside me yet again. When I squirm and struggle, he only fucks me harder.

"Still fighting me on this? You're not going anywhere. You're going to lie there and take my cock and think about how much better your life is going to be when you belong to me, totally and utterly. I've been merciful until now, Vivienne, and you haven't even thanked me. Now I'm done. Being. *Merciful.*" He emphasizes these words with vicious thrusts of his cock.

Merciful? He calls turning my life upside down merciful? My life was quiet before he invaded my home and stole Barlow away. Now it's chaotic, and I'm sinking deeper and deeper into the chaos with every stroke of his thick shaft. My core is blazing with pleasure around him. I'm tightening and tightening on his length and when he feels it, he utters a victorious groan.

"You love it when I'm cruel to you, angel," he seethes in my ear. "You love me controlling every little thing about your life. I'm the only one who can protect you. I'm the only one who gives a damn about you. Feel my cock? Feel those ropes? You're so fucking protected."

Tyrant forces my knees wider and his cock deeper, and I shatter around him.

As I climax, he hammers into me faster and harder than ever, making the bed shake and thud against the wall. Tyrant doesn't seem to give a damn about being heard now. He comes with a brutal thrust of his cock and a snarled curse.

He stills but doesn't pull out, and he traces his fingers over the spot where we're joined.

"So full of me, angel. My cock, my cum. Beautiful."

A warm feeling swells through me, and I close my eyes.

Tyrant pulls out and spreads me open. He rubs his thumb over my lips again and again as if admiring the sight. "Oh, fuck yes. That's a well-used pussy." Then he shoves himself back inside me again. "Hold still. I'm getting you pregnant this time."

In the silence that follows, there's a knocking on my door and someone calls, "Vivienne? Are you okay in there?"

I feel Tyrant glance toward the door. That's Julia out there. If she comes in here and sees Tyrant, it won't be good for her. I don't know what Tyrant would do to someone who tries to stop him from doing exactly what he wants to do.

Tyrant hooks a finger into my gag and moves it away from my mouth. "Scream for help if you want to."

A man has forced his way into my bedroom, tied me up, and started screwing me in my sleep. I should be screaming the place down.

"I-I'm fine. Sorry about the noise," I call, sounding more than a little shaky and out of breath. "I was just, um, doing some yoga."

"Okay. Talk to you later." Footsteps retreat down the corridor.

Tyrant laughs under his breath. "I'm yoga now?"

His hands are braced on either side of my head, and I watch the thick vein on his arm and the muscles of his forearm flexing.

"Can I have the gag back, please?" I miss the comforting fullness in my mouth.

"Of course you can, angel," he murmurs lovingly and pushes the gag back into place. My eyes slowly close. Bliss. Trussed up, mouth full, and pinned down by Tyrant's cock is the safest I've felt in a long time.

"What's this?"

I crack open an eye as I feel the bed shift. Tyrant has leaned down and picked up something off the floor. It's my sketchbook, which I left open to the drawing of my pregnant belly and his hand covering mine. I couldn't reach out and snatch it away from him even if I wanted to.

"Angel, this is fucking beautiful," he breathes.

I feel Tyrant's cock swell inside me. He drops the sketchbook and grasps my hips, surging deeper. He hasn't even pulled out and he's going again. Lowering himself onto his elbows, he pushes his hand beneath my body and his fingertip grazes my clit.

Lips against my ear, he groans in an achingly horny voice, "I'm going to make everything perfect for you, angel. You and this baby are going to have everything you want. All you have to do is give me your life and soul when I ask for it. Are you ready for that? Never question me. Never doubt me. Do everything I say, and I'll give you everything you want."

I moan against the gag, his voice and his fingers driving me headlong into pleasure.

Tyrant laughs softly and runs his tongue along my throat. "Of course you will. You're Tyrant's good girl, aren't you?"

Tyrant's good girl is being helplessly fucked into the mattress. My pussy is tightening hungrily on his cock. I'm whimpering against the gag.

I'm your good girl.

I'm your good girl.

I love being yours.

He fucks me so hard that my bed bashes against the wall, but I'm too far gone to care. Let them all hear. It doesn't matter anymore when I belong to the most dangerous man in Henson. They're all going to find out. They're all going to judge me. The world can't turn its back on me any more than it already has. Tyrant will always be there for me, and he's all I need.

My core lights up, and I cry out into the pillow. Tyrant sinks his teeth into my shoulder with a growl as his thrusts grow sharp and urgent. Warm liquid gushes between my thighs. I'm a slippery mess of my own wetness and two of Tyrant's climaxes.

He pushes himself up and looks down between us, breathing heavily. "You should see me buried inside you, angel. I'm covered in us." Pleased by the sight, he fucks me slowly with his still-hard cock. "I'm so deep inside you. I want to be even deeper."

The aftershocks of my orgasm and his movements have me crying out against my gag as I listen to the wet sounds of his thrusts. He strokes my hair, traces the long line of my spine with his forefinger, and reaches beneath me to squeeze my breasts.

"All mine," he whispers. "Don't do anything to make me angry, and it will always be like this, angel."

I crack open an eye and raise a questioning eyebrow. Make him angry how?

"Exactly. You wouldn't even know how. That should about do it." He pulls out, loosens the bindings on my wrists and the gag around my mouth, and covers me with a blanket. Leaning over me, he whispers in my ear, "If I'd known it was so easy to come in here and fuck you while you sleep, I would have done it months ago."

An illicit shudder goes through me as I wonder if he's going to do the same thing tonight. The next night. And the next night.

"It should take you a few minutes to untie yourself. Lie there and think about me and our baby, angel. I'll be deep inside you all day."

I hear a noise behind me at the window, and then he's gone.

CHAPTER SIX

Vivienne

On Saturday morning, I wake with a gasp of shock that has nothing to do with Tyrant for a change. The university dress-up ball is in one week, and I—a costume design student—have no costume to wear.

I throw the blankets aside and hurry over to my sketchbook, relieved that I have something pressing to distract myself with all weekend. Choose a design, find or create a pattern, buy the fabric, and sew and tailor the dress.

The ball is to celebrate one hundred and fifty years of Henson University. The Performing Arts Department is running the committee, so of course the ball is a masquerade, and the ballroom will be decorated lavishly for the occasion. Part of the college is an old nineteenth-century mansion, and it has a real ballroom where I imagine debutantes took their first hopeful spins around the dance floor.

I've known about the ball for months, but I've agonized over what to wear. I know a lot of the girls are renting frothy, hooped ball gowns or purchasing skintight catsuits, tails, and ears online. Many of the boys will be wearing tuxedos, Zorro capes, or their Halloween costumes.

I turn the pages of my sketchbook, silently begging for inspiration to strike. This is the one thing I should be able to handle easily, and yet my anxiety is doubling by the second.

I glance in fear and longing at the place where my little box of pain and freedom is hidden.

I shake my head and look determinedly at the sketchbook pages. I don't need to do that. I haven't done that in a long time. I don't ever need to do that again, and yet I haven't thrown the box away. For some reason, I can't make myself take the box down to the dumpsters out back and throw it in. Some compulsion always stops me and whispers, *Are you sure you want to do that?*

You should keep it.

Just in case.

My gaze falls on the weeping stone angel that I was drawing last Sunday before I was attacked in the cemetery. I nearly finished the drawing, and the angel stands out in delicate gray pencil on the white page. I even included the name that's carved onto the stone casket. Cecelia Henson, the daughter of Henson University's founder. She died tragically at age twenty, and it's said her family never got over the loss. They commissioned the stone angel to perpetually grieve for their lost daughter.

I trace my fingers over the picture, envious of Cecelia for experiencing love that has endured for over a hundred years.

"Angel," I whisper.

The strange endearment that Tyrant has bestowed on me. God knows why. I neither look nor act in an angelic way. I'm an anxious, frazzled mess most of the time, filled with insecurities. Every time Tyrant vanishes from my life, I become more and more certain that it's the last time I'll ever see him. Someday soon he'll tire of me, and then he'll forget about me like everyone else.

I can't tear my eyes away from my drawing. Maybe I could attend the masquerade as an angel. A weeping stone angel with crystal tears on my mask. If I can find the right fabric for the dress…

I reach for my phone and text Julia and Carly.

Me: *Anyone free to come shopping with me? I think I've decided on my costume.*

Carly: *Finally!! I wish I could but I have to study. *sobbing**

Julia: *I'm with family but I'm so excited to see your costume. It's going to be epic.*

Carly: *Can we see now?*

I text them a photo of my drawing, and they both reply with enthusiasm and heart and angel emojis.

Energized by their excitement, I leap to my feet and grab my washbag, and head for the communal shower room. It's okay that they can't come. I enjoy shopping by myself because that means I get to daydream.

Twenty minutes later, I'm dressed in a short A-line skirt and vintage blazer, a white blouse, and brown brogues, with a lilac beret over my long dark hair for a pop of color. My satchel thumps against my thigh as I hurry down the street. There's a bus that will take me where I'm going, but I wince at the thought of spending nearly five dollars on the round trip when I can barely afford to eat. The sky is overcast, and wet, orange leaves are stuck to the sidewalk, and more fall around me as I cross the road.

My favorite fabric store sometimes has sales on the ends of rolls, and I cross my fingers in my sleeves as I enter the building and begin the hunt for something ethereal and angelic. It's not long before I find a stunning silver-white georgette that flows through my fingers like water.

I check the price on the roll. Ninety dollars a yard. There's forty-two dollars in my bank account. Even if I'd wanted to buy Plan B the other night, I realized when I checked my balance earlier that I wouldn't have been able to afford it.

It's really hard to get pregnant, right? Women agonize for months, even years, about conceiving. I don't know whether that thought lightens my heart or makes it heavier. If I were pregnant, I'd have no choice but to turn up on Tyrant's doorstep and make myself and my baby his responsibility.

Oh yes? says a nasty voice in my mind. *And give him the opportunity to laugh in your face and reject you, wrapped up in a satin bow? He doesn't want to take care of you. He's just horny, and his fetish is unprotected sex.*

Sadly, I put the fabric back and head out of the shop. I guess I'm going back to my usual trick of turning old curtains into clothes.

There's a thrift store down the street, and in this wealthy district, it often has good quality donations that I can upcycle. Inside, my fingers dance across pantsuits and blouses, T-shirts, and jeans. There are probably pieces here and there that would fit me, but I head straight for the back of the store where the home furnishings are. There's a heap of curtains and duvet covers in a large bin, and I dive in with both hands. Polyester chintz curtains. Some blue netting. My fingers brush against something soft and lustrous, and though I can't see it I instinctively grasp hold of it and pull it out.

I can't believe what I'm feeling. What I'm *seeing*. White silk satin, finely woven and glimmering with subtle silver strands. Lots of it as well. Not as much as a set of curtains, but two very long, narrow pieces.

The shop volunteer, an older lady with her glasses around her neck on a gold chain, glances over my shoulder. "Isn't that lovely? A retired wedding planner brought all her props and accessories to donate last week. I think that piece was to hang over an arch where the bride and groom say their vows."

"It's beautiful," I murmur, stroking the fabric. It looks angelic. It even feels angelic.

I check the price tag and see that it's ten dollars. My heart soars. All this beautiful fabric for ten dollars? It's a steal. I bite my lip. This is a charity store, and I'll feel guilty later if I don't say something.

I show the volunteer the price tag. "Are you sure this is priced correctly? It's silk."

"Yes, but it's such an awkward shape, and how many people need to decorate an archway? I've been wondering how we'll get rid of it."

It is awkward, but I could make it work. Perhaps something strappy and backless so it doesn't use too much fabric. There aren't any scars on my back or on my arms. I scored all my cuts into my ribs, where I could wrap my arms around them and hold them tight.

I purchase the fabric and leave the shop, unable to believe my good luck.

As I'm walking down the street, my phone rings, and when I take it out, I see that it's Dad. Happiness flickers through me. Dad hasn't called me since I moved into the Henson dorms. Maybe this is a sign he's ready to mend our relationship.

I press the accept call button and attempt to sound carefree and casual, unlike the desperate and needy that I suddenly feel. "Hi, Dad, how are—"

"What the hell is wrong with you, Vivienne?" His voice is shaking with fury.

I stop dead in the street, my mind racing. There's plenty wrong with me, but his tone makes it sound like there's one specific thing to which he's referring. "Sorry, what do you mean?"

"Come to the house. Now." Dad hangs up.

There's a cold, leaden feeling in my belly as I turn and walk the other way, toward home. My footsteps drag, desperate to avoid the confrontation awaiting me there. I even hesitate and nearly run the other way several times. If I don't have my family as my anchor, then what? I'll be driftless and alone. My father isn't much of a father and Samantha has been a mediocre stepmother, but I'm Barlow's sister. I love being Barlow's sister. I never had anyone to look up to or rely on or love unconditionally, and I desperately want to be that person for him.

The moment I turn onto my street, I stop dead with a gasp of horror and start to shake.

How could they know? No one's supposed to know about us.

Sprayed across the front of the house, in three-foot-high neon orange letters, are two words.

Tyrant's slut.

Blood rushes in my ears. My body feels clammy.

He's said that word to me over and over again as he fucks me.

That's my good little slut.

Who's Tyrant's little slut?

My helpless slut.

From his lips, the words felt forbidden and decadent. His slut. *His.* He loved me wet and panting for more.

This time, the words feel vicious. A brutal slap across the face. Someone knows I'm sleeping with Tyrant when it should be a secret.

Dad has a bucket of soapy water at his feet and he's aggressively scrubbing at the paint with a sponge, but it's useless. The paint is indelible, and it's going to need strong chemicals to take it off.

He glances over his shoulder and sees me, and his face transforms with rage. "Who did this?"

Dad's voice is loud enough for all the neighbors to hear. I sense twitching curtains all around me. They've probably been twitching since the sun came up and revealed this pretty piece of graffiti.

"I don't know," I whisper, wishing he'd stop shouting at me in the street.

"Have you been seeing that piece of shit?"

I feel like I've been slapped. I feel like he's just called *me* a piece of shit. "Don't call him that."

Dad's eyes widen and his nostrils flare, and his expression fills with righteous indignation. "I knew it. You've been seeing that man when you swore there was nothing going on between the two of you."

"Can we just go inside?" I plead, tucking my hair behind my ear.

"You want to enter my house when you're a filthy goddamn liar and you're involved with a criminal?" He points at the graffiti. "Are you sleeping with him? Are you one of his whores?"

My chest hurts. His words feel crueler than knives.

"Tell me that you hate that man, and you can see Barlow. Swear that even the thought of him touching you makes your skin crawl. Promise you'll call the police if you ever see him again."

There's movement out of the corner of my eye. Samantha has come to the window with Barlow in her arms and her expression is accusatory as she peers out at me. I gaze at my baby brother with longing.

Dad is clenching the sponge so hard that water drips down his leg. "Choose. Your brother or that low-life bastard."

I don't understand why I have to choose one or the other. Tyrant never hurt Barlow. I never hurt Barlow. The only one who ever hurt this family is Dad.

"None of this would have happened if you hadn't run up a debt in his club," I whisper tearfully.

Dad's face transforms from angry to incandescent, and he shouts at the top of his lungs, "I will not be talked back to on my own property. You are so ungrateful, Vivienne. Depraved. You disgust me. I put a roof over your head when your waste-of-space mother died. I excused your strangeness, your unwillingness to fit into this family, but now you've gone too far. You're not safe to be around us."

My strangeness? My unwillingness to fit in? I wasn't trying to be the family weirdo. I was trying not to take up too much space in their lives. Cause any problems. I was afraid of Dad's irritation. Samantha's disdain. That they might get sick of me and throw me out. The only one who's ever smiled at me is Barlow, but now even he's being taken away from me.

I step forward, reaching desperately for my father. "I wanted to fit in. If I thought you liked having me around—"

He steps back sharply. "You live in a make-believe world, and you always have, and now it's making you dangerous. Leave. Get out of my sight."

My chest heaves in a sob. "Dad. Please don't do this."

He speaks slowly and loudly like he's talking to a very stupid person. "I. Don't. Want. You. Here. Vivienne. Ever. Again."

Each word hits me like a bullet.

"But Barlow," I whisper through my tears. I can survive if Dad and Samantha don't want to talk to me, but I can't lose my brother as well. He and I have been through so much together. If I can't visit, he's so young that he'll forget all about me. I'll have no family to my name whatsoever. "I'm his sister."

"Stay away from Barlow. I have no daughter." Dad throws his sponge into the bucket of soapy water and storms into the house, slamming the door behind him.

The silence that surrounds me is the loneliest sound I've ever heard.

I don't know how I make it back to the dorms, but somehow I do because the next thing I know, I'm on my knees by my chest of drawers, pulling the bottom one out so I can get to the box hidden underneath.

The hurt. It's too much. I need to let it out.

I open the box and my shaking fingers pick up a slender, pointed knife that's been sharpened to a wickedly gleaming edge. I want to stab the knife into my arm. My thigh. Anywhere that bleeds. I have just enough grip on my senses to pull my top off and then seek a fresh spot on my ribs. There isn't one because they're scored with dozens of scars. It doesn't matter if I go over old ones. I'll still bleed. I'll still hurt.

As I hold the blade to my ribs, there's a ragged shout and running footsteps. "Vivienne. *No.*"

A hand closes around mine on the knife, and I'm dragged back against a broad chest. We're fighting with the knife, me to pull it closer, him to push it away. Tyrant's much stronger than I am, and after a full minute of struggling, all the fight goes out of me, and I hang loosely in his grip, panting.

Tyrant's black velvet voice is in my ear. "Tell me what it is, angel. Do you feel nothing, or do you feel too much?"

"Too much," I cry. "Dad said—Dad said—" I can't even get the words out.

"The graffiti," he snarls. "I will find whoever did this, and I will make them pay. Your father disowned you?"

I nod, anguished tears rolling down my cheeks. "I'm not allowed to see Barlow anymore."

Tyrant doesn't say anything, but I can feel the anger racing through his body. With his hand still over mine, he forces the blade toward himself. His shirtsleeves are rolled back, revealing the muscles and tattoos on his forearm.

The knife is headed right for his flesh.

"Tyrant, don't," I cry desperately.

"If you need to bleed, then I'll bleed for you."

Tyrant is a perfect work of art, and he can't sully himself with my misery. "But your arm. Your tattoos."

"Fuck my arm. Fuck my tattoos."

He forces me to cut him. A long, blazing red line up the edge of his forearm. I start to shake, but Tyrant is as steady as a rock. Blood wells up and runs down his arm, over his fingers, and drips onto my thighs.

When it's done, Tyrant pulls the knife from my nerveless fingers, throws it aside, then wraps his uninjured arm around my waist and holds me against him. We both watch his forearm bleeding freely, bright red blood running over black tattoos.

His lips are against my ear. "Your pain is my pain. It's inside me. It's flowing out of me. I'm bleeding for you, so you don't have to."

Tyrant kisses my neck, and I take a shaky breath and close my eyes.

He goes on kissing me, and I feel some of the pain inside me ebb away. His erection is a thick rod against my ass, and my core clenches in response. I need the sweet pain of his first, hard thrust. Tyrant knows I need it. He turns me around and pushes me onto my back.

While he's unbuttoning my skirt and pulling it and my underwear down my legs, he asks, "Did you buy this bra, or make it?"

"I bought—"

He grasps it in the middle and pulls. The lace rips, and it comes off in tattered pieces. With his jaw grit tight, he unfastens his shirt and pants and shrugs out of them. His cock is a thick, hard rail that he grips tight in his blood-covered fist. As he spreads me open with his fingers, I can feel how wet I am already.

Tyrant gathers saliva on his tongue and spits it onto my inner lips. He squeezes his fist and blood from his cut drips down and splashes on my clit.

He pins me with a steely glare. "I'm going to fuck my spit into you. My blood into you. My cum into you. All of me, angel. You're so far from being alone. I'm going to fucking suffocate you."

With one thrust, he impales me with his cock right to the hilt. I gasp in shock, pain, and pleasure, and hold on to his muscular shoulders.

Tyrant groans like he's been as desperate to feel this as much as I have. With his blood-covered hand, he squeezes my breast, palms my belly, and then cups my jaw, all while hammering me with his cock and leaving smears of blood all over me.

He pushes his thumb into my mouth, and as I suck I can taste his blood.

Holding on to his wrist, I pull his hand away and gasp, "I'm too much for everyone. You'll leave me, too."

His punishing rhythm doesn't stutter. "Shut your fucking mouth."

"You will. Everyone always does. I'm weird. I'm crazy."

Tyrant reaches for the bloody knife, puts it in my hand, and then grabs my wrist and holds the blade to his throat. "Do you really think I'm scared of you? Angel, I'm not scared of anything. Now, hold that blade right here while I fuck you, and if you don't come, you can slit my throat."

CHAPTER SEVEN

Tyrant

I force her to hold the knife right where it is while I thrust deep inside her. I can see why she loves knives. It's never felt so good before. Knowing she's bare and unprotected makes me absolutely feral, and the scent of blood is making me insane. She's decorated with my blood, my vulnerable little angel.

Her eyes are huge and scared. "What the hell are you doing?"

"I'm going to let go. If you move the knife away from my neck, I will take it from you and stab myself in the heart."

"Are you fucking crazy?" she whispers.

I grin malevolently and raise my chin, baring my throat to her. "Will you make our baby fatherless before they're even born?"

Slowly, I let go of her wrist, and she keeps the knife where it is.

"That's my good fucking girl." I drag my thumb along the cut on my arm until it's wet from my blood and then apply it to her clit. Masturbating her with it. Pleasuring her with it. The prick of the blade against my throat is making my balls ache. I want more.

"Cut me, angel. Make me bleed."

She shakes her head. "I'll kill you. I don't know where's safe."

"I said cut me," I snarl in her face.

Vivienne jumps in fear, and the knife scores my collarbone and sinks into the muscle of my shoulder.

"Jesus, *fuck*." Pain blazes in my flesh, and I squeeze my eyes shut. Vivienne pulls the knife out with a horrified gasp and warm liquid drips down my chest and onto her. "If you lower that knife I will fucking kill you."

Vivienne puts the blade back against my throat with a shaking hand.

I open my eyes and see that her soft, pretty tits are spattered with fat drops of blood. Blood is running down my chest. I groan and push her knees up to her shoulders, pounding her even deeper. She whimpers as I fuck her closer to her climax, all the while my blood drips down on her. When she comes, the knife tumbles from her fingers. I snatch it out of the air before it can hurt her, and stab it point-first into the floor by her head as my own orgasm rips through me.

After, it's silent except for our gasping breaths.

Vivienne glances around. "It looks like a murder scene in here."

My blood is all over her body. My body. Her clothes and her satchel. There are drips on the carpet. She says murder scene. I say a really good fuck.

I keep her on her back for several more minutes with my cock buried deep inside her and then slowly pull out of her. I'll never get tired of the sight of her brimming with my cum. She's such a good girl for not fighting me this time and lying there full of my seed.

There are wet wipes and bandages in her cutting box, and I fish them out and start cleaning up my arm. The wound has clotted, and I wipe the blood off and wind some gauze around it. I don't know why Vivienne was so upset by the thought of a wound or a scar on my body. There are scars all over me from old fights, stabbings, even a bullet wound on my thigh. My tattooed knuckles are crisscrossed with white lines from being slashed against other men's teeth. I love that now I'll have a scar that makes me think of her.

Vivienne sits up and hugs her knees, watching me. "How did you know to come here?"

She's a smart girl. She'll figure it out.

"You heard about the graffiti on my house and knew what Dad would do," she guesses.

I reach for another wet wipe, glance at my blood smeared over her naked body, and change my mind. I like my blood all over her. Instead, I take a notebook and pen from her desk, prop my back against her mattress and the notebook against my knee, and start to write. Just a sentence or two, and then I rip the strip of paper off, fold it, and drop it in her cutting box. Then I do it again. And again.

"What are you doing?" Vivienne asks.

I don't answer. I just keep writing and ripping.

"You don't like me having that box."

It's not that I don't like it. I'd rather she didn't need it, but my girl needs dark things to cope right now, and I'm not going to take that away from her. Other people have already taken so much. Soon she won't need the box at all because she has me.

I'll be your dark thing, angel.

"Why don't you just throw it away?" she asks.

I keep writing. A few minutes later I'm finished, and I close the lid on the box and put it back in its hiding place.

Taking her face between my hands, I tell her, "Because you'll only buy another. At least when you open this one, you'll see that someone gives a damn about whether or not you're bleeding."

"Tyrant. I want my brother," she whispers, tears filling her eyes.

She's said that to me a dozen times. Angrily. Desperately. Defiantly. But never as brokenly as she sounds now. I wet my lips, wondering whether it's finally time to offer her everything she craves.

I can get her brother like *that*.

I take hold of her jaw and make her look at me. "This is Henson. My town. I'll fix everything for you, angel. All you have to do is trust me. Do you trust me?"

Vivienne sucks slowly on her lower lip, gazing up at me.

She still not sure? Then I'll keep convincing her. Vivienne needs to start thinking about our future.

I fish something out of my pocket, show it to her, and place it on her pillow.

Then I press my mouth to hers in a hungry kiss. "Be a good girl for Tyrant and take the test. I'm aching to know if I'm going to be a daddy."

I leave the dorms via the stairs and the front door, drawing several wide-eyed looks from random students. It doesn't matter if they recognize me and tattle to security. The moment Vivienne tells me she's pregnant, I'm taking her out of this place and bringing her home. I can picture the moment. I can *taste* it. Everything will change, and she'll finally be mine.

But that's for later.

Right now I'm going to do something about all those tears she shed.

The closer I come to the Stone residence, the stronger my anger surges. When I'm parked across the street, the house looks silent. Night has fallen and the road is in darkness except for intermittent pools of streetlight. *Tyrant's slut* is still scrawled across the front of the house, and it makes my blood boil as I wonder who's going out of their way to hurt my woman.

I glare at the house for going on forty minutes, and then a car comes down the street and turns into the Stones' driveway. It's Owen Stone, and he's alone when he gets out of the car, collects a can of paint from the trunk, and heads over to the graffiti scrawled on his house.

I get out of my SUV and approach him silently. I don't speak until I'm three feet behind him. "Doing some home maintenance?"

Stone whirls around and his eyes widen in fear. He starts to back away, but there's nowhere for him to go. "I've got your money. I'll give you your mon—"

I grasp him by the front of his shirt and yank him to me, snarling. "You're a liar, Stone. You haven't got shit."

"I'll have it soon. Any day now."

He couldn't pay back what he owes me—what he owes Vivienne—

if he shat solid gold for the rest of his life.

"Do you know how I deal with people who don't pay their debts? First I break their legs. Then I slit their throats. Do you know why I haven't done that to you?"

He swallows hard.

"I said *do you?*"

"V-V-Vivienne?" he stammers.

Like it's a fucking question.

I pull back my fist and smash it across his face. When he crumples onto the ground, I pull back my foot and kick him in the stomach. His groan is almost satisfying.

Standing over him, I wonder where I'll inflict more pain.

"I'll get you your—"

I kick him again, this time in the balls. I don't want his fucking money. I want him to stop punishing his daughter when she's already punishing herself enough. I want him *dead*. Him and his fucking wife, and then there'll be nothing stopping me from giving Vivienne everything she wants.

Leaning down, I grab hold of Stone, pull him to his feet, and shove him face-first into the graffiti.

"You're a coward, Stone. A piece of fucking scum. I had a low-life shit like you for a father as well and nothing was ever his fault. I'm here to give you an education. Whose fault is it you owe me money?"

"Mine, but I didn't—*ahh.*"

I grab his arm and twist it high behind his back when I hear the *but*.

"Stop whining," I seethe, twisting his arm harder and harder. "You racked up that debt in my club, and so I stole your son to motivate you to pay. Vivienne wasn't part of this until she tried to help the people who hate her guts by rescuing her brother. An angel who came to the devil's door. I saw her, so sweet and perfect with a baby in her arms, and my dick stood to attention. I fucked your daughter. I've fucked her so many times, and now I'm going to keep her because she's mine. The question is, am I taking your son from you as well? Barlow Mercer. That has a nice ring to it, don't you think? What a happy family the three of us will make. How long before he's calling Vivienne and me Mommy and Daddy and forgetting he ever had two pieces of shit for parents?"

"No, please, leave us—"

"I said stop. Fucking. *Whining*." I push his arm even higher. There's a crack. Stone lets out a bloodcurdling scream, and I can't help but grin at the beautiful pain in his voice. When I let go of him, he falls to the ground. I step back and enjoy the sight of him rolling around like the worm he is.

"My arm, my arm," he moans, clutching himself. "What do you want from me?"

I straighten the cuffs of my shirt and step on his neck. Harder and harder until he starts to choke. "There's one person preventing me from killing you right this second. I hate to see her cry, and right now she'd cry over your dead body, even though you don't deserve it. If my angel ever comes to me in tears over something you've done again, next time I won't just break your arm. I'll break your fucking neck, and your wife will get a bullet."

Stone makes some kind of choking reply that I take to mean he understands me, and so I reluctantly lift my foot. I won't kill him tonight.

But soon.

I'll make Vivienne love me so hard that she'll barely feel a flicker when I finally kill her father and stepmother. Until then, I'll have to put up with them breathing the same air in this city as her.

I turn and walk back up the darkened street. It's up to Stone what happens next. If my girl is smiling, I'm smiling, and they get to live a little longer. If she keeps crying, then I'll have to fix this problem quickly for her. I hope with all my heart Owen Stone fucks up soon, because killing him and his wife and rolling them into shallow graves?

I can't fucking wait.

CHAPTER EIGHT

Vivienne

I work like a demon all week to get my costume ready for the ball, and when I'm not measuring, cutting, sewing, unpicking, and resewing, I'm hanging decorations in the ballroom with the decoration committee to get everything ready for the big night. The committee has chosen a classic masquerade theme, taking inspiration from *The Phantom of the Opera* and Venetian masked balls. Several enormous crystal chandeliers are hanging from the high ceiling, which is festooned with colorful banners and hundreds of fairy lights.

On Tuesday, I borrow some angel wings from the drama department to go with my unfinished dress.

By Wednesday, I'm in tears in my room because I can't make the silk fabric flow how I want it to over my body.

Thursday night sees me finally getting the dress right—and then I panic when I remember I haven't started my mask.

On Friday, I'm frantically hot-gluing crystal tears to a stone-white masquerade mask with a golden ivy halo.

When Saturday afternoon rolls around, my costume is as ready as it's ever going to be and I sit down to put my makeup on. I'm so exhausted that I've barely thought about Tyrant and the things he said the last time I saw him. Now that I have a moment to breathe, the things he said come rushing back.

Be a good girl for Tyrant and take a pregnancy test. I'm aching to know if I'm going to be a daddy.

I glance at my bedside table drawer where I stashed the pregnancy test. I really could be pregnant. I haven't had my period for more than three weeks, but I don't know exactly when to expect it because it can be unpredictable.

Do I *want* to be pregnant? I imagine Tyrant's face as I put my arms around his neck and whisper to him that we're having a baby. His quicksilver eyes gleam and a smile spreads over his beautiful lips. He'll kiss me, and whisper against my lips that he's never loved anyone before, but he loves me and our baby so much he can barely breathe.

My eyes sting and my throat burns. Being loved that much is impossible. That kind of all-encompassing love is only in the movies, but as hopeless as it is, my mind runs away with itself, imagining Tyrant getting down on one knee and proposing with a diamond ring. Watching me walk down the aisle toward him to take my hands in his strong ones. Drawing a white veil back from my face and kissing me. Caressing my baby bump. Holding our baby. Swearing that I'll never be alone again, and our child and I will always, always be his family.

It's such a beautiful dream. It can't possibly be real. I berate myself for being so sentimental. Tyrant isn't a Hallmark movie kind of man. If he wants a baby, it's because he wants a baby, not because he wants me.

Tomorrow. I'll take the test tomorrow. I don't feel pregnant, so I feel pretty confident that it will be negative. When I see that it's negative I'll be able to put Tyrant out of my mind forever and get on with my life.

Unless I call him up and tell him that it's negative. I pause, the sponge of white makeup I'm using to make myself look like a statue pressed against my neck, wondering whether I should tell Tyrant the results, even if they're negative. If I do, maybe he'll appear and try to do something about me not being pregnant. I meet my gaze in the mirror and realize I'm blushing.

At seven, I'm ready for the ball, and I meet Carly and Julia outside in the hall. Carly is dressed as a sixteenth-century plague doctor with a black corset, a long flowing skirt, and an unnerving hooked-nose mask. Julia is wearing a green-and-purple Poison Ivy catsuit and mask, with glimmering lights in her curled and teased hair. We gush over each other's outfits for several minutes, all of us declaring that the other two have put together the best ones and theirs is nowhere near as beautiful or interesting.

The halter neck of my dress needs smoothing down, and when I run my fingers over the fabric, my fingers pass over a lump on the back of my neck. Frowning, I rub the spot and feel something moving around beneath my skin.

"Vivienne?" Carly asks me while tugging her corset into place. "Is something wrong with your costume?"

"No, I just thought…do you feel anything here?" I lift my hair and turn away from her, pointing to the spot.

Carly rubs it. "Maybe something's there," she says, but she doesn't sound certain.

"Have you got a birth control implant?" Julia asks.

I don't have a birth control implant. I should probably have one. Reality suddenly comes crashing down on me, and I swing violently from not believing I'm pregnant to panicking that I might be. What the hell am I going to do if the test is positive? I can't have a baby. I *can't*. Whenever I'm around Tyrant, I crave the moment he fucks me full of his cum, but that's not a sane reason to start a family with a man.

"It doesn't feel like a birth control implant. It's hard, like metal," Carly says.

I finger the lump, frowning. What the hell could it be?

I shake my head. Now is not the time to figure it out. "Come on, we're going to be late."

When we walk into the ballroom at Henson University, it's filled with magic. Music plays beneath the lit chandeliers, and golden light dapples the dancers who are moving in a riot of color, silk, sequins, velvet, glamour, and secrecy. I barely recognize anybody behind their masks as I move among the crowd.

After a few moments, I turn to Julia and Carly to exclaim to them how wonderful everyone looks, only to find I've lost them among all the dancers. I turn this way and that, trying to find a plague doctor and a Poison Ivy. Only, I don't find them. I find someone else, who's instantly recognizable despite his mask.

The crowd parts, and there he is.

The devil himself.

He's wearing black on black. A black tie and shirt with a black suit, with his hands casually in his pockets as he smiles a wickedly pointed smile at me. His eyes are covered with a black mask decorated with gleaming, pointed horns.

My heart pounds in my chest. Three girls move in front of him as they cross the dance floor, and when I look for him again, he's gone. The devil has vanished.

I pick up my skirt with both hands and hurry toward the spot, my head turning this way and that as I hunt for the elusive figure.

An arm snakes around my waist, and I'm drawn back against a broad chest with a thud. I gasp and hold on to the man's wrist. A tattooed wrist. The scent of blackcurrant, cedar, and blood fills my nose. I'm in Tyrant's arms, and everyone here can see it and later tell my family about it. I feel a thud of panic until I remember that we're both masked. Tonight we can be anyone we want. Do anything we want.

I turn slowly in his embrace and wrap my arms around Tyrant's neck. "I should have known you'd come, and as the devil."

He flashes his smile at me again. "I'm an angel too, only I've been locked out of heaven lately. How about you help me find my way back in?"

There's something strange about his eyes. As the lights flash over his face, I realize he's wearing contacts and his eyes are demonic red.

"Why would you want to find your way back in?"

His head dips closer to mine and he murmurs against my lips, "If that's where you are, angel, I'll break down the fucking door."

The music changes and swells. Tyrant wraps his arms around me and draws me against him. In this crush of bodies and with the masks over our faces, I can do something I've never dared before. Be with Tyrant out in the open. Touch him. Adore him. We dance together, our gazes locked. My body feels hot and pleasant and light in his arms. I'm floating in a warm ocean with him and a nameless score of people.

Tyrant's lips brush over mine, and I find myself smiling. His fingers trace the nape of my neck, circling right over the lump.

The smile dies on my lips. "Do you feel that? I've been wondering what it is."

"Feel what?"

His fingers are right on top of the bump. He can't not feel it. Is it just my imagination or is there a gleam in Tyrant's red eyes?

Something is trapped in a box at the back of my mind. It's been rattling all evening, desperate to get out. I'm missing something important. "I…"

There's a peal of laughter behind me, and it echoes in my ears, growing more and more shrill. Someone calls my name. Tyrant glances past my shoulder, seizes my wrist, and pulls me through the crowd, and the voice fades away behind us.

I glance over my shoulder as he drags me along. "Wait, I think I heard my name."

But Tyrant doesn't wait. He pulls me to the edge of the dance floor and then out through heavy velvet curtains and onto the terrace where it's dark and the air is fresh and cool.

He pushes me against the terrace railing and traps me with his arms. "Forget about everyone else. Listen to me." His expression and tone are suddenly urgent. "I'm tired of waiting for you to ask for it."

"Ask for what?"

Tyrant seizes my wrists. "Everything. I can give you everything you want. All you have to say is *I wish*."

What I want is Barlow, and for the world never to hurt me again. Tyrant might as well promise me the moon.

His eyes narrow behind his mask. "You think I can't give you what you crave, but I can. All you have to do is name it, and the devil will get to work."

"But then the devil would own me."

"Body and soul," he agrees, caressing my wrists with his thumbs. "But you get your heart's desire. A fair trade, don't you think? Say it, Vivienne. *I wish Tyrant Mercer would give me my heart's desire.* Say the words and everything you want is yours. You'll wake up in the morning and your whole life will be different."

My heart aches with longing. He's promising me the moon, and as it hangs over us, silvery and luminous, it suddenly feels within reach.

"I wish…"

A wicked smile spreads over Tyrant's face. There's danger and blood in that smile. For a moment, over his shoulder, the ballroom turns an ominous red and the dancers are suddenly screaming and writhing as if they're trapped in the depths of hell.

Why does it feel so ominous that Tyrant is offering me everything I want on a silver platter? Shouldn't this be the most romantic moment of my life?

"I'm afraid of you sometimes," I whisper.

He leans down and his lips ghost up my ear. "Good."

There's someone behind Tyrant. A figure lurches toward us, moonlight sliding over his bruised and battered face. His arm is in a sling and he moves like it's painful to walk. The man's face is swollen so much that I barely recognize him, but when I do, I gasp in shock. "Dad?"

Dad sees me in Tyrant's embrace, and his face transforms in disgust. "I knew I'd find you here with him." He gestures at his wrecked body with his good hand. "Do you see what he did to me, Vivienne? Do you see what happens when you choose a monster over your own family? Our lives are ruined, and it's all your fault."

CHAPTER NINE

Tyrant

Vivienne has turned pale and her fingers are digging into my shoulders as she stares in horror at her father. She almost said the words. I was so close to everything I crave, and then up pops this piece of shit, laying all his crimes at his daughter's feet. Owen Stone ruined his own life.

"Dad, what happened to you?" Vivienne cries. She tries to go to him, but I don't let her leave my embrace.

Stone glares at her. "As if you don't know. Your fucked-up boyfriend here beat me up."

Vivienne shakes her head. "Tyrant wouldn't do that."

I smile and press a kiss to her temple, just behind her mask. Oh, my little angel. Still believing that I have a shred of conscience just because I'm sweet to her. She's so vulnerable and soft-hearted, but that's one of the things I love about her. The world has treated her cruelly, but she hasn't lost her innocence.

"Ask him. Go on, ask him," Stone demands as I give him a gloating smile.

"Tyrant is merciful," Vivienne insists. "He let Barlow come home to us. He hasn't demanded that you pay back his money. He hates to see me suffering, so I know he wouldn't hurt my family."

I hate to see Vivienne suffering, so I have to kill her family. As soon as she asks for it, as soon as she's safely living with me, I'll slit Stone's throat.

"You're deluded, Vivienne. He stole Barlow. He beat me up. He already killed Lucas. They found his body not far from one of Mercer's clubs. He'd been beaten to death. That's because of you as well, isn't it?"

Vivienne's hands tighten on my shoulders after hearing that little piece of news. I wrap my arms around her waist, soothing her surprise by stroking her bare back. Lucas Jones screamed, wet himself, and sobbed for his mother as I beat him to death with a heavy chain. What a wonderful moment that was. Almost as wonderful as killing Stone and his wife will be, and then taking Barlow for our own.

"Dad," Vivienne says in a shaky voice. "I've only ever wanted to be your daughter and Barlow's sister. How can you say that everything's my fault?"

"You're next, Vivienne," Stone warns her. "He'll beat you black and blue the moment you make him angry. He's an animal."

"My angel knows I wouldn't lay a finger on her in violence." Running my thumb along her jaw, I smile. "Unless she wants me to."

"You're a sick bastard," Stone accuses.

"Dad, don't speak to Tyrant like that," Vivienne tells her father.

I give Vivienne an admiring smile. My kitten is unsheathing her claws to defend me.

"Why do you care if I'm a sick bastard or not?" I ask Stone. "You disowned your daughter, and I'm picking up the pieces." I stroke Vivienne's nape, right over the lump in her neck. I can't help but caress that lovely spot. "Don't worry, angel. I told you I'll always take care of you, and I will."

Vivienne rubs the back of her neck. "What *is* that?" She's frowning at me, and I don't look guilty because I sure as hell don't feel guilty. "Tyrant, you do know what this lump is, don't you?"

There's no reason to hide it anymore. After tonight, she's coming home with me forever. It's time she understood how deadly serious I am about her.

"Yes. I know what it is," I say calmly. "It's a tracker."

Her eyes widen. "How do you know that?"

"Because I put it there."

"You what? When?"

"The night you slept in my bed and in my arms."

Her hand drops from her neck and she pulls herself out of my embrace. "Please tell me you're joking."

Vivienne has seen my obsessively secure home. She's heard what I say to her when I fuck her. My possessiveness. My desire for her. I haven't hidden who I am from my woman. It may be a slight shock to find out just how far I'll go to protect her, but she'll understand that it was necessary soon enough.

"This town is full of vipers, and I need to know where you are at all times so I can keep you safe." I take her hand and draw her back into my arms. She's trembling as I murmur, "All those times you needed me, aren't you happy I was there? I couldn't have let you leave my side without knowing I could get to you at all times. Do you think me so careless that I'd lose sight of my little lamb?"

Past her shoulder, Stone is gazing at her in disgust. "Enjoy your psychopath. You two deserve each other." He turns away and limps through the doors.

Anger flares in my chest, and I nearly follow him, prepared to break his other arm and his stupid fucking neck as well, but I'm not leaving Vivienne here on her own.

I turn back and pull her against me once more. "Your father can rot in hell, and so can your stepmother, but don't worry, angel. You're not going to lose Barlow. I'll take care of everything. You want me to do that for you, don't you?"

Vivienne gazes up at me, perplexed. "What do you mean, take care of everything?"

"You don't need to know all the gory details. If you want Barlow, just ask me, and I'll go and get him for you."

"Get Barlow? How? Steal him again? Dad and Samantha will be heartbroken."

After everything that's happened, she must have realized that I can't let these people live. They've made her too unhappy. "Hearts that don't beat, can't break."

Vivienne gasps and shakes her head. "Tyrant, you can't be serious. Dad doesn't want me, but as much as that hurts, I don't want him or Samantha to be killed."

I take her face between my hands and say urgently, "I'm deadly serious. It was always going to be this way the moment I saw those scars on your body. *They* put them there. They hurt you. They're going to pay for each and every cut, and then I'm going to take Barlow and bring him home for us."

Vivienne rips my hands from her face and backs away from me, breathing fast. "Are you *crazy*? You can't kill them just so we can take their son."

"Did they hurt you?"

She raises a hand and touches her ribs. Her stomach. All the scars that she bears because of them. Pain is etched on her brow as she remembers all her loneliness, all their cruelty. "Yes, but…"

"Will you ever forgive them?"

"No, but…"

"Then they have to die."

Vivienne drops her hand. "Tyrant, no. If you really think they deserve death for neglecting me, then you're a monster."

Her angel wings are luminous in the moonlight. Her halo gleams atop her long, glorious hair. She's everything a devil like me craves.

I take a step toward her. "A monster? Is it monstrous to want to make a family with you? I'm giving you everything you've ever wanted. You said it yourself, those people never made you feel like you belonged. I can do that for you. It's the only thing I want."

Vivienne backs away from me, and anger flares through me. How dare she try to escape while I'm offering her dreams on a silver platter. I reach out and seize her throat and drag her close.

"You belong with me," I seethe, and she struggles in my grip, holding my wrist with both hands.

That's right. Cling to me, angel. I'll never let you go.

"Tyrant, please," she whimpers.

She needn't be afraid. I'm not going to choke her. I just need to be sure she's not going to run. "You're the only one who matters to me. Tell me you love me, and everything you want is yours. Say it, angel. Say, *I love you, Tyrant.* Then your every wish is my command."

Tears fill her eyes. "You're crazy. Why didn't I see it before? It took you wearing that mask for me to see your true face."

I pull her into my arms and hold her tightly. "This is who I am, but I'll always be sweet to you, angel. It's everyone else who should be scared. Be a good girl and say you fucking love me."

Vivienne whimpers and struggles for a moment and then gives up. Her body softens against mine, and she takes a shuddering breath.

A smile spreads over my face, and I gather her against my body. "That's it, angel. See how easy this is?"

Her arms wrap around my waist. Her cheek falls against my chest. She's stroking me. Feeling me. My angel has always loved to touch me, and my eyes close as warmth cascades through my body.

Her seeking hands slip beneath my jacket, and when she finds what she's looking for, she pulls it out and backs away from me.

I open my eyes and see that I'm staring down a metal barrel.

My gun.

She stole my fucking gun.

Vivienne points the weapon at me with shaking hands. "I'm not going anywhere with you. I'll kill you before I let you hurt anyone else."

I watch her through narrowed eyes. Calculating. I could snatch the weapon from her before she gets a chance to fire it. Her grip is terrible. I don't think she's ever held a gun before.

There's no reason to grab it from her. My angel won't hurt me. She doesn't have it in her.

I open my jacket, giving her a clear shot at my heart. "Then shoot me. I'm never letting you go, and I'm going to destroy everyone who's ever hurt you, so killing me is your only option if you want to stop me."

The gun trembles in her grip. Her eyes sparkle with tears.

She doesn't shoot.

Vivienne hasn't got any violence in her heart except toward herself.

I snatch at the gun, and she sobs and jerks it away from me. Aiming into the air, she pulls the trigger, and a shot explodes in the darkness, making her flinch.

Was that supposed to scare me? A warning shot isn't going to make me back off. I reach for Vivienne again, and she cries out in anguish and throws the gun over the terrace into the garden below.

"Don't ever come near me again, Tyrant. I don't want to see you anymore."

She dashes toward the ballroom, and I lunge for her and miss. Anger bursts through me, and I roar, "Angel, don't you run from me. You fucking love me."

She poises on the threshold, outlined against the dancers in that silvery dress, her angelic wings spread. "I don't love you, Tyrant. I could never love someone like you."

I grab her hand, but her slender fingers slip through mine, and she disappears into the crowd. I run inside and turn on the spot, peering over the heads of the dancers, through plumes of feathers and wings and headdresses. Vivienne is nowhere in sight.

Frustration and anger race through me. *I could never love someone like you.*

Never?

Never love me?

After all I've done for her?

Spite and rage roar in my heart. I promised Vivienne the moon, and she threw it in my face. I fought for her, bled for her, made myself *feel* for her. I have thought of nothing but her since the moment we met, and she thinks she can toss me aside?

Decide all by herself that it's over?

This will never be over.

I'll have her, or I'll end this world and everyone in it.

Outside, something white and sparkling is lying on the stairs. I pick it up and turn it over in my hands. Vivienne's angel mask. She was running from me so fast that it fell off, or she tore it off in her haste.

I hurl it away from me with a snarl of rage and stride down the steps. I'll find her. She can't hide from me for long when I've put a fucking tracker in her.

CHAPTER TEN

Vivienne

I run through the deserted streets, blinded by tears and the crushing weight of despair in my heart. I thought there was some goodness in Tyrant. I thought he was only a little bit crazy. A little bit violent. A little bit obsessed and unhinged.

Dad telling me that everything bad that's happened to our family is all my fault killed my last scrap of love for him, my last pitiful hope I had of ever winning his approval, but can Tyrant really believe I want him and Samantha dead for the pain they've caused me? I keep picturing them both dead on the kitchen floor, and Barlow wailing between their blood-spattered bodies.

Barlow can't be orphaned because of me. It's too cruel. A baby needs his parents.

At the front door to my dorms, I'm panting as I push the code into the lock. It opens with a beep but I take a furtive look behind me before I cross the threshold. The street is deserted. No Tyrant. Yet.

But he must be following me, which means I can't stay here. I can't rely on my family for help and protection, which means I should probably leave Henson for a little while at least. I need some breathing space from everything that's happened. I don't trust myself not to give in to Tyrant's dangerous seduction the moment he pushes me against a wall and slams his mouth over mine. I'm too addicted to that man.

The next ten minutes are critical if I'm going to slip away where he can't reach me. I hurry upstairs, and for the first time in my life as I reach my room and pull out my cutting box, I'm not thinking about the sweet agony and release of blood and pain.

I feel around for the lump in the back of my neck and press it down and hold it in place. With the sharpened edge of my knife, I make a small cut in my flesh and try to squeeze the tracker out. A drop of blood runs down my back, but the tracker won't budge. I cut deeper this time, wincing as the knife slices into my flesh. After digging painfully around with my nails, I grasp hold of something small and hard, and pull it out.

In my blood-coated fingers is a small piece of plastic embedded with an electronic chip. I drop it onto my desk and stare at it in horror. There it is. Undeniable proof that Tyrant has been tracking my every move since the first night we met.

I pick up a high heel and use the metal spike to crush the tracker into an unrecognizable mess of splintered plastic and twisted metal and then throw it out of the window.

The back of my neck is bleeding, and I reach into my cutting box for a bandage, but instead, I draw out a small piece of paper. The box is filled with them. Little folded notes.

It takes me a moment to remember what they are. Tyrant put them in my cutting box the last time he was here, but I was too far gone in a post-sex and violence haze to wonder what he was doing.

I unfold the note and read his elegant, slanted handwriting. I read another and another.

Say the word, and I'll make them bleed for you.
If someone hurts you, I will make them suffer tenfold.
Knives cut deep, but my obsession for you cuts deeper.
Your pain doesn't control you. I do.

The notes flutter from my shaking fingers and onto the floor. Why couldn't I see what was in front of me all along? Not an intriguingly dangerous man, but a psychopath. My loneliness made his obsession seem romantic. My damage turned him from a villain into a hero. I should have known that I'd fall for the first toxic man who came my way and that the sweet words he said to me about starting a family weren't sweet at all. He held me down and fucked me raw against my will, and my twisted heart mistook that for love.

Screw my bleeding neck. I don't care. I just want to get out of here. I grab a backpack and begin stuffing clothes and toiletries inside. I take off my masquerade costume and pull on jeans and a sweater. My face and hands are ghost-white from makeup, but I haven't got time to wash them right now.

My knife is lying on the carpet, and I take a moment to tape it to the inside of my wrist with bandages, inside my sleeve. You never know when you might need a weapon.

With the backpack over my shoulder and my hand on the door, I take one last look around my room. This has been my happy place since I started college. In this room, I've felt safer and more myself than I ever did living with Mom or with Dad and Samantha. All my favorite things are on the walls. Drawings. Pictures. Swatches of colors and fabrics. It hurts so much to leave it all behind.

I take a deep breath and harden my heart. If I stay, Tyrant will continue to hurt and threaten my family because he thinks he has a chance with me.

And if I'm pregnant? What then?

I hurry back to my bedside, take out the pregnancy test that Tyrant bought me, and shove it into my backpack.

Leaving my room and the dorms behind, I walk out into the silvery darkness of a night with a full moon. The bus station is a mile or so away, and that's where I head. I don't know where I'm going, but I'll buy the cheapest ticket for whichever bus comes soonest and takes me the farthest away. After that, I don't know. I barely have any money, so I'll try to get a job and find some way to put a roof over my head.

At the bus stop, I contemplate the noisy, smelly buses, wondering if I'm making the right decision. Maybe I should stay in Henson and go to the police instead. Tell them I have a stalker. Tyrant is powerful, but the police can do something to protect me, can't they?

I gnaw on my lip, hesitating by the curb. I'm not sure about the police. Tyrant has been right under their nose for decades, and from what I've heard, they've never so much as issued him a speeding ticket.

I should know everything before I make a decision that affects my future. Am I only looking out for myself, or do I have a baby to protect as well?

The restrooms are dingy and leaky, and I'm hit by the sour smell of stale urine. Sitting on the toilet in an empty cubicle, I take out the test and read the instructions. Pee on this end, wait three minutes. Seems easy enough.

A short while later, I'm holding the test in my fingers as I wait for it to develop, my phone in my other hand so I can keep an eye on the time. The seconds seem to crawl by. I'm not pregnant. There's no way I can be pregnant. I've got too many things to worry about, like Tyrant and what he's doing right this moment. Probably tearing my dorm room apart in a rage because the tracker has gone dark.

After three painstaking minutes, I glance down at the test and examine the indicator window. I gasp in shock, and the test drops from my fingers and clatters onto the concrete floor.

Oh, fuck.

Oh, *fuck*.

I consider picking up the test and checking it again, but what would be the point?

I'm pregnant.

I'm having Tyrant Mercer's baby.

For a long time, I stare blindly at the graffiti on the back of the stall door until the grinding of gears and the roar of a bus engine outside draws me back into myself. I have to run. Get far away from Tyrant before he can find out about the baby and become even more insane. He'd make his child just like him. If he finds out I'm pregnant, he'll probably try to take my child from me the moment they're born.

Feeling disconnected from my own body, I scoop up the test and throw it in the trash, pull on my jeans, and flush the toilet. This doesn't feel real. I'm only nineteen. I can't have a baby.

I don't have to have this baby.

Do I even want this baby?

In a flash, at the thought of getting rid of it, I immediately know the answer. I want this baby. I was half in love with the idea when Tyrant was fucking me without protection. I was playing with fire on purpose, and I didn't even try that hard to get ahold of some Plan B when one pharmacist told me they were out of stock.

Being a mom means having a family at last. My family. Someone who I can love unconditionally. I'll protect this child in all the ways that Mom, Dad, or Samantha never protected me.

I wash my hands and splash water over my face, dry them on my sweater, and head back out into the fresh air. I need a bus schedule and then I need to sit down and make a plan.

"Where do you think you're going, angel?"

I freeze, fear racing down my spine. I want to run, but Tyrant spoke so close behind me that he could reach out and grab me in less than a second. Slowly, I turn around and see him leaning against the wall, the top half of his body in the shadows.

"How did you find me? I cut the tracker out."

Tyrant pushes away from the wall and saunters into the light. The flickering neon bulbs highlight his cheekbones. The cruel curve of his mouth. Those dark, threatening eyes. He's taken out the red contacts and removed the horned mask, but he still looks like the devil. "You forgot to check if you were being followed when you left your dorm. You're not a naturally deceptive person, Vivienne. It's useless trying to hide from me."

My shoulders slump. I forgot to glance around even once.

Tyrant glances suspiciously at the restrooms. "What took you so long in there?"

My stomach lurches. Remembering what Tyrant just said about me not being naturally deceptive, I force myself to put on the performance of my life. As nonchalant as I can, I tell him, "I was trying to take this makeup off."

"It's still on your face."

"I said trying. I need makeup remover."

He steps closer until he's looming over me. His height and strength always made me feel safe. Excited. Turned on. There's a threatening aura about him tonight, and I realize how easily he could destroy me without breaking a sweat.

"How dare you run from me," he seethes.

"I was frightened. I still am." I take a steadying breath and decide for the first time in my life to ask for what I want.

Demand it.

"I want you to leave me alone. Forever. I don't want to see you anymore."

"Vivienne, you're only making me angrier."

His brutal expression makes my knees tremble. There's so much violence in his heart, and he's going to unleash it all on me. "Tyrant, please just let me go. I need some space to think."

His hands curl slowly around my elbows, and he jerks me toward him.

"I'll give you one last chance to come willingly. Don't forget that I love you, Vivienne. I've never loved any woman before. If you throw that back in my face, I'll be very fucking angry." He caresses my cheek with the backs of his knuckles and his eyes are narrowed in fury.

One last chance? That sounds ominous. That sounds *deadly*.

It might get me killed, but I have to speak the truth. "I'm not real to you. I'm just an obsession."

Tyrant seizes my upper arms so tightly that I can feel myself bruising. "You're choosing them over me?"

The ultimate betrayal. Siding with my family over him.

I shake my head. "No, Tyrant. I'm not choosing them. I'm choosing Barlow. He has to stay with his family. He's innocent in all of this, and I want what's best for him."

"They don't love you," he snarls. "They despise you."

I dig my nails into my palms and will myself not to sob. "I *know* that."

"Then I don't understand why you're being so stubborn, unless you want to suffer."

"I don't want to suffer. I just don't want anyone to die."

"We can't always get what we want. Or rather, you can't. I'm taking what's mine."

He glances past my shoulder and nods at someone I can't see. From behind me, a bag comes down over my head and pulls tight. I'm lifted by strong arms and slung over a shoulder. Tyrant's shoulder. I can feel his expensive suit beneath my fingers. I'm about to scream when he takes a few steps and pushes me onto a broad leather seat. Someone gets in beside me and the door slams. A moment later, my hands and feet are bound with zip ties. I didn't even have time to reach inside my sleeve to grab my knife.

I lay sprawled across the leather, the same place where Tyrant held me down and screwed me. I've been so stupid, and now it's too late. I danced with the devil, and now he's never going to let me go.

"What do you want from me?" I whimper, my voice muffled by the bag.

"You owe me," he seethes.

"I've never taken anything from you. The only thing you ever bought me was one pregnancy test."

Tyrant laughs as the car moves off, and the sound is cruel and cold. "I bled for you, angel. That's a bigger debt than money, and I will be repaid in full for every last drop."

PART II: THEN

CHAPTER ELEVEN

Vivienne

TEN MONTHS EARLIER

"Julia, these are just stunning."

I look up from the sewing in my lap and see that Carly is examining a dozen or so black-and-white photographs that are spread out on a table in front of Julia. We're in the near-empty common room on a Saturday afternoon, attempting to make some progress on our art history projects. The assignment is on local Henson history, and I'm deep in the throes of recreating the beaded debutante dress worn by Cecelia Henson in 1921. A portrait of her wearing the dress hangs in the main entrance to the university. I've studied the painting and found drawings of the dress, which was designed just for her, in the university archives.

Carly is painting a map of Henson as it was in the year 1900, and Julia has been photographing gardens in Henson that were first planted in the late nineteenth and early twentieth century.

Julia arranges one of her photographs next to a printout of a much older photo. "I'll display my pictures alongside these ones from the past, so people can see how much the gardens have changed. Or haven't changed."

"That will be beautiful," I tell her, carefully adding a silver bead to the bodice of Cecelia's dress and tying off the thread.

"You know whose garden I'd really like to photograph?" Julia asks with a mischievous smile.

"Don't even say his name," Carly says, catching on right away.

"Why, will he appear and kill us all? Tyrant Mercer is just a man, and I've heard his garden is beautiful."

Beautiful and deadly, if the rumors are true. Apparently Tyrant loves to lock people in the maze of his garden and hunt them down for sport.

"Yes, but not very old because he put it in himself, so it's no good for your project," I tell her, glancing at the time on my phone. "I have to go. I told Dad and Samantha I'd be home for dinner."

I pack my sewing away and tell Carly and Julia I'll be back later, take it upstairs, and then grab my satchel and coat and head out of the dorms and across the university grounds. It's only a fifteen-minute walk to my home.

A cold wind ruffles my hair as I make my way along my street. The temperature is crisp but the sky is clear, and it's the kind of winter afternoon that makes the heavy, invisible burden of life feel lighter. For a little while at least.

I'm huddled in my coat, anticipating an evening with Dad and Samantha and my baby brother, Barlow. He was born six months ago, and he's the most adorable baby who's ever existed. There's a baby romper in my satchel, one I sewed for Barlow myself. It's made from fuzzy white cotton and printed all over with little yellow ducks. I can't wait to dress him in it at bedtime and lay him in his crib. Just picturing him makes happiness and warmth flood through me.

When I reach the house where Dad and Samantha live, which was my own home for four years until I moved into the dorms at Henson, I remind myself that Barlow might be napping. I enter quietly rather than throwing open the door and calling, *It's me.*

As I leave my satchel on the sofa and take off my coat, I hear voices coming down the hall. Dad's, Samantha's, and another man's. With a lurch, I wonder if it's Lucas. I haven't seen him in some time, but I suspect he still comes over occasionally. The sight of him makes all the scars on my ribs ache, and then I crave to add more.

The man speaking has a deeper voice than Lucas, and it's not one I recognize.

Suddenly, Samantha cries out, shrill and tearful. "What do you want from us?"

I freeze, just a few feet from the coat stand. I've never heard Samantha sound so terrified before. Who is in our house?

I step into the shadows beside the coat stand and peer carefully around it. From here, I can see into the kitchen. Dad is standing by the wooden table, holding a ladle as if he had been in the middle of stirring soup. Samantha is behind him by the sink, clutching it for support. Both of them are wide-eyed with fear as they stare at a man in a black suit. A startlingly tall, muscular man with broad shoulders, long legs, and large feet in stylish leather shoes. His fine, fair hair is swept dramatically back from his angular face, revealing cold eyes, malevolent brows, and sharply handsome features. There's a faint smirk on his lips as if he knows that his mere presence in this suburban kitchen is terrifying the hell out of my father and stepmother.

He knows it.

And he's enjoying it.

I've only crossed paths with him once before, years ago, but I know exactly who this man is. Everyone in Henson knows this man.

Tyrant Mercer.

Officially, he's a club owner and a businessman, but unofficially? There's not one murder, assault, robbery, illegal gambling den, or counterfeit scheme in Henson that's not rumored to be connected to him somehow. He rules the dark, dank locales of this city's underbelly. So what's he doing in our kitchen?

Barlow sits in his high chair, his big baby blues gazing innocently up at Tyrant with no understanding that he's gazing upon a killer. To Dad and Samantha's horror, and mine, Tyrant lifts a tattooed hand and runs his forefinger over Barlow's plump cheek.

"Such a pretty baby. You must be so proud."

I nearly shout, *Don't touch him*, but stop myself just in time. I have to call the police before Tyrant realizes I'm here. I glance toward the sofa where I left my satchel.

"Get out, or we're calling the police," Samantha tells him in a shaking voice.

Tyrant laughs. "Be my guest, Mrs. Stone, but if you do, your parents will be calling a funeral parlor next. For your husband, for you, and for your baby."

I wince and forget about trying to reach my phone in my bag.

"You wouldn't hurt a baby," Samantha whispers in horror.

Tyrant pretends to look mystified and points at Barlow. "What, this baby?" He lifts Barlow out of his high chair and settles him against his hip while Samantha covers her mouth in horror. Tyrant smiles at Barlow, revealing strong, white teeth, and my skin crawls. "What a sweet little man he is. Do you suppose it would be difficult for someone like me to hurt a baby? I've never tried before. There's a first time for everything."

Samantha cries out and lunges for Barlow with both hands, but Dad holds her back. She falls to her knees, sobbing, and Tyrant watches her with that cruel, mocking smile on his face.

"Babies are just so defenseless, aren't they? Look, he trusts me already." Tyrant wiggles a tattooed forefinger against Barlow's cheek, and Barlow wraps his chubby baby hand around it and stares in fascination at the ink.

I have to cover my mouth with both hands to keep from bursting into tears.

"Owen, *do* something," Samantha shrieks.

Dad opens and closes his mouth, and when he speaks his voice is wheedling. "Please. What do you want from us?"

Tyrant drops his smile, and the room turns even colder. "What do you think I want?"

"I don't have the money."

Oh, no, not Tyrant as well. In the past, Dad has owed money to banks, payday lenders, his family, various friends, but to get into debt to a dangerous criminal like this man? What was Dad thinking? He probably wasn't thinking at all and was on one of his benders. I thought with a new baby and a family relying on him, Dad would want to turn over a new leaf and be a better man.

"Owen, please. You didn't. How much?" Samantha asks in a trembling voice.

"You haven't told your wife?" Tyrant sneers. "Your husband owes me twenty-nine thousand. I normally wouldn't come personally to collect such a small sum, but Mr. Stone called me a few names when the bouncers were throwing him out of my Yancy Street club. Apparently I'm a prick?" He arches a questioning brow at Dad.

The horror I feel is echoed on Samantha's face. Twenty-nine *thousand*, and he insulted Tyrant Mercer to the men who work for him.

"We have savings. The joint account…" Samantha trails off as Dad shakes his head, telling her that the money is gone. He must have drank and gambled it away. Tears well up in her eyes. "Owen, how could you?"

The silence is crushing.

Tyrant glances between them. "No more ideas? Then perhaps this will motivate you. You can have your brat back when I have my money." He holds one of Barlow's hands and makes him wave at his parents. "Bye-bye, Mommy and Daddy. I'm going home with Daddy Tyrant."

With a laugh, he turns toward the door. Toward me. I quickly pull back into the shadows.

Samantha screams and reaches to grab her baby, but Tyrant pulls a gun out of his jacket and aims it at her head, his mocking expression turning ferocious.

"Back the fuck off. I have no mercy for you, and no mercy for this child. If I don't get my money, I will rip your lives apart, and what's left will be a blood-soaked mess. Right now, no one's been hurt, but if I'm still waiting this time next week, that will change." He presses a kiss to Barlow's temple and smiles at them once more. "Piece by piece."

I have to do something. I can't call the police. I don't have a weapon. Dad doesn't have that kind of money and neither do I. Barlow's only hope is if someone breaks into Tyrant's impenetrable mansion, grabs him, and sneaks out again. Tyrant's home has high surrounding walls and presumably more security systems than a bank vault. Once Barlow's inside, there'll be nothing we or anyone can do to get him out.

I glance over my shoulder toward the front door. The glossy black car out front must be Tyrant's car. Stealing Barlow back from Tyrant will be a hell of a lot easier if the person doing the stealing only has to break out of that mansion, and not into it as well.

I turn and hurry as quietly as I can back down the corridor.

"You're a monster," Samantha sobs behind me as I slip out the door and pull it closed behind me.

With blood roaring in my ears, I run to Tyrant's car, hoping with the full force of my desperation that he's left it unlocked. To my amazement and relief, the rear door opens when I tug on the handle, and I slip inside.

There's a coat on the back seat of his car, long and dark and made of wool. I dive onto the floor of the car and cover myself with the garment, and I'm enveloped in a fragrant but cold scent. It fills my lungs with each breath I take, and I realize I'm breathing in Tyrant Mercer's scent. The wool against my cheek is warm and soft. I should be feeling nothing but terror at this moment, but I'm distracted by the sensation of this man and his tastes. Expensive. Subtle. Dangerous.

The driver's side door slams, the engine starts, and I feel the car start to move.

My hands clench on the wool in horror. What have I done? How is it any better that I've essentially been kidnapped along with my brother? My breaths come faster and faster. Tyrant will hear me if I keep this up. I bite the inside of my cheek, and the pain cuts through all the noise in my head. For now, Tyrant doesn't know I'm here, which means I have the advantage.

I wish I'd brought a hammer, a knitting needle, anything I could use as a weapon. I don't know how capable I am of hurting another person, but if it's to save Barlow, I think I could grab whatever is on hand and use it against Tyrant. I imagine picking up a lamp or a flowerpot and smashing it over his head. That could work, though I feel ill at the thought of hurting anyone, even a criminal like Tyrant.

"No tears? Don't I frighten you, little Barlow?" Tyrant says, and I wonder if he has my brother on his lap as he drives.

Barlow makes a baby talk sound that I know means he's curious about something.

"Are you trying to help me drive?" Tyrant utters a soft laugh.

"You're a trusting little fellow. Let's hope your father comes through with my money by the deadline. I'd hate for anything bad to happen to an innocent little baby."

There's not a shred of mercy in his laughter. Tyrant won't think twice about hurting Barlow if he doesn't get what he wants, so why should I agonize over whether it's wrong to hurt him? A monster like him doesn't deserve to go on breathing. I won't feel a shred of remorse as he lies bleeding at my feet.

CHAPTER TWELVE

Tyrant

I realize that someone is hiding in the back of my car when I'm still eight blocks from my home. My coat has slipped from the back seat to the floor, which isn't where I left it when I got out of the car.

I'm driving one-handed, with one hand around the baby to keep him on my knee. My free hand grips the steering wheel as my eyes narrow at the road ahead. Could it be an assassin? There are plenty of people who want me dead. Or is it Merrick's daughter? My annoying little stalker. Irritation washes over me at the thought. My men have told me that the Merrick girl has been turning up at my clubs, hoping to catch my eye. The last thing I need is a desperate, weak little idiot who wants to give me incompetent blowjobs and spend my money, and I'll slit my own throat before I'm linked for life to a politician.

As I take a right-hand turn, I glance into the back of my car. As the streetlights move across the coat, I see a foot poking out the far end.

A slim foot in a pointed ballet flat.

Not an assassin. If this is Merrick's daughter, I will drag her home by her hair and slit her throat in front of her father. As I turn into the long, winding driveway that leads up to my home, the wrought iron gates slide open, revealing gardens with high hedges. My house with its white columns and long windows rises beyond.

"Call the housekeeper," I say to the voice recognition software on my phone, and when Angela answers, I tell her to meet me down by my car. The garage is separated from the house, either by a long walk through the garden, or a shortcut via an underground passage and a locked door.

The garage doors roll up, and I park in an empty place. Angela, a woman in her fifties and wearing a neat gray dress with a white lace collar, is waiting for me.

I open my door and get out with the baby in my arms. "Take this up to the house."

"Yes, Mr. Mercer." Angela doesn't even blink as she accepts the child from my hands and carries him up to the house via the shortcut. I've asked her to do stranger things than this in the past. Once she had to feed a leopard for a week. Most days she has to clean bloodstains off my clothes. Like everyone else in my employment, she's well-paid and fiercely loyal.

The garage door grinds as it closes, and now we're locked in together, my little stowaway and me.

I pretend that I'm going up to the house by entering the code for the shortcut and opening and closing the door. Then put my back against it and wait. The automatic light in the garage flicks out, and the only illumination is the moon coming through the skylight.

Several minutes pass, and then there's the sound of fumbling inside my car. The passenger door opens, and a cautious foot reaches toward the floor. Like a scared rabbit emerging from her burrow, a dark-haired girl peeks out. With exaggerated care, she closes the door quietly behind her and glances around. She looks around eighteen or nineteen years old, and she's wearing a short, pale slip dress that looks like it was made about fifty years ago. The small, faded T-shirt underneath has been washed a hundred times or more. Her shoes are dated, but cute. Everything about this girl is neat and pretty, but vintage or secondhand, right down to the cream satin bow in her long hair.

I doubt this is Merrick's daughter. The photographs I've glimpsed as he's waved his phone in my face are of a glamorous and very modern blonde.

I slowly reach into my jacket and unfold a knife. Girls don't need to be threatened with guns. They're more afraid of knives, especially pretty girls who care about their lovely faces. When her gaze pans over me, I smile in the darkness. She gasps as she sees the gleam of my teeth.

I step forward into the light, twisting the knife in my fingers. "Well, hello. Who the fuck are you?"

The girl has her mouth open, and for a moment she's frozen in shock. Then, in a surprisingly determined voice, she straightens up and says, "That's my brother you took."

Her brother? This is Owen Stone's daughter. I didn't see anyone else at the house, so she must have hidden from me and listened to our conversation, the tricky little bitch.

I put the tip of my blade under her chin, forcing it up. "You've intruded on my property. What did you even think you were going to do here?"

There's fear in her moonlit eyes but she remains calm. "I was going to steal my brother back, of course."

I put some weight on the knife, enough to threaten that I will break the skin and plunge it into her throat. To my surprise, Miss Stone reaches up and wraps her hand around the blade.

"If I pull, I'll slice your hand open," I point out.

"But you won't be able to cut my throat if I hold on like this. I don't care if you hurt me, but I do care if you kill me because then there will be no one to save Barlow."

My gaze drops to her pretty, lush mouth. What a strange girl she is, holding on to my blade like she's never been scared of a knife and she's not about to start now. "How badly do you want him?"

Miss Stone swallows against the blade, and it nicks her skin. A single drop of blood runs down her throat and soaks into the neckline of her tee. I twist the blade again, and another droplet runs down her perfect skin. My tongue moves against the roof of my mouth as I imagine gripping her tightly by the hair and licking it up.

"You…you can have me instead. I'll trade places with him."

"You do realize that your father hasn't got any money, and at the end of the week, I'll kill you." I lean down toward her, smiling coldly. "I think I'll hunt you down for sport. You must have a beautiful scream."

Miss Stone's fearful breaths come a little faster. "Fine. Just don't hurt Barlow. I'll trade places with him."

My gaze slips down her body. So reckless for one so young and pretty. "It doesn't seem like a fair trade. You for a precious baby? Do Mommy and Daddy love you as much as him?"

Miss Stone flinches. "They'll be…motivated to get the money for you if they have Barlow back."

I laugh softly. "You're saying they don't give a shit about you? Then I'll never get my money."

"Barlow is just a baby, and as much as you're laughing, it's not funny. Don't treat this like a stupid game."

Fury sweeps over me. She snuck in here and now she's getting mouthy? If she's so desperate to die, then I'll throw her into the labyrinth of paths and hedges around my house and watch her run herself to exhaustion. With the moving walls and locking and unlocking gates, it's impossible for anyone to make it in or out without my say-so.

"A game, you say?" I ask coldly. "I love games. You can have your brother back if you manage to discover where he's hidden. I'll give you a fair chance. I'll even tell you that he's up at my house. Reach him, and you can both go home."

Miss Stone's tongue plays with the corner of her lip as she considers this. "The house on this property? What's the catch?"

"No catch. I'll leave the front door unlocked for you."

"That should be easy enough," she says uncertainly, letting go of my knife.

I snicker softly. She fucking thinks. I lower the knife, get my phone out, and call my head of security. "Close gates one, three, four, seven, nine, and ten. Open two, five, six, eight, eleven, twelve, and thirteen. Set them to randomize every fifteen minutes."

A moment later, a mechanical sound fills the air. The grounds leading up to my house are a series of walled gardens within walled gardens. A labyrinth that I can change with the opening and closing of thirteen gates. When you're the most hated man in Henson, you need to take a creative approach to security. It's a good thing I did, otherwise, this pretty little stowaway might have skipped off to wherever she pleased.

"You have forty-eight hours." I glance at my watch. "Starting now."

"But you gave Dad and Samantha a week," she exclaims.

I pull out my phone and press the screen. The garage door rolls up, and the gate at the end of the drive opens. There's a tantalizing glimpse of the street beyond. "Don't like it? Leave. This is your only chance to get out of here alive, and you'd be wise to take it. Once that gate closes..." I give her a cold smile. "You're mine. You and your brother."

Miss Stone glances longingly toward freedom, tendrils of her dark hair blowing across her face.

She shakes her head and turns back to me. "I'm not leaving without Barlow. We're not yours if I manage to find him, and I don't care what happens to me. Do your worst."

I lean down until my lips are tantalizingly close to hers and murmur, "I plan to. Tick-tock, Miss Stone."

Leaving her standing by my car with blood on her throat, I enter the code into the locked door, and leave via the shortcut up to the house, closing it firmly behind me.

As I walk along the passage, I examine the ruby beads of blood on the tip of my knife. Then I lick them off.

Miss Stone is a pretty girl, and she tastes delicious. Such a pity that she won't live beyond the next two sunrises.

CHAPTER THIRTEEN

Vivienne

Forty-eight hours to get my brother back, and the clock is ticking.

I emerge from the garage and look up toward the house. It stands on a hill with ornamental gardens sloping upward toward it. Complicated gardens with densely packed hedges and walls. The man who's holding Barlow captive holds all the power, and he isn't going to play fair. I try not to think about the fact that Barlow is in danger right this second. If he cries too much or screams too loudly, what's to stop Tyrant Mercer from losing his patience and hurting my brother?

There are footsteps behind me, and I whirl around, expecting to see Tyrant marching toward me with that knife in his hand.

It's not Tyrant. Instead, a man in his fifties with a dark beard and a neat white shirt emerges into the garage and closes the pin-code door firmly behind him. He ignores me as he gets into the black Cullinan, drives it out of the garage, and parks it by a hedge. Still ignoring my presence, he gathers a bucket, a sponge, and a bottle of wash and wax, and sets about cleaning Tyrant's scrupulously clean car.

I suppose it's not unusual for bleeding young women to appear in the grounds of Tyrant's estate. I don't warrant a first glance, let alone a second one. Fine by me. I don't want anyone getting in my way while I'm trying to reach Barlow.

I walk around the garage and into the garden. A pristine lawn runs up to a high stone wall covered here and there with ivy and evergreen shrubs growing in the flower beds. I'm not actually in the labyrinth yet, so there must be a door somewhere, and if it's closed, I'll wait for it to open. I'll only be waiting fifteen minutes at the most.

Only there isn't a door. Not where I'm looking, at any rate. The stone wall is uninterrupted. No obvious door, and no concealed one, either. Just stone. Even hunting among the ivy gets me nowhere.

A few minutes later, I hear a grinding noise from within the maze, and I freeze, waiting with bated breath for a door to swing open, showing me the way forward. Nothing happens. Tyrant told security that the gates should change configuration every fifteen minutes, but if there isn't a gate here, how am I supposed to get inside? Unless he tricked me and made it impossible for me to proceed.

With a sigh of frustration, I turn and head back to the garage, wondering if I missed something there. The door Tyrant disappeared through is still firmly locked, and it doesn't seem like that's the way I'm supposed to go anyway.

I'm hesitating by the black Cullinan when a voice speaks, making me jump.

"Can I help you with anything, miss?" The man washing the car is watching me with an expression of concern on his face. He wrings out the sponge and shakes the water off his hands. He has friendly eyes and a trustworthy beard. I'm not sure how a beard can be trustworthy, but his is. Neat but bushy and a glossy brown color.

If someone doesn't help me, I'll probably be stuck out here forever. "Hello. Um. Maybe you can, if it's not too much trouble. I'm Vivienne, by the way," I add hastily, realizing I haven't introduced myself.

"Pleased to meet you, Miss Vivienne. I'm Mr. Mercer's driver, Liam Summers." He offers me a polite nod. "Is there something you need?"

I point toward the mansion. "I'm trying to reach Mr. Mercer's house. He said that the path up there is difficult, but I can't even seem to find the path so I can begin."

Mr. Summers glances up toward the house, and is it my imagination or is there a worried flicker in his eyes?

I back away, holding up my hands. "Wait. Never mind. You shouldn't help me. Mr. Mercer will probably punish you."

The driver snorts. I can't tell if it's in amusement, derision, or agreement. "Go back."

"I'm sorry?"

The driver dunks his sponge into the bucket of soapy water and applies it to the car once more. "Go back."

"I'm not giving up."

The man shrugs and keeps soaping Tyrant's car.

I stand around for several more minutes, waiting for something to happen. The only thing that happens is Mr. Summers finishes soaping the car, rinses it with a power hose, puts it back in the garage, and disappears back through the locked door.

A cold wind sweeps across the driveway, making me shiver. I wrap my arms around my body and realize that I left my coat back at the house. I'm freezing, and I'm hungry as well. What am I going to do, stand here waiting for my forty-eight hours to be up? Maybe a better idea would be to escape the grounds and fetch help for Barlow some other way. I'm not sure calling the police is a good idea, but maybe Dad or Samantha have thought of something by now. I don't want to give up. I hate giving up. I don't tackle fiendishly difficult sewing projects just to throw them aside when they get challenging.

I go back to the stone wall and explore it with my hands as well as my eyes. I do it again. And again.

Nothing. No doorway. I can't get into the labyrinth. Tyrant tricked me by making it seem like it was possible, and he's probably watching me right now through a CCTV camera and laughing at me.

Disappointment is a cold stone in my belly, and I turn and head down the driveway. If there's a way in, I can't find it. Tyrant wins this round, but I'm not giving up Barlow. I still have a week to find some other way to get him back.

I don't know what makes me glance to my left when I'm halfway down the driveway, but I do.

And I stop in shock.

There, between some slender cypress trees and surrounded by rose bushes, is a metal gate, standing open. Beyond the gate, I can see hedges, ornamental stone pots, and a water fountain.

A garden. Tyrant's garden.

I can barely believe my eyes. For a second I don't trust the way the gate seems to be beckoning me to enter. It doesn't seem safe. But of *course* it's not safe. Passing through that gate means getting closer to Tyrant, but it's also one step closer to reaching Barlow. Before the fifteen minutes is up and the gate closes on its own, I dash through it.

The temperature seems to change once I'm in the garden. The wind doesn't blow so hard, and I feel a little warmer. A shade more hopeful. I walk slowly through the gardens, admiring their moonlit beauty. Who would have imagined that a man like Tyrant, with his heart full of darkness, money, and violence, would own a garden as beautiful as this. I'm reminded of Renaissance paintings. The Pre-Raphaelites. Classical Rome. I make a left by a hedge, the vista opens up, and I get my first real look at Tyrant's house. It's as beautiful as the grounds, with white columns and long windows through which I can glimpse gilded mirrors and chandeliers.

Someone is standing in one of the second-floor windows. A tall figure with broad shoulders, lit from behind. He appears to be holding something in his arms.

Anger races through me when I realize that it's my brother. I can't see Tyrant's face from here, but his smile is probably gloating as he watches me.

As I'm glaring at Tyrant, a gate to my left grinds open. I dart through the gate and jog along the garden path, unable to stop a satisfied smile spreading over my face. Two gates down, eleven to go.

I don't know why I was panicking. This is too easy.

CHAPTER FOURTEEN

Tyrant

I laugh as I turn away from the window, bouncing the baby in my arms. I caught the smile on her face as she passed through the second gate. After being hopelessly stuck and wasting so much precious time, she stumbled across the first gate by accident, and now she thinks she has my whole labyrinth solved already. What Miss Stone doesn't know is that it's not only the gates that change. As soon as she disappears around a corner, walls will move. Markers like lamps and other decorations shift around. It amused me to design a garden that would confuse anyone who doesn't understand its secrets. I find it fun watching people stumbling around in it, hopelessly lost.

I tickle Barlow's cheek. "Shall we go and watch your sister on the security monitors? It won't be long until she bursts into tears from sheer frustration because she's hopelessly lost, and I can't wait to see it happen."

I walk out of the drawing room and down the passage to a smaller room filled with monitors. Most of them show no movement, but on three, there is the girl, moving through my garden, her head turning left and right as she goes.

Her dark hair tumbles down her back, and her pale dress gleams in the light from the moon, making her look like a lost nymph clothed in spider's silk and starlight. She's already pretty, but she looks beautiful in my garden. Soon she'll be pretty and dead on the grass with her throat and dress shining with blood. Her arms and legs will be sprawled out. Her thighs will feel soft and smooth against my fingers. I imagine Miss Stone will leave behind a beautiful corpse. Meanwhile, I'll watch as she exhausts herself in my labyrinth, take note of where she curls up and goes to sleep, and then go down there and play with the doll-eyed girl. With her hands bound and a gag between her teeth, she won't be able to scream.

I groan and shift on my feet, and I have to adjust my pants which are suddenly tight around my hardening cock. I wonder how wet she'll get as I lick her. How hard she'll cry as I force her to get turned on against her will. I would bet my fortune that if I fuck her, there'll be blood all over my cock after that first thrust.

Imagining all this is doing nothing to quell my raging erection.

I glance at Barlow with narrowed eyes. "I think I kidnapped the wrong sibling. Your sister and I could have more fun, don't you think?"

Barlow looks back at me with wide, trusting eyes. He pats my jaw with his chubby hand, right over my tattoos, and I can't help but laugh. "It's a good thing you can't understand a word of what I'm saying."

Glancing at the monitors, I'm pleased to see that she is headed in completely the wrong direction. From the way she keeps doubling back, I'd say she was thoroughly fucking confused once more.

"Your sister still hasn't made it past the third gate," I murmur to Barlow. "It's almost like she's not trying to get you back."

Barlow grabs a fistful of my shirt before looking restlessly around. He squirms against me, making frustrated little noises, and I realize what's about to happen. It's been a long time since I held one of my siblings when they were this age, but you don't forget.

Barlow starts to cry. Big, open-mouthed wails at a volume to wake the dead. He might be lacking a fear response to strangers, but there's nothing wrong with his lungs.

Angela hurries into the room, her arms outstretched, a warm bottle of formula in her hands. "I was just coming to find you, Mr. Mercer. I'll take him off your hands so you can—"

I turn my body protectively aside so she can't take the baby from me. "Ah-ah. I can do it." I pluck the bottle from her fingers. I enjoyed doing this once upon a time. I forgot how much I missed it. "Did you get everything else I requested?"

Diapers. Romper suits. Wipes. A bassinet. Angela nods, watching with surprise as I settle Barlow in my arms. "Everything is set up in the room down the hall. A proper little nursery. I must say, it's lovely having a baby in the house."

"Don't get used to it. Barlow's only here because his father owes me money."

Angela reaches out and tickles his cheek. "Still. Now that he's here, it makes me realize that a baby is what this house needs. It's time you were married, Mr. Mercer."

I jerk my chin at the door. "Go. You've got work to do."

Angela leaves the room, but she comes back a moment later with a clean white cloth which she lays over my shoulder. "So you can burp him without worrying about your nice shirt."

Barlow finishes the bottle, and I pass it back to Angela before lifting the baby against my shoulder. "Hungry little fellow, aren't you?" Barlow answers a moment later with a burp that seems to make his entire little body quake.

Angela beams at me. "You're a natural. You'll make a wonderful father one day."

I open my mouth to tell her I doubt I'll be a father when I've never met a woman who doesn't irritate the hell out of me, but I'm distracted by Barlow's wriggling. He's been fed and burped, but he's still not happy. "Do you need changing? Is that it?"

"I can do that for you, Mr. Mercer." It's clear my housekeeper is dying to pry the baby away from me and make a fuss over Barlow.

I should just hand him over, but I find myself reluctant to deposit him in Angela's capable hands.

I stole him. He's my baby.

I stride past Angela and carry Barlow down the hall to the makeshift nursery.

She hurries after me. "Mr. Mercer, are you sure you don't need any help?"

"Didn't I ever tell you I have four younger siblings? I've done this a thousand times." I lay the baby down on the changing table and examine his little suit with a frown. "It's been some time. I might be a little rusty. Let me see…"

After a few false starts and some clenched fists and howls from Barlow, I manage to change his wet diaper and get him into a fresh romper.

Angela's worried frown softens into a smile. "Look at that. I've been thinking lately that you're the ideal age to become a father. Not so young you're hot-headed. Not too old you don't have the energy to run after them. This big house needs a woman and babies, and so do you."

I don't need a woman or any babies. I need my fucking money. "This is a hostage situation, Angela. Stop getting clucky."

"Ahh, whatever you want to call it, you do look lovely holding a baby," she says, gazing fondly at me. "If only the pretty little miss down in the garden could see you like this."

I catch sight of myself in the mirror across the room. My hair is falling over my brow. My shirt is rumpled. Barlow is holding on to the silver chain around my throat. The pretty little miss down in the garden would gouge my eyes out if she had the chance.

"I wonder what she's doing now." I glance at Barlow in my arms. "Let's go find out, shall we?"

Back in the security room, Miss Stone is walking in circles, growing more agitated by the second. I smile nastily at the monitors, enjoying the way she's pushing her hands through her hair. Backtracking and second-guessing her movements. Worrying on that plush lower lip with her teeth.

It's not enough anymore to watch her from afar as my garden torments her. I want to torment her myself.

In my arms, Barlow is growing sleepy. His eyes are half closed and his wriggling is slowing down. "Here. I'll be back soon."

Carefully, I deposit him in Angela's arms, and her face diffuses in delight as she cuddles him close. I leave her cooing over the sleepy baby.

As I promised Miss Stone, my front door is unlocked, and I leave it that way as I walk out into the crisp night air. Using the security app on my phone, I open several of the garden doors and close them behind me. I can hear her moving up ahead, coming this way.

I glance around at a stone folly with white benches. An archway with climbing roses. A low wall that she'll see the moment she comes around the corner. Where would I like her to catch sight of me?

The wall. I stretch out, my back propped against bricks, ankles crossed loosely. My clothing is black, and I melt into the shadows as I stand as still as stone.

Miss Stone comes around the corner and casts a dejected gaze over what looks like another dead end. She barely tries to locate the hidden gate next to me before she's turning away and going back the way she came.

"You're terrible at this," I speak quietly, but my voice travels in the still night air. Miss Stone jumps and whirls around. At first, she doesn't see me, and then I smile, and my teeth must gleam in the darkness.

Her expression flattens from fear into dislike. "You remind me of the Cheshire Cat, posing like that. It's cliché."

This girl has a sharp tongue for one who's so desperate and afraid. I stay where I am, enjoying the sight of her covering up her shivers with false bravado. "You wound me. Next you'll tell me that my garden is derivative."

She glances slowly around. "Clearly you've watched *The Shining* one too many times, or maybe you've read the story about the Minotaur and the Labyrinth and loved the idea of being the monster in the maze. Does the maze make you feel clever? Enigmatic? I hate to tell you this, but you're not as complicated as you think. You're just a thug."

I've made this girl angry, and now she's going in for the kill. "Oh, you've read a book of myths and watched a movie. Congratulations on your literature degree."

"Art history and costume design, actually. Do you know what always happens to the monster in the maze? He's killed."

I smile and let my gaze travel down her body. "Eventually. But he fucks a virgin sacrifice first." To my delight, her cheeks flush in the cold air. "You're not as brave as you're pretending to be."

"At least I'm not a pathetic, grandiose bully who's more in love with himself than anyone will ever be with him," she snaps back. "You're not interesting. You're not charming. You're not good-looking."

"I never claimed to be any of those things."

She gives a short, sharp exhalation. "Everyone in Henson talks about you that way. It drives me mad."

"But you're too wise to believe any of that," I guess.

"Of course. And now I see I was right all along."

"Oh, no. A little college nobody thinks I'm cringe. Hashtag sobbing."

She clenches her fists by her temples and makes a frustrated noise. "I can't believe I'm having this stupid conversation. I'm letting you distract me." She turns around and starts to walk away, but a moment later she hurries back, interest and excitement gleaming in her green eyes. "No, wait. If you're here it means that I was going the right way."

Shit. I gave away the answer.

That *is* cringe. Or bad vibes. Or basic. Whatever the eighteen-year-olds in my crew say.

While she hunts for the hidden door, I hunt for a way to distract her. "Your little Bradley has the most irritating scream."

Miss Stone immediately ceases her hunt and turns her focus back to me. I nearly grin in delight. She's so much fun to manipulate.

"Barlow? Why is he crying? Are you hurting him? Please just let me see him. He must be hungry by now and need changing as well. Who's going to do that?"

"He was. I did it."

Miss Stone blinks. "What?"

"I fed him. I changed him." I give her my coldest smile. "When you and your family are dead, I think I'll adopt him. Raise him to be just like me."

She stares at me in shock, and then she slowly shakes her head. "You're not really going to do that. His crying is going to wear on your nerves, and then you'll lose your temper and hurt him."

"Probably. You'd better hurry up and get to him. Otherwise, it will be all your fault when something terrible happens."

I anticipate her screaming at me and having a complete breakdown at my feet. It will be just wonderful when it happens. Any second now.

Only Miss Stone doesn't scream or sob. She steps closer and presses her hands imploringly against my chest. I'm lounging atop the wall and our eyes are at the same level.

"Please," she whispers, and her heartfelt expression makes the nasty words I was about to say freeze in my throat. "You don't understand. I can't lose Barlow. He's innocent in all this. He's the only good thing I have. I'll die if something happens to him."

I drop my gaze and look at her hands. Such small, pretty hands. She's touching me the way a woman might touch her lover right before she leans in to kiss him. If I was shirtless, it would be how she touches me when she's imploring me to fuck her. I picture myself capturing her hands against my chest and slamming my mouth over hers.

Her green eyes are huge and liquid as she supplicates me. "Take me instead. I won't talk back. Well, I'll try not to, but you're very annoying, and—" She takes a calming breath. "I promise I won't talk back. I'll do whatever you want me to. Just please, *please* let Barlow go."

What is it about Miss Stone, dangerously close to tears and pleading for her brother, that's turning me on so much? My gaze drags up her body to her beautiful face. I want to fist my hand in her hair and flick her lips with my tongue, but I keep my hands forcefully in my lap.

I never wanted a woman. My own woman. The mother of my children. A fierce, beautiful little thing to fuck my babies into, who will protect them to the ends of the earth and back. There's no woman I've met that I would trust to be as insanely overprotective as I would be. Miss Stone begging for her baby brother and running herself to exhaustion to save him is the hottest thing I've ever seen.

"Mr. Mercer?" she whispers when I don't say anything.

I'm meant to be distracting and tormenting Miss Stone, not the other way around. "I just took two hours off your time limit. You have forty-one left."

She rips her hands off my chest and steps away from me. "What? Why?"

"For pissing me off," I growl.

Anger bleeds into her expression. "You *bastard*."

"Name-calling? There goes another four. Keep talking and I'll keep taking away hours."

"It isn't fair if you keep changing the rules."

"Who said any of this was going to be fair? I'm letting you play the game. I'm giving you a chance. Am I not merciful?"

Miss Stone's eyes flash, and she really loses her temper. "You're a power-hungry asshole who expects everyone to roll over at your feet out of pure fear. *Yes, Mr. Mercer. Thank you, Mr. Mercer.* I'm not afraid of you. You're a bully, just like all tyrants are. Just like your name. Do you know what happens to tyrants? They're toppled. Their regimes end. Their statues are torn down. Read some history."

Oh, this girl is mouthy. I stand up and push past her as if I'm leaving her behind, but I'm only pretending to go. I whip around, grab her by the throat, and slam her into the wall. Miss Stone gasps and her eyes grow huge. She grabs my wrist and struggles against me, but she's not going anywhere.

My hand tightens mercilessly around her slender throat. Such a pretty neck. So very chokeable.

"You're doing everything right to make me lose my temper," I growl through my teeth, my nose an inch from hers. I crave her pitiful surrender like oxygen. She's so fucking pure. So *good*. I hate it. "No one asked you to sneak into my home and enact a daring rescue. If you're just going to whine, you should give up and go home."

Desperately, Miss Stone shakes her head.

"Why not?" I demand. I'll figure out her buttons and press every one of them until she's a crying mess at my feet and she loses to me.

"Because—" she wheezes around the grip I have on her throat. "Because you don't abandon family. Please, I can't breathe."

I want to throw up. You don't abandon family? How honorable. How *admirable*. What total fucking bullshit. People abandon family all the time. She's probably been abandoned herself in one way or another. Her father's had another child well over a decade after she was born. Replaced her with a new family. She must feel angry about that.

In fact, I'll prove she does.

"You're a pathetic little child." I let her go and stride through my labyrinth, and behind me, I hear her gasping for breath. A moment later, the hidden door opens with a mechanical whir. There's a shocked cry, and then the sound of footsteps receding.

For *fuck's* sake. She's made it through the fourth gate. I keep walking, angry at myself as well as at her.

Miss Stone isn't here out of loyalty or love. Something else is driving her, and I'm going to find out what it is. At the very least, I'll discover that she's not the ever-adoring sister she pretends she is. No one likes a half-brother that much. She's had jealous and petty thoughts, and I'll find out what they are and throw them in Miss Perfect's pretty fucking face.

The best place to discover her secrets is in her bedroom, so I get into my car and drive to her home.

The Stone residence is in darkness and the car isn't in the driveway. I wonder where Owen Stone and his wife are. Presumably out somewhere trying to get my money if they know what's good for them.

In their haste to do what I've asked of them, they've left the back door unlocked, so I don't even have to smash a window to get inside. Their dinner has been left on the kitchen table and it's grown cold. A glass is smashed on the floor. A coat is lying in the hall, and I pick it up and breathe in the scent of spring blossoms.

I throw the garment away in disgust. I shouldn't have to know what that girl smells like. She's in my labyrinth, focused on her task, and I'm in here to dig up dirt on her.

Upstairs, I find her bedroom at the end of the hall. There's her made bed, her paperback novels, her desk covered in knickknacks and papers. I discover her name is Vivienne and turn the pleasing syllables over in my head. Of course she has a pretty name. How predictable.

There are cardboard boxes and random junk that doesn't belong to her, like golf clubs, stacked up in the middle of the room. Vivienne sleeps here sometimes, but she doesn't live here. Presumably, she lives at Henson University. I hope she hasn't taken everything important with her, but what I'm looking for isn't the sort of thing a young woman would take to college.

In the third drawer of her desk, I find what I'm looking for. Vivienne's teenage diaries, and I pull them out with a smirk on my face. Inside these covers, I should discover every nasty thought she's ever had about her father's new wife, the pregnancy, and the injustice of being replaced and neglected because of a new baby. There are three diaries, the first beginning five years ago when she moved to Henson at age fourteen. Turning the pages, and reading Vivienne's loopy cursive, I murmur, "What secrets do you have for me, Miss Stone?"

Words like *Henson*, *school*, *weather*, and *friends* jump out at me. Boring. Irrelevant. I want complaining. I need *spite*.

A familiar name catches my eye, and as I stop to read the entry, a smile spreads over my face. By the time I'm done with two pages, I'm grinning with glee. This is not what I was expecting. It's got nothing to do with Barlow, her stepmother, or even her father, but what I've found in Vivienne's diary is far more humiliating than anything I'd hoped for.

I snap the diary shut and head for the door, laughing as I leave the house and head back to my car. This is going to destroy Vivienne.

CHAPTER FIFTEEN

Vivienne

"What the hell?" I whisper, gazing out across serene, still waters reflecting the silvery light of the moon. A lake. Tyrant Mercer has a *lake* on his property.

It's not a big lake, granted, but it's too big to be called a pond. You could get in a boat and row across it, and it would take you several minutes to reach the other side. Of all the rumors I've heard about Tyrant over the years, no one's ever mentioned that the grounds of his home are big enough for a lake and a labyrinth.

That he keeps a menagerie of tigers, lions, venomous snakes, and other predators? I heard that rumor, and I'm overwhelmingly grateful that so far nothing here has threatened to kill me except Tyrant himself. There's also the rumor that he killed five men in one day when the car they were traveling in splashed muddy water all over him, ruining one of his suits. I can imagine how an incident four years ago may have spiraled into that particular rumor. The most notorious rumor about Tyrant Mercer is a lot bigger than lions and tigers and killing strangers who ruin his Italian wool suits.

It's the rumor that he killed his own father.

Some versions of the story are that at nine years old, he walked in on his father having sex with a woman who wasn't his mother, and he immediately shot him in the head. Another version is that once he was a grown man, Tyrant tracked down the father who abandoned him as a child and killed him with his bare hands. I happen to know that the suit-ruining story has a grain of truth, which makes me wonder if the same goes for the patricide rumor. I glance at the serene surface of the lake, wondering if it conceals any anacondas, alligators, piranhas, or other predators.

I'm not wearing a watch, so I don't know how much time has passed since I entered Tyrant's labyrinth, but it feels like it's been many, many hours. My body is tired and cold, and there's so much farther to go before I reach the house. I need to rest for a little while.

A boathouse is visible among the rushes and trees to my left. It might be a good idea for me to attempt a short nap there if the door is unlocked.

When I walk over and try the handle, the door sticks a little, but it opens. Inside it's illuminated by moonlight coming in through the windows, and it feels like the rafters are probably full of spiderwebs, but the wooden floor is dry and not too dusty.

I sit in the corner with my back propped against the wall and my arms wrapped around my knees. Even inside away from that labyrinth, I don't feel safe. This is Tyrant's home, and he can get to me anytime he wants. Lying down on the floor and letting my guard down seems like an invitation for something terrible to happen.

It must be hours past midnight, and my eyes burn with fatigue. Slowly, against my will, my head nods forward. I'll just rest my head on my knees for a moment…

"Dear diary, you won't believe what happened today. I barely believe it myself."

My head snaps up at the sound of a deep, gloating voice cutting through my slumber. I glance around in confusion, wondering where the hell I am. I'm sitting on a wooden floor. There's the sound of lapping water from outside.

Tyrant Mercer's labyrinth. The boathouse. Barlow. I remember now. My stomach fills with dread as I realize I'm not alone. Someone is moving in the shadows, and from their mocking voice, I know exactly who it is.

"My heart is still racing and my palms are sweating as I write this."

Tyrant Mercer steps toward me out of the shadows with a taunting smile on his lips and a pink book in his large, tattooed hand. For some bizarre reason, he's holding one of my teenage diaries and reading aloud from it.

This can't be happening.

I'm still asleep and having a nightmare.

"There will never be a day more wonderful than this one as long as I shall live. Let July seventeenth mark the occasion of the best day of my life. I will be thinking about these moments until I die."

My body flushes hot and cold as I realize which entry he's

reading from. I was fifteen when I wrote those words. The events of that day—and worse, how I gushed about them—are excruciating to remember considering where I am now. It's bad enough what's on those first two or three pages, but the confession I wrote after? It's the last thing I want anyone to know, and I would rather tie rocks to my ankles and hurl myself into Tyrant's lake than have him discover my most shameful secret.

I get slowly to my feet, my palms pressed against the wall behind me while my mind races. Tyrant is nearly twice my size. There's no way I'll be able to wrestle that diary away from him, and he's probably dying for me to try. If I'm not here, if I refuse to listen, he'll lose interest in reading it aloud.

Pretending that I'm bored by this new turn of events and not inwardly panicking, I head for the door with what I hope is a nonchalant expression on my face.

When I try the handle, I find that it's locked.

"Ah-ah, Vivienne. You're not getting out of here so easily, and that door isn't on a timer."

I turn around and see that Tyrant has a set of keys dangling from his forefinger.

I swallow down a wave of anxiety. "You can keep my diary. Go nuts, read as much of it as you like if you're that interested in the ramblings of a teenage girl. I've finished my nap, and now I'm going back out there to your labyrinth. I'm on the clock, remember? I don't have time for this."

Tyrant tucks the keys back into his pocket with a smirk. "You'll do whatever I want, Vivienne, and right now you are going to listen to every glorious detail of this fascinating diary entry."

Not the whole entry. Please, God, no.

My despair must show on my face. Tyrant laughs, raises my diary, and keeps reading.

"It's been so hot these past few weeks. Too hot to go home and be a nuisance to Dad and Samantha until it's dinnertime. If I'm late, they don't care much. I think they prefer it when I'm not around so they can talk about what they're most excited for, which is starting a family of their own. They don't need to hide the fact that they want a baby. I'm not jealous. I'm excited. I love babies, and I've always wanted a little sister or brother. If Samantha has a baby, there'll be all sorts of things for me to do to help like wash tiny itty bitty baby clothes, mash up fruit and vegetables for baby food, and sing the little one to sleep. It will be wonderful if Samantha is able to get pregnant."

A pang goes through me at the memory. The anticipation I felt that Samantha might get pregnant. The joy when I discovered she was. After Barlow was born, for whole hours at a time, I was able to forget the terrible thing that happened when I was fifteen. I never thought I would make it through all that pain, but Barlow saved my life, which is why I won't give up trying to get him back from Tyrant Mercer. Barlow saved me, and now I'm going to save him.

Tyrant turns the page and keeps reading. *"Anyway, this evening I was sitting on the edge of the fountain down in the big park. That side of the park is usually pretty quiet, but you can still hear the traffic on the main road. I was enjoying the way the hot breeze would blow spray from the fountain across my back and watching the occasional person walk by.*

"About forty feet from me, a beautiful girl in a tight, coral-colored dress was standing at the curb like she was waiting for someone. She was my age or maybe a year older, but we were not similar in any other way. I would never be brave enough to wear such a tight dress. I would never be allowed to wear such a tight dress, but I was vividly imagining what I'd look like in something so daring."

Tyrant glances at me, his head on one side as he assesses my body. "That sexy, coral-colored dress? It wouldn't suit you, little ingenue."

I narrow my eyes in hatred. That was unnecessary. I know now that such a garment would make me look like a little girl playing dress-up with her mother's sophisticated clothes, but give me a break. I was wondering about it to my diary, and I was fifteen.

Enjoying that he's pissed me off, Tyrant smirks and keeps reading. *"The fountain had been leaking and there was a puddle in the road—"*

"Wait," I call. Tyrant pauses and raises one of his eyebrows at me. "I know what happens next. You know what happens next. Why are we wasting time with this?"

"Why would I remember anything about events that you wrote about in your diary? I'm on tenterhooks to find out what happens next. Don't interrupt me again or I'll take six hours off your time limit."

I grit my teeth and clench my fists. I hate him so much.

"The fountain had been leaking and there was a puddle in the road right by where the girl was standing. Just then, a car came along, and from the way it slowed down, I thought it was the car the girl was waiting for. Suddenly it swerved, sped up, and drove right through the puddle, splashing dirty road water all over the girl. She gasped in shock and jumped back, but it was too late. Her dress was ruined, her hair

was dripping, and so was her makeup. She couldn't do anything but stare down at herself in shock and despair while the men in the car all laughed at her.

"They were so busy laughing that they didn't notice someone striding across the road with murder in his eyes. He came out of nowhere, reached in through the car window, and pulled the driver out of the car. Just yanked a whole person through a car window and threw him to the ground. The driver was young, only nineteen or twenty, and probably very stupid if he thought it was funny to go around humiliating girls in the street. But he wasn't too stupid to know that he'd made a huge mistake when he saw who was standing over him, angrier than a bull with a red flag being waved in its face.

"I gripped the edge of the fountain with both hands, knowing I should flee, but my heart was pounding so hard, and I had to know what happened next. I recognized the man in the black suit. Tyrant Mercer, and he was furious.

"The man on the ground tried to flee, but as soon as he was on his feet, Tyrant punched him, a brutal blow that made the driver crumple to the ground, unconscious. One of the other men jumped out of the car and tried to run, but Tyrant pulled out a gun and shot him in the thigh. The crack of the gun echoed off the buildings. The road. Blood spattered everywhere. The gunshot should have brought people running, but suddenly everyone was minding their own business.

"The last man emerged from the car holding a knife. He and Tyrant stared each other down for a moment. Attack, or flee? His two friends were bleeding in the road, but apparently, this man thought he could take Tyrant because, a moment later, he attacked.

"Tyrant got the knife away from him and stabbed the man in the thigh, right above his knee. Gripping the handle, he forced it into his knee until the man screamed in pain. 'Say you're sorry, or I'll pop your kneecap off and you'll be crawling for the rest of your life.'

"The man was shaking in pain and staring at the knife embedded in his leg, but he managed a stumbling apology. 'I'm s-sorry. I won't do it again.'

"'Don't apologize to me, moron. Say you're sorry to her.'

"The girl in the dripping coral dress was standing on the sidewalk, watching the scene unfold.

"'I'm sorry, I'm sorry, I'm sorry.'

"But it wasn't enough for Tyrant, and he twisted the knife until the man screamed again. 'You can do better than that.'

"'I said I'm sorry!' the man shrieked.

"Tyrant yanked the knife out and straightened up while the man clutched his leg. It was a blistering hot day, but Tyrant hadn't even broken a sweat. There was blood all over his hands and dripping from the knife.

"Apparently, Tyrant wasn't satisfied with the apology, or maybe he still had some anger to work through, because he leaned down, grasped the man's left ear, and sliced it off in a blur of silver and a spurt of blood.

"The man screamed louder than before, one hand clutched to the side of his head. Tyrant pushed the dripping ear into the man's mouth, shoving it so deep that he choked.

"'I won't remember your face. But I will remember some cunt without an ear. Cross me again, and I'll break every bone in your body and bury you alive.'

"Then he walked over and gave the other two men the same treatment. The one who was unconscious didn't notice when Tyrant sliced off his ear, while his friend vomited his up behind him. The one with a bullet in his thigh tried to get up and run, but he fell right back down again as Tyrant loomed closer with the knife.

"'No, no, n—aah!'

"Schhk. Splat. Tyrant tossed the ear onto the asphalt and then he threw the knife in the other direction.

"Finally, he approached the girl, and the fury on his face melted into concern. He took off his suit jacket and wrapped it around her. She was crying, and he kept his arm tightly around her waist, comforting her with bloodied hands. He put her into his car, and they drove off together.

"I stared after them for a long time. I didn't even notice the bleeding men limping back to their car and driving away. The way he held her. The way all he cared about was the fact that she was crying. Who was she to him? Who was he to her? If they were on a date, has he kissed her?"

Tyrant meets my gaze over the top of my diary. "How envious you are. Shall I satisfy your curiosity and tell you who she is?"

"That was a lifetime ago. I don't care who she is."

His smile widens. "Liar. You cared then, and you care now. I can see it written all over your face."

Yet Tyrant doesn't say anything. He's enjoying the fact that I'm trapped in a hurricane of emotions.

"Her name is Camilla. It was her sixteenth birthday, and I was taking her out to dinner."

"You were a grown man and dating a sixteen-year-old? Creep."

"And yet you hoped I would date you. You hoped I would do all kinds of things to you," he says, his gaze caressing my body.

"You're disgusting," I whisper, my nails digging into my palms. At the same time, I'm picturing Tyrant kissing that girl in the coral dress, his hands running over her, fingers pushing possessively into the peachy cleft of her ass.

"Whatever you're imagining, stop it. Camilla is my sister."

I blink in surprise. The vision of Tyrant kissing that girl snaps out of existence. His sister? I feel relieved, and then annoyed at myself that I feel any such thing. Not one ounce of that relief, not one whisper of it, better be showing on my face.

"You're pleased she's my sister," Tyrant says with a wicked smile.

"I couldn't give a damn who she is."

"You're a liar, Vivienne," he says and returns to perusing my diary, trying to find his place.

My blood pressure ratchets up. No more. This can't go on.

"I can fill you in on the rest," I tell him quickly. "I'll say it out loud so you can enjoy my complete and utter humiliation in person instead of from my diary. I…" I swallow hard, because even though I have to say this, I really, really don't want to. "I touched myself thinking about you," I say in a rush. "The first orgasm I ever had, I was thinking about you. I came home from seeing you beat the shit out of those men and it turned me on." Heat erupts in my cheeks. I've never admitted that shameful secret to anybody. I wish the ground would swallow me up, but I force myself to look at Tyrant. "Now you know every demeaning thing about that day. Are you happy? Are we done?"

Tyrant studies me through narrowed eyes for a long time. In his hands, my diary starts to close. Only by a millimeter at first. Then another and another. Relief washes over me. He's losing interest, or I'm making him realize how disgusting he is to peruse the sexual fantasies of a teenage girl.

"Most teenage girls fantasize about pop stars and tortured werewolves," he says. "What made a good little girl like you crush on a violent asshole like me? It wasn't pretty what I did to those men. You should have been throwing up. Did you even wince? Feel a little sick?"

Not once, but why is none of his goddamn business.

Tyrant waits, eyebrows raised. "Nothing to say? Then I'll keep reading."

My heart leaps into my throat. He can't keep reading. He *can't*. I've kept what's written in that diary buried so long that I'm more terrified of it than anything Tyrant could do to me. His fingers move to turn the page, and I lose my last shred of self-control. With a cry of desperation, I run across the boathouse and try to snatch the diary from his fingers.

He holds it up out of my reach, his expression mystified. "You're panicking, Vivienne. What could be on these pages that's worse than what I've already read aloud? What you've already told me? Did you become my stalker and I didn't know it? Did you steal my trash? Wipe your pussy juices on my front gate?"

If only it was something stupid like that. Tears spring into my eyes as I attempt to snatch the diary from his fingers, and my voice cracks. "I already told you everything. There's nothing else that's even about you. Why are you doing this to me?"

The diary is hopelessly far over my head. I cling to the sleeve of his suit, trying to drag his arm down, but he doesn't move even one inch. It would be easier to snatch a star from the sky.

"Why? Because I'm having so much fun."

A sob rises up my throat. *Fun.*

I look around for a weapon through tear-blurred eyes. Something sharp, or something heavy and blunt. Anything. This is a boathouse, but there isn't even an oar I can hit him with over the head. I have nothing to stop Tyrant, so I can only turn away from him, squeeze my eyes shut, and cover my ears. If he wants to read, then I'm not going to listen. I'm not here. I'm far away, sitting on my dorm room floor with something beautiful and silky in my lap that I'm sewing with a needle and thread.

A strong hand seizes my wrist and drags it away from my ear.

"You're going to listen," Tyrant snarls. "You broke into my home. You invaded my privacy. It's your turn to know what that feels like. Stop being a fucking baby and acting like I'm destroying your life with the nonsense you wrote about me four years ago."

I can feel the bones of my wrist grinding against each other in his grip. I try to pull away, but it's useless. I'm leashed to him.

"Where was I? Oh, yes."

He reads aloud my detailed description of how I masturbated to thoughts of him. What I thought it would be like to be kissed by him. Touched by him. Fucked by him. Most important of all, adored by him.

"Stop, please," I whimper, twisting my arm as I struggle to get away.

Tyrant continues without mercy. "*I think what I like best is fantasizing about him hurting Lucas. Maybe I shouldn't, but seeing Tyrant defend the girl in the coral dress makes me wonder what he'd do if I told him what happened."* Tyrant slows down, his gleeful expression fading as his brows draw together. *"He's the only one who would believe me. I would never ask anyone to hurt Lucas, but thinking about it isn't so terrible, is it? I don't know what hurts me more, that it happened, or that Dad didn't believe me."*

All the malice has vanished from Tyrant's face, and he's frowning at my diary. He's not going to stop now. He's going to read every last word. The fight goes out of me, but he's still holding on to my wrist. I slump in his grasp, a marionette held up by a single string.

"He said that I must have misunderstood Lucas, but later I heard him talking to Samantha, and he told her I was lying. He's known Lucas for years, and Lucas would never do anything like that. Besides, Lucas is good-looking and he's always got women falling over him, so what would he want with me?

"I cried and cried when I heard that. My insides felt like they were on fire. It was worse than all the times that Mom forgot about me. It's worse than finding her dead body, cold and covered in vomit. I thought I couldn't feel more alone than I did at that moment. I didn't think there could be anything more terrifying in the world than that.

"I need to stop thinking about all this and writing it all down, but I can't make myself stop. Lucas came around again tonight. I need my box to make the pain stop. There are already so many cuts. Sometimes when I catch sight of myself in the bathroom mirror, I'm terrified by what I see. I don't know how to stop. I feel like I'm going to cut and cut until there's nothing left of me."

Tyrant trails off into silence, but his eyes are still moving, absorbing every humiliating, painful thing that I poured onto the page. The silence is excruciating. He knows everything about my secret, and he's the only one who does. I should have burned that diary so no one could ever find it.

As he keeps reading, he slowly lets go of my wrist. I flee to the other side of the boathouse, slump against the wall, and slide down until I'm sitting on the floor with my arms wrapped tightly around my knees. I want the world to end. I want to die.

Tyrant drops his hand so my diary is dangling by his side. He stares straight ahead for a moment. Then he turns to me. "Lucas who?"

When I don't answer, he walks over and stands in front of me. I stare at his large feet in their polished shoes.

"I said, Lucas who?"

"None of your business."

Tyrant hunkers down to my eye level. He lifts my diary and reads aloud, "*I want Tyrant to cut me and let all the ugliness out. Deeper than I cut myself. I'm such a coward. He could do it so much better than I could.* That sounds like my business."

I shake my head, my fingers clenched on my knees. "I don't care what I said when I was fifteen. I wasn't talking to you. I was talking to an idea of you. You've hurt me as much as you possibly could. Take two or six or twelve hours off my deadline, unlock that door, and let me go and find Barlow."

"Lucas. Who."

Those two words hammer into my brain, and I can't take it anymore. I shoot to my feet and scream. I shriek every curse word I can think of at the top of my lungs. My fingers are in my hair, pulling as hard as I can. Pain is the only thing that I crave.

"Vivienne. Don't." Tyrant seizes my wrists and forces me to stop. He traps my hands against his chest, and so I scratch his throat with my fingernails until I feel wetness beneath my fingers. If I can't hurt myself then I'll hurt him until he lets me go.

"You only want his name so you can tell me you don't believe me as well," I shriek at him as I struggle back and forth in his iron grip. "I'm not giving you that power. You've already stolen everything else from me. I won't let you take one more thing."

The diary has fallen at our feet, and seeing it laying open like that and displaying all my secrets feels obscene, and I moan at the sight. Tyrant kicks it away and it skitters into a dark corner where we can't see it.

I've disgusted him. *Him*. Tyrant Mercer, who maims and kills people for a living.

"Look at me," he commands.

"Don't touch me. I *hate* you."

He releases one of my wrists and shoves my chin up, forcing me to look at him. His harsh good looks are emphasized by the shadows, and his blue eyes blaze with cold fury. "Show me what you're hiding."

"I'm not giving you his name."

He glances down at my ribs, and I realize with horror what he means. He doesn't just want a name. He wants to see my scars.

"Never." There's no way in hell that's happening. I've never shown them to anyone before. Not a friend. Not a boy. Not even a doctor. Tyrant might be able to strip my secrets from my diary, but he can't have what's on my body as well.

"You asked for my help," Tyrant says. "You begged for me to know all about your pain four years ago. That's not a lot of time. Things can't have changed that much. So show me."

"I was fifteen. A lot changes in four years."

"Oh yes? Like your father suddenly believing you when you tell him that his friend is a predator?"

I want to spit in his face. I scream again and struggle in his grip. When I was fifteen, I was miserable enough to comfort myself with a fantasy about Tyrant, but this man isn't anyone's savior. He's a violent criminal who stole my brother and terrified my family over a gambling debt. The scars are *my* ugliness, and I'm not sharing them with anyone. If I show him, then I'll be handing him the power to make me feel even more worthless than I already do.

"Vivienne. Show me."

"One flicker in your eyes will be enough for you to tell me I'm disgusting. I'm not giving you that kind of power."

"Do you really think that after all I've seen and done, anything that you can show me will be too much for me?"

A lump rises in my throat. I never wrote that in my diary, but it's what I always hoped, that a man as monstrous as him wouldn't even flinch. Tyrant wouldn't have to psych himself up to tell me that it didn't matter to him that I had scars. He wouldn't expect me to be slavishly grateful to him that he's able to stomach the sight of me. He wouldn't even see my scars. That was the fantasy.

"I need to get to Barlow," I whimper.

"The clock has stopped in here."

I squeeze my eyes shut. Now he stops the clock? Why did the first person who found out about my scars have to be him? The overwhelming love I had for Tyrant is etched into these scars. My fantasies about him are carved into my body.

"Please stop tormenting me. Just let me fail at your labyrinth and then kill my family. It will be easier for me to bear."

"This isn't about tormenting you."

Tears collect on my lashes, and I brush them away. "Then I don't understand why you want me to show them to you."

"Because I really did think you were perfect."

I look up at him. "What?"

"I hate perfect." Tyrant cups my jaw in his large, warm hand. His velvety voice caresses me. "You wanted me to hurt you. Show me what you wished I could do better."

This feels like a seduction, or what I've always imagined a seduction must be like. Doing anything Tyrant wants is a mistake, but in this darkened boathouse with him standing over me, speaking so coaxingly, I feel dangerously tempted.

"I'm not showing you anything," I whisper.

"Are you so sure about that?" Tyrant dips his head so close that I feel his lips ghost over mine as he murmurs, "I believe you, angel."

I believe you.

The tears that have gathered on my lashes spill down my cheeks. Tyrant brushes his mouth over mine again, and I breathe unsteadily. I've never been kissed before, but my lips seem to know what to do, and they part for him. He seems surprised by my surrender. Then he smiles, looks at me through half-lidded eyes, and slants his mouth hungrily over mine. He kisses me slowly, and it's not an innocent kiss. He parts my lips and sweeps his tongue into my mouth, caressing me.

This is dangerous.

I'm too far gone.

I don't care what he does next if only he keeps believing me.

When he breaks the kiss, he runs his teeth over his lower lip as if enjoying the way I taste.

Then he waits.

"You thought I was perfect because I wanted to save my brother, and that annoyed you so much that you went and found my diary. Now you know I'm so far from perfect. I'm completely broken, and I'll never, ever be put back together. No one's going to find out about these scars for the rest of my life, but seeing as you already know, fine. Let me look into your eyes as you see something that no one else ever will."

Before I can change my mind, I grasp the hem of my dress, pull it up over my head with my T-shirt, and throw it aside. Terrified by what I've just done, I stare straight ahead at the bloody fingernail marks I scored into Tyrant's collarbone. Cold night air touches my flesh and I shiver. I'm standing in front of the most dangerous man in Henson, if not the whole state, in a triangle lace bra and tiny little briefs, every single one of my scars on display.

But I've done it now.

It's too late to take it back.

Slowly, I raise my chin and look into his face.

Instantly, I know I've made a huge mistake. Tyrant's eyes are filled with the horror of what I've done to myself. Things I'll never be able to undo. Things I'll probably do again and again because I'm too weak to stop. There aren't a handful of scars. There are dozens and dozens of them, all over my abdomen, from beneath my breasts all the way down to my pubic bone.

Anger sweeps over Tyrant's face and he seizes my upper arms. "Vivienne, what the fuck is wrong with you?"

"I don't know," I whisper, my voice shaking with tears. He's right in my face, and I try to pull away from him, but he's holding me too tightly. I condemn myself for this every day. I don't need his revulsion as well. "Let go of me, please. I want to leave."

Tyrant gives me a shake, and now he's shouting at me. "Why did you do it? What possessed you?"

Fresh tears spill down my cheeks, and I start to sob. "I know I'm disgusting. You don't have to look at me."

"I don't mean your scars." His jaw pulses in anger and his blue eyes are burning. "Those people. Your father. Your stepmother. They did this to you, and you're here killing yourself trying to save their child. Are you completely insane?"

CHAPTER SIXTEEN

Tyrant

"When you saw me standing in your home, why didn't you step out of your hiding place and tell me to kill them?" I demand of Vivienne.

"Tyrant, you're hurting me," she whimpers, struggling in my grip.

I realize I'm squeezing Vivienne's upper arms so hard that I'm leaving bruises on her tender flesh. I don't know what I expected to see when Vivienne took off her dress, but I wasn't ready for the pure rage that swept over me at the sight of her scars. Now I'm unloading all my anger onto a naked, crying, scared girl.

I take a deep breath and make myself loosen my grip, but I don't let go of her. I shouldn't have said, *What the fuck is wrong with you*, because it's obviously something she's asked herself again and again.

I try again and lower my voice so I'm no longer shouting at

her. "Why are you helping them get their child back? Why are you suffering even more for those people?"

Vivienne takes a few moments to compose herself while she wipes the tears from her cheeks. "Because I had to save Barlow. Dad and Samantha must be losing their minds with worry."

"You should have been jumping for joy that someone was finally hurting them like they deserve."

Of all the startled looks Vivienne has given me, this has to be the most horrified of all.

"Look me in the eye and tell me they don't deserve it," I demand.

"They don't deserve to have their child stolen from them, and Barlow doesn't deserve to be ripped away from his family and used as a pawn."

I hunt Vivienne's expression for any sign that she doesn't believe what she's saying, but she means every word. God fucking dammit. I won't accept that. "Admit you're enjoying that they're finally being punished for what they've done to you."

Vivienne looks at me like I'm crazy. "I don't feel any such thing! All I've felt since I wound up in your labyrinth is stomach-churning anxiety."

"You liked what I did to those men who humiliated my sister. Your father and stepmother deserve far fucking worse."

"Only according to you." She gazes at me in silence for a moment. "You killed your father, didn't you?"

I feel a jolt of surprise at her sudden question, and then I laugh softly. I haven't thought about that cherished memory in years. "I made that man cry for his mother, and she'd been dead for twenty years. How do you know about that?"

"I heard a rumor. Why did you do it?"

Vivienne is trembling before me in her underwear. She looks so vulnerable, and I'm feeling so turned on all of a sudden. It must be all this talk of violence.

I take her jaw in my hand and smile, my lips close to hers. "I don't like it when people abandon me, angel. It makes me crazy."

"A lot of things seem to make you crazy."

Her nipples are standing out in little points through the white lace, and her arms are protectively wrapped around her ribs. I'm no stranger to violence, and I've heard of self-harm, but I've never seen it for myself. In my experience, people go to extraordinary lengths not to bleed and feel pain.

Vivienne notices me gazing at her scars. "I've never shown anyone before," she whispers. "How…how does it look?"

"Move your arms."

She drops them, and I take a good, long look at her. I stroke my forefinger over her collarbone and down over her chest. I tweak one of her nipples through her lace bra, and she makes a gasping sound that goes straight to my dick. This girl would look stunning trapped beneath me as I fucked her into my mattress. I want her innocent wetness all over my fingers. Coating my dick.

"Tyrant, please," she whimpers. "Just tell me how it looks."

Her scars? I don't know. I'm too transfixed by the sight of her.

"You're really fucking sexy," I say huskily.

Vivienne's face transforms in disgust. "Don't patronize me. Don't *lie* to me." She shoves my chest with both hands, and I let her do it because this girl has only ever directed violence at herself. She should inflict it all on me because I can take it.

When she's done pushing me, I step toward her once more and take her in my arms. "I'm not lying."

"You told me I'm not sexy just ten minutes ago," she says, as I plant kisses along her collarbone and up to her throat.

"I said you wouldn't be sexy in that coral dress, not that you're not sexy at all. Your body looks incredible in…softer things. You're like a fairy." I run my finger under the lace strap of her bra. "An angel. You're beautiful, and I'm not lying to you. The fact that no one's seen these scars but me?" I hum my appreciation against her throat. "That makes me want to be all your firsts."

"You're so full of shit," she tells me. "You'll say anything to win. I'm not forgetting about Barlow."

This is about so much more than Barlow. She shouldn't be thinking about Barlow right now. She should only be thinking about me.

I grip her throat and squeeze, and her eyes go wide. Lovingly against her lips, I murmur, "I could hurt you, angel. I could make you bleed with one hard, deep thrust."

This time, Vivienne doesn't try to grab my wrist and pull my hand away. Her green eyes are filled with fear and longing, which is the sexiest thing I've ever seen.

I smile and flick her lips with my tongue. "What a good girl you are." I lift my hand to her ribs, but she cries out in horror and shrinks away from me.

"Don't touch my scars. I can't bear it if you touch them."

"But I want to feel you."

"I feel disgusting," she whimpers.

"I'll make you a promise," I whisper, my lips ghosting over hers. "I'll touch your body, and the only thing either of us will feel is how much we want to fuck."

Vivienne still looks afraid, but she doesn't stop me as I put my hand on her and caress her ribs. She feels warm, and her heart is beating wildly. I run my knuckles over her belly and she gasps against the hand I have wrapped around her throat.

"Mm, that's better. Who's Tyrant's good girl?" I murmur, running a finger around the inside of her panties. Vivienne is so caught up in what I'm making her feel that she doesn't answer. I squeeze her throat tighter. "Say it."

"Um—me?" Vivienne asks uncertainly.

"That's right, angel. I love to be sweet to my girl." I push my finger deeper into her underwear until it slides between her pussy lips.

Slides easily.

Christ. She's so fucking wet.

Vivienne rises up on her toes and her eyelashes flutter as I caress her clit. I press my forehead to hers and groan, "Oh, fuck. You're soaking wet for me. I've never felt anything like it. How many times in your life have you been this wet and turned on by me?"

"Hundreds," she confesses in a whisper.

"Good thing I'm finally here so I can do something about all your sweet, dripping frustration."

I pick her up in my arms and carry her to the door, unlocking it while she holds on to me, and take her out into the night. I know every twist and turn in my garden, every hidden spot, and I find a secluded place and lay her down on the grass.

There's just enough starlight for me to see her beautiful body. I lean over her, bracing my hands on the grass by her head.

"Kiss me," I command.

Vivienne's breathing is shallow and fast, and her pupils are blown in the darkness. "I don't know how. We shouldn't do this."

I ignore that second part. "Yes, you do. Kiss me."

Tentatively, Vivienne puts her hands on my shoulders, raises her chin, and presses her mouth to mine. A shy kiss. I slip my fingers into her briefs and caress her clit.

Vivienne moans and inhales deeply, opening her mouth wider and giving me a horny, fuck-me-daddy kiss. I groan against her lips as her tongue moves against mine, and then I yank her underwear down her legs and spread her open with my fingers. Breaking our feverish kiss, I look down at her slippery, shining sex, and my balls ache at the sight. She's just so pretty, and I crave to fuck her more than I've wanted anything in my life.

"I mean it. We can't do this. You're holding my brother captive."

I need to get my mouth on her. I move down her body until I'm between her thighs and take a long lick of her. Fucking *delicious*. I find her clit with my tongue and massage her slowly and firmly.

Vivienne sinks back on the grass, her eyes closing as she takes unsteady breaths, and lets her thighs fall open. "That feels amazing…" Her back arches. She moans so sweetly for me. Then she sits up with a gasp. "Tyrant, this is crazy."

"Let me do this for you, angel. No one's ever made you feel good, and I can't stand it."

Vivienne's head falls back with a cry as I go on licking her, and soon she doesn't sound like she's thinking much of anything anymore. Finally she whimpers, "Aren't you supposed to say something like, *I'll give you your brother if you sleep with me?*"

I laugh softly. Why bargain for what she's so hungry to give me? Besides, if I have Barlow, I keep her. Vivienne won't be going anywhere without him.

She buries her fingers in my hair. Caresses my ears. Wraps her legs around my shoulders. "None of this counts," she insists breathlessly. "It hasn't got anything to do with why I'm here. This is between you, me, and what I wrote in my diary when I was fifteen. After this, I'm going right back to looking for Barlow."

I smile and slowly suck on her clit. She can tell herself whatever she likes. I know why I'm doing this. A pretty angel getting wet over me beating the shit out of some lowlifes is the best thing I've ever heard.

I sit up and take my jacket off and start unbuttoning my shirt. While I'm doing that, Vivienne reaches out and puts her hand on my dick through my pants. I groan and close my eyes as she touches me. Her fingers slide along my length and feel the thick ridge around my head.

"You're a bold little thing."

"I'm a stupid little thing," she whispers and unthreads my belt.

Heat and desire pump through me as she undoes my pants and pushes her hand inside my underwear to grasp my shaft.

She really wants me to fuck her.

I watch her small, slender hand moving on my cock. She caresses my stomach and then my chest. She pushes my shirt from my shoulders and stares at me in wonder as she runs her hands over my torso. "You're so beautiful."

I laugh. "Me?"

"Yes, you. I thought so the moment I saw you. Don't laugh at me."

I lean down and kiss her, pulling her naked body closer to mine. "I'm laughing because I'm surprised. You've seen me all but kill three men, and you still think I'm beautiful."

"Maybe that was beautiful as well," she says, then takes my face in her hands and kisses me.

I haven't forgotten about the terrible thing that happened to her that made violence so alluring to her. We'll circle back to that later, and I'll fuck up this Lucas so hard that he'll wish he'd never been born.

Later. Right now, I need her so much I think I'll explode.

I take my cock in my hand and line it up with her pussy, and glance up at her. "You want me?"

She nods rapidly.

I'm looking right in her eyes as I sink half my shaft into her. Vivienne cries out and grabs my shoulders, pleasure-pain flashing over her face. Slowly, I draw out of her, and there's a crimson smear of blood on my cock. I run my thumb over it, groaning at the beautiful sight.

"You're only allowed to bleed for me from now on, angel. You hear me? Only for me." I sink into her once more, and thrust again and again, deeper each time, making her stretch around me.

Her whimpers change to moans. Her fingers are no longer

clenched on me in pain but soften and caress.

"You're so thick," she whispers, looking down and watching me fuck her.

"Too thick?"

Vivienne shakes her head and breathes, "Perfect. I love the way your body moves. You're so strong. I should be scared of you, but I'm not."

I smile and kiss her, our mouths open and breathless with each kiss. Each thrust.

Vivienne reaches up and touches my face, and says wonderingly, "I don't feel ugly when I'm with you."

That's the most beautiful thing anyone's ever said to me. "How do you feel?"

She traces my jaw, my lips, as she carefully thinks about her answer. "Like nothing bad ever happened."

Her glossy hair is spread out around her on the grass. Her cheeks are flushed. With each thrust, every inch of me is buried inside her. When I pull back, her wetness is glistening on the veins of my dick. This is where I'm meant to be. Right fucking here. I lick the pad of my thumb and swipe it over her clit, making her cry out. "Is this how you touched yourself thinking about me?" I rub her in slow circles, watching the pleasure flicker over her face.

She grips my shoulders, her nails digging into my muscles. "Yes. Yes, God, just like that."

Her clit swells against my touch, and she gets even more slippery as I glide in and out of her.

"Are you going to come on my cock, angel?"

She bites her lip and nods, her arms locked around my neck. "Tyrant. Oh, God, Tyrant, please."

Her inner muscles are strong. When she climaxes, she clenches so tightly that she nearly pushes my cock out of her, but I don't let her. I pound her harder as she cries out from pleasure. I wrap both my arms around her body and bury my face in her neck as my own orgasm rushes up my cock and fills her to bursting.

I pull back slowly and kiss her panting mouth while I'm still buried deep inside her. Vivienne's lying on her back with her arms flung over her head, her eyes closed, her whole body surrendered to mine. My angelic little virgin, full of cock and cum, without a care in the world.

That was the most incredible experience of my life. Hers too, from the looks of it.

As much as I want to stay where I am, I pull out, and dress Vivienne in my shirt, pulling it tightly around her so the night air can't touch her. Then I pull on my pants and shoes and toss my crumpled jacket over one shoulder.

Vivienne has her arms wrapped around her as she watches me dress with huge, luminous eyes. "What now?"

I hold out my hand to her. "Come up to the house. Barlow misses you."

CHAPTER SEVENTEEN

Vivienne

I'm walking hand in hand with Tyrant through his labyrinth. This must be a dream. I fell asleep in the boathouse and my mind conjured up the horniest, most improbable thing it could imagine. Any moment now, I'll open my eyes to find a fully dressed and sneering Tyrant standing over me and telling me my time is up.

He stops when he reaches the front door of his mansion and turns to me, and the expression on his face is anything but sneering. He cups my face and kisses me.

I'm a slippery mess inside my underwear. He helped me put them on, but now his cum is slowly oozing out of me.

I slept with Tyrant.

I slept with *Tyrant*.

This is too crazy to comprehend, and I don't understand how it happened, but right now I can't process anything because Barlow is here. I'm going to get my brother back.

"I've made it to your house before the time limit is up. If I go inside, it means I win."

"I think we fucked the rules away, angel. But sure, you win." He grasps my hand with his huge, strong one, and draws me up the steps and inside his house.

There's a grand entrance hall and a sweeping staircase. Tyrant takes me upstairs and along a hall. I peep into bedrooms, sitting rooms, a security room with CCTV monitors, and then finally a bedroom with a changing table, baby paraphernalia, and a bassinet.

In the bassinet, sleeping soundly and being watched over by an older woman in a maid's uniform, is Barlow.

I gasp and rush over. My brother looks even more adorable and peaceful than he ever has before. I want to pick him up and cuddle him, but I also don't want to wake him up.

"You can go to bed now, Angela. We'll take the baby to my bedroom," Tyrant tells the woman.

Angela nods and gets to her feet. "Thank you, sir." She casts only the merest glance in my direction without an ounce of judgment in her eyes, but my face turns red as I realize I'm wearing nothing but Tyrant's shirt and there's probably grass sticking out of my messy hair.

We'll take the baby to my bedroom. Wait, does that mean—

Tyrant grasps the handles of the bassinet with one hand, me with the other, and walks us both out of the room and down the hall. He sets the bassinet on a desk by the window while I gaze around the room. At the enormous bed. The walk-in wardrobe off to the right.

The man seems to love his clothes.

"I think he's waking up." Tyrant turns to me, moonlight burnishing his bare shoulders and tattoos with silver. "What are you waiting for? Pick him up."

"Really?" I take a hesitant step toward Barlow, hope swelling inside me. This feels too good to be true.

Tyrant folds his arms across his chest and watches me. In the bassinet, Barlow stirs, rubbing his little hands against his chubby cheeks and opening his eyes. My heart lurches, and I can't hold myself back any longer. I reach for Barlow and hold him tight in my arms.

I rock him back and forth, happy tears crowding my lashes. "Hey, baby boy. I missed you so much."

His diaper feels dry, and he's wearing a new romper with baby owls on it that I don't recognize. Should I thank Tyrant for taking such good care of Barlow? Or should I feel angry that he stole him in the first place? In Tyrant's room with Barlow in my arms, I have my brother all to myself for once. Tyrant wants me to hold him. I can tell that from the intense feeling in his eyes. No one is going to tell me I'm in the way or resent me for spending time with him.

I keep rocking Barlow in my arms until he falls asleep. When I glance up, I see that Tyrant is still staring at us with hungry eyes. Devouring me. Like he can't get enough of how I look and he's about to snap and do something crazy.

"Why are you looking at me like that?" I whisper.

Tyrant takes a sleeping Barlow from my arms and puts him carefully back in the bassinet before pulling me into his arms and slamming his mouth over mine. His kiss is wild and hungry, and he pushes his tongue into my mouth at the same time he yanks his shirt from my body.

"Angel," he says between kisses. "I need to fuck you again. Are you sore?"

My nipples brush against his chest, and suddenly I'm even more turned on than I was in his labyrinth. We can't have sex again so soon, can we? Apparently we can because Tyrant's cock is hard and pressing against my belly, and my core is aching with the need for him to sink every inch of himself inside me.

"I don't know. I don't feel sore."

He slides two fingers straight up inside me, and I see stars and moan his name. If it hurts, I can't tell because being filled by him feels so incredible.

My arms come around Tyrant's neck. He lifts me up against him as we kiss each other frantically, and my legs wrap around his torso. He walks me over to the side of the room and we fall clumsily against a side table as we both undo his pants. I get one look at his cock before he grasps hold of himself and impales me right to the hilt.

"Fuck," I cry out at the top of my lungs before gasping in dismay and clapping a hand over my mouth. "Oh no, Barlow."

"He's too young to know what he's hearing. Eyes on me while I fuck you, angel."

Tyrant pulls back and thrusts into me again. I don't need to be told twice. Tyrant's beautiful, brutal face is just inches from mine, and I cling to him as he fucks me. The table thumps against the wall, and we're probably waking everyone in the house.

Tyrant's got me. All I want is him. I alternate between kissing him and watching his cock slide in and out of me.

My oversensitive sex responds so fast to the primal way he's pounding me. My body races ahead before I can even comprehend what's happening. I bury my face in his shoulder and bite down on his flesh against my cry of pleasure as I come. Tyrant fists my hair, holding me tight as he pounds me faster and harder, his flesh burning hot, until his orgasm breaks over him and his rhythm becomes uneven and then slows down.

We're both breathing hard as we draw apart.

"I can't help myself when you look like that," he says, swiping his thumb over my wet mouth.

I'm so dazed from sex that I have no idea what he's talking about. "Like what?"

"Holding Barlow. That does something to me."

"Does what?"

Instead of answering, he picks me up and carries me over to his bed, which is enormous with soft, dove-gray bedding. So many people don't care about good fabrics. This man knows quality. When I'm settled on the sheets, he gets into the bed with me and draws the covers over us, holding me tight against him. My hands are pressed against his muscular chest, and I suddenly feel shy from the intense way he's staring at me. I have no idea why any of this is happening or what Tyrant wants from me. I can't stay because I have to leave with Barlow. It's insane that Tyrant thinks I'm going to…what? Snuggle against his body for the rest of the night and fall asleep?

Apparently that's exactly what Tyrant wants because he's stroking his fingers through my hair and relaxing his head onto the pillow.

"So beautiful," he murmurs. The gentle rumble in his voice sends hot sparks swirling through me. "Did I hurt you?"

I squirm my legs a little, trying to feel if there's a sore spot. There's an ache deep in my core, but a pleasurable one.

"Yes and no."

He studies my face, and then a slow smile spreads over his lips. "Yes, but you liked it?"

Exactly that. I'm suddenly overcome with shyness, and I wrap my arms around his neck, wriggle closer, and tuck myself beneath his chin. I'll sleep, but just a few hours until morning, and then I'll take Barlow home. That's safer than carrying a baby across town in the middle of the night.

I feel a guilty pang as I think of Dad and Samantha worrying about Barlow.

Tyrant kisses the top of my head, and a wave of warmth and sleepiness washes over me. Lying in Tyrant's arms is the safest and most comfortable I've ever felt, and I drift off to sleep.

I'm awoken sometime later by the sensation of my legs being moved. I'm on my side and hugging a pillow, and someone pushes my knees up toward my chest. Between my thighs feels so slippery, and I drowsily remember that I've been having sex with Tyrant.

Something plush and blunt slides against my inner lips, and then pushes inside. Somewhere over my head, Tyrant groans.

"*Mmf*," I moan into the pillow, hugging it tighter, but I'm too sleepy to drag my eyes open. There's a delicious stretching sensation as that thick object bottoms out inside me, and I whimper into the pillow.

"Shh, angel. I couldn't wait till morning. You just sleep." Drag. Thrust. Drag. *Thrust.* "You look so perfect with your eyes closed. Fast asleep. So helpless." His voice is roughened with desire.

The thick object is Tyrant's cock.

"You're insatiable," I whisper into the pillow. I pull my knees higher so he can go even deeper.

"You should see what I can see from here. Your pussy looks fucking amazing stuffed full of me."

I moan in response to his filthy words, and my hand snakes down between my thighs. I trace my fingers over his thick cock pistoning in and out of me and then draw them up and over my clit, circling slowly.

"I'm not letting you go, angel," he whispers, hammering me harder. "You're all mine. Barlow as well. I'm going to keep you both because fuck everyone else and what they want. I want you."

I want to tell him he's crazy, he can't keep us, we're not his to keep, but the rough way he's fucking me and the pleasure I'm chasing makes me moan, "Yes, Tyrant, please, *please.*"

A hand clamps around my throat and holds on tight. Blood rushes to my brain. It's a struggle to draw air into my lungs, and that little bit of panic has my orgasm rushing up, even stronger than before.

"Oh, fuck yes, angel, I love when you come on my cock," Tyrant seethes through gritted teeth, hammering me so hard he fills me with stars, and then he groans with his release.

Tyrant slowly lets go of my throat and eases back before drawing out of me and dragging his fingers along my oozing slit.

"I love fucking you raw. Making a mess of this pussy is my new favorite thing."

I'm so boneless and heavy with pleasure that all I can do is lie there as Tyrant admires me, strokes me with his fingers, and plays with the cum leaking out of me by pushing it back in. His fingers make squelching noises as he delves slowly in and out of my pussy and hums with satisfaction. I moan softly and revel in the heavy weight of the hand he has on my hip. No one's ever admired me before. I've never wanted anyone to look at me before.

"How long was I asleep for?" I whisper.

Tyrant takes his time answering. He's too busy chasing a droplet of cum down my thigh, drawing it back up again, and pushing it inside me. "About an hour."

"Did you sleep?"

Tyrant laughs in a way that tells me he absolutely didn't sleep.

"Are you having fun back there?" I ask as he goes on playing with my pussy.

"The time of my life, angel."

In his bassinet, Barlow stirs and makes a squawking sound. I raise my head and start to open my eyes.

"I'll go," Tyrant says right away, getting out of bed and pulling his pants back on. "I think he's hungry. You stay in bed."

I listen to the sound of his footsteps descending the stairs. What a crazy night this has turned into. Tyrant Mercer has gone to prepare a bottle of formula for my baby brother.

I cuddle the pillow closer and close my eyes. How peaceful and cozy everything feels. I imagine how Tyrant, Barlow, and I wouldn't have to leave this house for days on end if I stayed. What a beautiful thought, just being here together looking after the baby. Not that I'm going to do that. It's just nice thinking about it. Like all the crazy things Tyrant says while we have sex. There's a small ache in the back of my neck, and I rub it. I must have hurt myself on my adventure through Tyrant's labyrinth.

I fall half asleep again, and when I hear a noise a short time later, Tyrant's standing by the moonlit window, still shirtless, with Barlow in his arms. His usually fierce brow is relaxed as he gazes down at the baby, who's nestled comfortably in his tattooed arms. Tyrant murmurs to the baby as he bottle-feeds him, shifting his weight slowly from side to side.

It's terrifying how good Tyrant looks doing that. There's a strong, inexplicable pull deep inside me. What a perfect little family we'd make, the three of us.

A stupid thought. An impossible thought. Barlow's not Tyrant's son, and I'm not his mother. Dad and Samantha must be out of their minds with worry while I'm here screwing a kidnapper and playing happy family.

I lay back down again, but this time my eyes are open, and I feel wide awake. Barlow must finish his bottle and fall asleep because I hear Tyrant settle him back into his bassinet and then I feel the other side of the bed sink.

A strong hand grips my shoulder and rolls me onto my back. Tyrant is looming over me in the darkness.

"Who's Lucas?" he murmurs, and he says it so quietly that, for a moment, I don't realize he's asked me a question.

Panic makes my belly swoop. "Don't worry about it."

Tyrant is silent for so long that I think he's decided to do as I ask, and in the back of my mind, I feel a trickle of disappointment.

"No, Vivienne. You don't tell me what I do and don't worry about. I'm going to have his last name from you. I want to hear the whole story, and then I'm going to find this Lucas and anyone else who's responsible for hurting you, and I'm going to make them bleed." His mouth captures mine in a kiss. "Just like you always wanted me to."

Tyrant can't possibly put anything right. I'll have these scars forever, the ones on the outside and the ones on the inside.

"Please don't make me talk about it anymore. The past few hours have been so precious that I don't want to ruin it by risking seeing one flicker of doubt in your eyes. I won't be able to bear it if you don't believe me."

Tyrant laughs softly, his teeth gleaming in the darkness. "Believe you? I'm not going to believe you."

Pain blazes in my heart. "Then why—"

"I'm going to reorder the universe by reordering his fucking organs. I'm going to make such a mess of his entrails, eyeballs, and fingernails that it will take a team of crime scene investigators to identify who he used to be and a dozen cleaners to bleach away all the blood. This Lucas, anyone else who hurt you? They're as good as dead."

CHAPTER EIGHTEEN

Tyrant

Vivienne gazes up at me with huge eyes. My perfect little nymph lying in my bed. Totally naked. All mine. A possessive thrill goes through me knowing I have her and the thing she most cares about in the world. My cock starts to thicken at the thought that she'll never leave me while I have Barlow. Jesus Christ, I could fuck her again, and it's only been twenty minutes since I last blew my load in her tight, liquid heat.

Her pretty hands flutter to my shoulders and squeeze. "It was so long ago. I don't want to go dredging up the past. Please, can we just forget about it?"

"This isn't about what you want. This is about what you need. You needed me four years ago, and I had no fucking idea. But I'm here now."

"Remember who I am? I'm Owen Stone's daughter. We owe you so much money."

"You owe me shit, angel. It's your father who's in my debt, and while I have his son and daughter under my roof, I'm not sending any debt collectors after him. If he knows what's good for him, he'll stay far away from us forever." I lean down, take one of her nipples in my mouth, and suck.

Vivienne gasps and buries her fingers in my hair. "Dad's not going to—"

I sit up and silence her with a finger over her lips. "Pretty girl, answer the question. I need to know everything that happened to you."

She gives me a desperate look and then covers her face with a moan. "I hate that I want to tell you everything. I blame that stupid diary and all those fantasies I had about you."

"You need to let me live up to all those expectations you had of me," I say, gathering her into my lap and sitting with my back against the headboard. "If I'd known you back then, I would have happily murdered anyone for you."

Vivienne touches my cheek, stroking my cheekbone with her thumb. "You're crazier than all my expectations."

I wait, watching her silently.

Finally, she sighs and drops her head onto my shoulder, and says dismally, "There's a reason I was sitting on the edge of that fountain for hours and hours the evening you were meeting your sister. I didn't want to go home. Dad and Samantha were angry with me over something that happened a few weeks earlier. Everything had been going so well. I nearly had one good year."

I frown. "One good year? I think I'm missing something, angel."

"Oh. I lived with my mom until I was fourteen. Down in LA." There's a troubled expression in her eyes.

"I think you need to go back and tell me everything from the beginning."

Vivienne glances at Barlow in his bassinet. He's still fast asleep. "From my childhood?"

"However far back you need to go to give me the full picture."

"Okay. But tell me if I'm boring you or taking too long," she adds doubtfully.

I settle my arms around her, loving the sensation of her naked body against mine in my bed. "You won't bore me. And spare no detail."

Vivienne traces her fingertips over the tattoos on my chest and begins speaking in a soft voice. She tells me of being born to two addict parents and knowing from a young age that she was a mistake. Her father cleaned up his act and left her. Left his fucking *child* behind. Rage burns in my heart as I remember my own father doing more or less the same to me and my brothers and sisters. Vivienne tells me about a childhood filled with neglect, darkness, loneliness, and fear. Burning herself trying to cook when there was food. Going hungry when there was none. Being alone in a huge, empty house. Keeping herself from starving too much or looking too neglected at school so that no one would know how bad things really were. Then the horror of discovering her mother's dead body and losing her last shred of hope that someone, even a ruin of a someone, in this world gave a damn about her.

Then her father came for her, reluctantly from the sounds of it, and Vivienne moved from chaotic LA to quiet, suburban Henson. It doesn't sound like she was particularly loved, but to someone like Vivienne who'd known only despair, her new life seemed like a fairy tale.

I tuck Vivienne under my chin so she can't see my furious expression and glare straight ahead. I sense where this is going, and I don't like it one bit.

"I tried not to cause trouble," Vivienne says. "Really I did, but I guess I made a lot of mistakes because Dad always lost his temper with me and Samantha seemed exasperated a lot. It's not their fault. They were trying for a baby and nothing was working."

Sure it wasn't. "Go on."

"I got to know one of Dad's friends who was always coming around the house. He and Dad would watch football together. Have nights out."

This must be the Lucas she mentioned.

"Tyrant, are you all right? Your muscles have suddenly gone rock hard."

I take a breath, but I can't relax. "Don't worry about me. I'm listening."

"This man was nice to me, I guess. Having someone's attention felt new. I was so hungry for any scraps of attention, and I think he could tell." She covers her face and moans. "Isn't that pathetic? None of this would have happened if I hadn't been so desperate to be liked by *someone*."

I hold her as tight as I can without actually crushing her ribs or cutting off her breathing. "This is Lucas?"

She nods. "Just after I turned fifteen, I snuck out one night to go to a party. I'd never done that before, and I had a terrible time, and then my friend left me stranded without a ride home, so I had to walk. I was sick with anxiety about being alone in the dark. It reminded me of being a child. As I was walking along some dark street, a car pulled up beside me, and it was Lucas. I was so relieved I jumped straight in and immediately confessed everything to him. I was out without permission. I'd had an awful time. I was stuck on the wrong side of town. He told me that he'd drive me home and everything would be okay."

She swallows hard.

"Only, he didn't. He drove to an underpass and parked there, telling me he just wanted to talk. Every time I asked him if we could go, he changed the subject, and things started getting creepy. I remember I was so confused by what was happening that I couldn't concentrate, and then the next thing I knew he'd pushed my seat way back and he was climbing on top of me."

I can picture it in my head. Fifteen-year-old Vivienne, vulnerable and afraid, while a man puts his hands on her and treats her like a piece of meat. A sick, angry sensation twists my guts.

"I could feel him ripping my clothes, and he was so frightening that I froze. One part of my brain was telling me to play dead and let it happen, but another part of me was *screaming*. I suddenly remembered that if you're attacked, you should go for their eyes. So I shoved my fingers in his eyes. He pulled back, and I had just enough room to reach for the door, open it, and scramble out. I didn't stop running until my lungs felt like they were about to explode."

I slide my hand into her hair and rock her against me, seeing that terrified fifteen-year-old in my mind's eye. Having two younger sisters means I've lain awake imagining the worst things happening to them. I've seen firsthand the cruelty of men toward women. What a horrible story, made no better by the fact that Lucas didn't actually succeed in what he set out to do.

"Did you tell your father about this?" I ask.

Vivienne nods, wiping tears from her face. "I didn't want to because they were such good friends, but Lucas came to the house a week later to watch football. I saw him standing in my living room and panicked. I was so scared. I couldn't breathe, and Samantha nearly called an ambulance. After Lucas left, they dragged the truth out of me." She hesitates, and I feel her hand clench on my shoulder. "Dad was so angry with me."

"Angry with *you*?" I exclaim. I would have been beyond furious if I saw my daughter panicking at the sight of one of my friends, but not with her.

"He told me I was mistaken and that Lucas wouldn't do that. Then he asked me if I made it up because I was worried I would be in trouble for sneaking out of the house."

The mental gymnastics involved to ask such a ridiculous question is astounding. Vivienne isn't a troublemaker, and she blames herself for everything, and you'd think her own father could see that. "Did Lucas keep coming around to the house?"

"Yes. And every time he did..." She touches her ribs.

I exhale heavily. So that's why. Every time she saw Lucas, she was flooded with misery and fear, and she had to let it out.

"I couldn't help myself. It was the only thing that made me feel sane."

I take her hand and press a kiss to her palm. After everything she'd been through with her mom, being attacked by a family friend and having her trauma thrown in her face was too much pain. Of course she had to let it out somehow.

"When was the last time you made yourself bleed?"

"Just before I moved out to go to college. I have a room of my own, and even though I know that Lucas can't get in, I still have my cutting box. Just in case," she confesses in a whisper.

The thought of sending her and her brother back to that shitty home is too much even for my bloodstained conscience. I gaze at the bassinet for a long time, my brain ticking over at a hundred miles a second.

"Stay."

Vivienne looks up at me in surprise. "What?"

"Stay. You won't ever be alone here. You and Barlow."

"I can't do that."

"Why not? You want me. I can make you fall in love with me. Everything you could possibly need is here, and if it's not, I'll buy it for you."

Vivienne stares at me like I've sprouted two heads. "Make me fall in love with you?"

I stroke my fingers along her throat, murmuring softly, "Yes, make you. I promise you'll enjoy it."

"The reason I want you so much is because I'm afraid of you, for good reason. Do you know what everyone in Henson calls you?"

"What do they call me?"

"A monster."

I brush my lips over hers. "Sure. I'm a monster. But there are monsters living inside your head, Vivienne. They tell you that everything that's happened to you is all your fault. If you stay, I'll make sure they're too afraid of me to ever tell you that again."

Her hands tighten on my biceps. There's so much yearning in her eyes. "How would you even do that?"

"Once upon a time, I had the same monsters, and so did my brothers and sisters. I chased them all away."

"Tyrant," she whispers. "That's impossible."

Not for me it isn't. And she can have a therapist or whatever. There's nothing wrong with some head-shrinking. The point is that Vivienne stays with me, and far away from those assholes she calls family.

I plant a kiss on her nose, gather her up, and lie down on the sheets with her, tucking the blankets around us. "I'll worry about what's possible. You just go to sleep."

"But—"

"Sleep."

Vivienne watches me for a moment and then she closes her eyes. Slowly, her body relaxes and her breathing deepens. My woman falls asleep in my arms, and my black heart feels strangely full. Tomorrow, I'm going to do what I do best, which is taking shit apart and putting it back together. I did it with my family when my brothers and sisters were young and Mom couldn't take care of us. I did it with Henson when I took over and threw out every lowlife piece of shit who wouldn't follow my rules. Now I'm going to do it for Vivienne. I'm going to do it for me as well. My life needs to be smashed apart and rebuilt from the ground up, just like hers. When I'm done, our pieces are going to fit so tightly together. Hers. Mine. Barlow's. Because fuck giving him back to those snakes.

I close my eyes, and Vivienne is a warm weight against my chest. Sleep is deep, and dreamless.

Hours later, I'm awoken by sunlight coming through the bedroom. Without opening my eyes, I reach out for Vivienne. The space beside me is empty. Confused, I lift my head and look around, but she's not here. My room is silent and still.

Panic slams through me, and I leap out of bed and grab the bassinet, only to find it empty. Maybe Vivienne is just in the bathroom or kitchen with Barlow. I check the en suite and then yank on my pants and race down the hall to check the room I was using as a nursery, but that's empty too. So are all the bathrooms. When I ask, none of my staff have seen Vivienne this morning.

I stand at the window and stare out onto the garden where I had Vivienne trapped just a few hours ago. I promised Vivienne the world, and now she's nowhere. She's gone.

CHAPTER NINETEEN

Vivienne

It's an hour past dawn when I walk up the front steps at home with Barlow in my arms. I left Tyrant's house before the sun came up. My bare feet are sore and muddy, and there's an ache deep inside me. An ache that's different from the one I'm sure I'll feel in my core later after the triple-pounding Tyrant gave my virginity in the space of a few hours.

As I raise my hand to knock on the front door, I swallow the lump in my throat. I was well within the time limit that he gave me. I won Barlow back fair and square.

I won, but I feel empty.

There's the sound of footsteps coming down the hall, and the front door is yanked open. Dad stands there with bloodshot eyes, and for a moment his expression is baffled. As if he's forgotten that I live here when I'm not at college.

Then his gaze drops to Barlow and he gives a ragged cry.

"Who's that?" Samantha calls, and her voice is high and stressed as she approaches us. Her eyes are red from crying, and she's wearing the same clothes as when Tyrant took Barlow last night.

Samantha screams when she sees that I'm holding their son and dashes forward to rip him from my arms. She's crying as she rocks Barlow back and forth. Dad's staring at his son in shock with his hand on Samantha's shoulder, asking over and over, "Is he all right? Are you okay, Barlow?" Barlow begins screaming because the noise and emotions are too much for him.

No one looks at me, and so I come inside, close the door, then stand here feeling like an uninvited guest.

Finally, Samantha turns her tearful gaze on me. "How did you get him back from Mercer?"

This is the part I've been dreading, but I gather my wits about me and resolve to keep my explanation simple. "I came home last night and was hiding in the hall when Tyrant took Barlow. I ran out and got into his car, and he drove to his house because he didn't see me. I waited until Tyrant was asleep, and then I grabbed Barlow and I ran."

Dad and Samantha both stare at me in surprise.

"When Tyrant wakes up, he's probably going to be very angry, so I hope you've got his money," I tell Dad.

Dad glances fearfully at Samantha, and my heart sinks. I know that look. He hasn't got the money. I wonder if I've endured the craziest night of my life for nothing and Tyrant is going to burst in here at any moment and take Barlow back.

Samantha frowns at me and wipes her eyes. "Vivienne, what are you wearing? Are those men's clothes?"

I glance down at myself. I'm dressed in an oversized black T-shirt and some sweats. Things I stole from Tyrant's walk-in wardrobe. "I fell in a lake, so I stole some dry clothes from Tyrant."

This is the part where they thank me for bringing Barlow back. I don't need their unending gratitude, but just a small acknowledgment for what I've been through would be nice. Dad is tiredly rubbing his eyes and giving his son a rueful smile. Samantha is still frowning at me as if she's trying to make sense of what I just told her.

They're not going to say thank you or that I did a good thing for our family.

A stupid, sad lump rises up my throat.

"I'll go shower," I whisper, and move past them toward the stairs.

Just then, the doorbell rings. All three of us turn to the front door at the same time, and my heart starts to race. It's Tyrant. It has to be. I can't see the outline of anyone through the frosted glass, but he's moved back or to one side, and he's going to burst inside as soon as someone opens that door.

"What are you going to do, Owen?" Samantha asks in a frightened whisper.

Dad's expression is furious as he moves over to the hall table, opens a drawer, and pulls out a handgun.

My mouth falls open. "Dad, you can't—"

He puts a finger to his lips and hushes me.

I watch, my heart in my mouth, as Dad moves toward the front door with the gun held behind his back. He's going to kill Tyrant, or more likely, Tyrant's going to see the gun and kill Dad.

Dad turns the front door handle and slowly pulls it open, and I can't help myself. I shout a warning to Tyrant. "He's got a gun!"

There's no one outside. Dad turns around and glares at me. "Whose side are you on?"

I'm on the side of no one dying on my front doorstep.

Samantha points past Dad. "Owen, there's something on the mat."

He glances down and picks up a large, blank envelope. It seems to contain some papers or cards, and there must be quite a few sheets because the envelope is nearly half an inch thick. With a puzzled frown, Dad comes back inside, closes the door, and lays the gun back in its drawer.

Then he opens the envelope. His frown instantly turns into surprise, and then his eyes narrow. "Vivienne. What are these?" His voice sounds strange like he's on the verge of losing his temper.

I go to his side and look at the photos, and so does Samantha. Instantly, she gasps.

As I gaze at the glossy rectangles, I feel like I've been punched in the stomach. I've lost the ability to draw breath into my lungs. The photographs are of Tyrant.

Me and Tyrant.

Having sex in his garden last night.

There are dozens of photos. *Dozens.* Dad keeps going through them, one after another. In all of the photos, I'm kissing Tyrant. Wrapping my legs around him. Touching his face. Crying out in pleasure. His feral beauty has softened into adoration as he gazes at me or watches his cock sink inside me. Even the way he holds me is brutally adoring.

His grasp on my thighs or my hips firm and possessive.

The last few photos are the worst. Tyrant picks me up in his arms and carries me toward the house. My arms are wrapped around his neck. Our heads are close together, and the shots are more intimate and emotional than any wedding photos I've seen. We're gazing into each other's eyes, and we look like we're in love.

"Are you going to explain this?" Dad asks through his teeth, brandishing the photos at me.

"I…" Forming words is suddenly impossible. My skin is flashing hot and then freezing cold. "I…"

"Did *he* force you as well?" Dad asks sarcastically. "Hurry up and answer, Vivienne, before you can make up a lie."

"I'm not a liar," I manage to whisper, but I sound guilty as hell.

"Really? Because your explanation to Samantha just now about how you got Barlow back didn't include you spreading your legs for Tyrant fucking Mercer."

I take a shaky breath. "I did what I had to do. I never wanted…" But I'm not a liar, and I can't say the words *I never wanted it to happen*, because it's not true. I wanted Tyrant so much. I still want him. If I had done as he asked, I'd be safe and warm in his arms right now instead of facing Dad's judgment.

Stay. You won't ever be alone with me.

I hear Tyrant's heartfelt words in my head, and I long for his arms around me.

Dad raises his voice and steps toward me. "I'm not doing this with you again, Vivienne. This time I have proof, so don't bother to lie to me. These photos don't show Tyrant forcing you to have sex with him. There's nothing forced about it. It's just like the time you threw yourself at Lucas. Admit it."

He's shouting in my face, and I flinch and can't reply because I'm so choked up.

"I knew it." He throws the photos at me and they scatter all over the floor.

I stare at a photograph of myself with my hands pressed against Tyrant's bare chest as I gaze up at him. Adoring the man who took my virginity. Who could have done this? Tyrant himself? For what purpose? The photos are taken from an angle slightly above us, and they're grainy as if the photographer has had to zoom in from a distance. Tyrant uses CCTV in his labyrinth. I saw the room, but these don't look like stills taken from a security video. Whoever is responsible, their purpose was to humiliate me in front of Dad and Samantha. Tyrant must be furious with me for sneaking away with Barlow, but I don't believe he would do something like this. It doesn't seem like his way of punishing someone.

I need the comfort of a cuddle with my brother. I reach for Barlow, but Samantha backs away to the other side of the room with him.

A fierce ache of loss opens up in my chest. "Why won't you let me hold Barlow? I'm not going to hurt him. I risked everything to bring him home to you."

Samantha shakes her head and turns away from me. "I don't want you here, Vivienne. You're hiding something."

Dad gives me a disgusted look. "Go back to your dorms. We can't look at you right now."

"But when can I come back?" I choke out, trying to hold on to my tears.

"When you're ready to tell the truth about what happened last night. We're so sick of your lies."

The unfairness of it all is making my stomach clench with despair. I collect my satchel and my coat from the places I left them last night. I don't know what to tell them. I just wanted my brother back, and then everything got out of hand.

Dad and Samantha don't say goodbye as I let myself out of the house and into the cold morning air.

I'm halfway down the street when someone grabs me, pushes me against a car with his massive body, and growls into my ear, "Got you, you little thief."

CHAPTER TWENTY

Tyrant

Vivienne's sweet scent blooms around us as I crush her against my car. Relief pours through me. She's back in my arms where she's meant to be. She stole my fucking hostage, but right this moment I can't even feel angry about it.

I turn her around to face me and find that there are tears pouring down her face. Vivienne throws her arms around me and sobs against my chest. She's crying?

"What the…" I pull open the rear door of my car and lift her inside, get in after her, and close the door behind us. Liam's in the front seat, and he drives off down the street.

Taking Vivienne's face in my hands, I ask, "What happened? Why are you crying?"

She's sobbing so hard she can barely get the words out. "Dad and Samantha told me to leave. I brought Barlow back to them and…and…"

I wipe the tears from her cheeks. Stone and his fucking wife. I spent all night making this girl come and smile and pour out her heart to me, and those assholes reduced her to a whimpering mess again in a matter of minutes. I vividly imagine Stone's windpipe beneath my foot as I crush the life out of him.

"Someone took photos of us having sex in your labyrinth last night. They delivered the photos to my home. Who would do such a thing?"

"Photos of us? How? Where are they?"

"I left them behind. I don't know how they were taken. It was humiliating enough, other people seeing us when we thought we were alone. I didn't say I didn't want you, but then Dad told me not to pretend again that I'd been forced."

A deadly, ice-cold sensation washes over me.

Pretend she was forced. Stone threw that in her face when she half-killed herself trying to get Barlow back for them? I would bet my fortune that they didn't even thank Vivienne for stealing Barlow back for them. She doesn't ask me if I took the photos, so she must understand that I would never be that petty. Not now, anyway. Stealing her diary and reading it aloud to her was pretty fucking petty, but I never would have done it if I'd known her story. Seeing those scars on her body changed everything.

Fresh tears run down her cheeks and her face crumples. "Samantha wouldn't let me hold Barlow. I have a terrible feeling that they're never going to let me see him again." Vivienne starts to cry in earnest.

I'll have my revenge on those two, and it will be bloody and brutal beyond anything they could imagine. I take Vivienne's shoulders in mine and force her to look at me. "Ask me to fix this for you."

Vivienne wipes wetness from her cheeks. "You can't fix this. No one can. All I can do is come back next week and hope that Dad and Samantha have calmed down enough to let me hold Barlow again."

She's wrong. I can fix this in a heartbeat. I narrow my eyes meaningfully. Come on, angel. You can figure out what I'm offering. You know exactly the kind of man I am.

"Say, *I wish Tyrant Mercer would give me my heart's desire.*"

Her heart's desire is her brother.

A home.

My undying love and loyalty.

Vivienne gazes up at me with a confused expression, unable or unwilling to understand what I'm offering. Is it too much for her right now to contemplate their deaths? Fine. She'll come around soon enough, when I've won all her heart and they've destroyed all her love for them.

"I'm sorry, Tyrant. I can't ask you for anything. Last night you made a fifteen-year-old girl's fantasy come true, but you and I...I can't keep making one dangerous decision after the other. Everything can't keep falling apart around me or I'll fall apart too."

"Vivienne, you didn't do anything wrong. None of this is your fault."

"Then why do these things keep happening to me?" she asks brokenly. "Please just let me go. I want to go home."

I feel a thud of alarm. Vivienne is in so much pain right now and she wants to go back to her dorm so she can cut. Over my bleeding corpse is she going to sit alone in her room with a blade in her hands, crying as she slices herself up.

I push her against the door of the car, looming over her so she has to tilt her head right back to look me in the eyes. "There's something you should know about me, Vivienne. I don't give up when I want something. I will bend the world until it breaks and rearrange it the way I want it to be."

"I'm not going anywhere with you," she says. "You can't make me."

Yes, I can, but if I force her to come with me, I'll be the bad guy and the reason she's never allowed to see Barlow. Vivienne needs to realize for herself that she's never going to make those people happy, and then she'll be all mine.

I stroke a finger under her chin. "You don't have to go anywhere with me. I already own you."

Vivienne's eyes widen. "What?"

"You can go home, but you're my property. I own every inch of you. No one hurts what's mine, even you. I'm very fucking serious about that."

"Wait, are you letting me go or not?"

I let out a dark laugh. "Letting you go? In Henson, where everything and everyone belongs to me? Where every person watching you from a car, a street corner, a bus stop, works for me? Angel, you're not going to be more than ten feet from someone connected with me from now on."

Thanks to the tracker I injected into the nape of her neck while she was asleep, I'll always know where she is. God, it turned me on to do that, and seeing the tiny bump beneath her skin. I had to fuck her again right then, and I did. I thrust myself balls-deep inside her before she could wake up. Now, thanks to that tracker, I'm always inside her, and I can get to her in a heartbeat.

I won't be telling her that, however. Vivienne would do something silly with her knife if she knew it was there.

"Don't even think about leaving Henson. I can and will find you anywhere at any time. If you flee, I will drag you back here and punish you. You don't leave Henson. That's your first rule."

Both her eyebrows shoot up. "I have rules?"

I'm not answering stupid questions. Of course she has rules.

"You go to class. You visit your brother. If you're hurting, you call me. If you want to talk, you call me. If you need me to fuck you, you call me. Unlock your phone and give it to me." I hold out my hand and wait.

"We won't be needing to talk or fuck, thank you," she tells me with a shake of her head.

"Unlock your phone and give it to me, or I will go to your house, steal Barlow, and we'll do this all over again."

"Dad has a gun."

I laugh softly. "So do I, and I know how to use mine. Does he?"

She thinks about this for a moment, sighs, then takes out her phone, presses in the code, and hands it to me. I call my own phone, let it ring once, and then hang up and pass it back to her.

"Finally, the most important rule of all." I take her shoulders in my hands and lean in close. "You're only allowed to bleed for me, angel. You want to hurt and scream and suffer?" I brush my lips over hers. "I'll make you suffer."

Vivienne watches me through half-lidded eyes as if what I've just said is the most alluring thing she's ever heard. She gazes at my mouth for a long time and then seems to come out of a trance and shakes herself off. She addresses Liam, who has been driving all this time and pretending not to listen to us. "Could you please take me to the dorms at Henson University?"

Liam meets my gaze in the rearview mirror, and I nod.

"Of course, Miss Stone. We'll be there in five minutes," Liam says, smoothly turning the wheel.

We pull up outside the dorms, and Vivienne turns toward the door to get out. I pull her back to me.

"One more thing before you go. Give me Lucas's last name."

She shakes her head. "Just leave the past buried, please."

I grab her throat, and I'm not gentle about it, and I seethe in her face. "I said give me his fucking name."

She squirms against my fingers. "Haven't you got other things to worry about? What about Dad and his debt?"

"What about everything I just told you? You're mine, and that means doing as I say, otherwise, I'll make you very fucking sorry."

Vivienne swallows hard against my hand. "Lucas Jones. I don't know where he lives."

Lucas Jones. Finally. It doesn't matter that she doesn't know where he lives. If he's still breathing, I'll find him, even if he's left town. I keep hold of Vivienne's throat and slant my mouth over hers. Good fucking girl. I'll take care of this asshole, and Vivienne will realize her family is a pathetic waste of space and cut them out of her heart.

If she thinks that anything is over between us, she's very much mistaken. I own Vivienne Stone, now and forever.

I break the kiss and seethe, "You're already mine. Don't you fucking forget it, and don't break my rules."

"Or what?" she asks, breathlessly staring into my eyes.

"Try not to find out, angel."

CHAPTER TWENTY-ONE

Vivienne

Three weeks have passed since my adventure through Tyrant's labyrinth, and my life is quiet.

Eerily quiet.

I never feel alone. Is it paranoia, or was Tyrant telling the truth when he said that someone would always be watching me? People are looking at me when I buy groceries. Footsteps follow me on dark streets. Even down here in the empty basement of the library as I attempt to concentrate on an essay, I feel someone's eyes on the back of my neck.

Last Sunday, I returned home for the first time since Tyrant stole Barlow and I returned him. Samantha didn't look surprised to see me on the doorstep, but she wasn't pleased to see me either.

"Please, just let me see Barlow," I begged her. "You know I'd do anything for my brother."

Her expression softened, and she relented. "Fine. But don't stay long."

I held Barlow in my arms in front of the living room window, bouncing him gently and murmuring soft words. Dad came into the room and stood behind me. I focused on Barlow and pretended not to know anyone was there.

"You have no shame." His voice was filled with revulsion. Without waiting for me to reply, he walked out of the house and slammed the door behind him. I couldn't even be angry with him. I felt pathetically grateful that he hadn't ordered me to get out and never come back.

When I returned to my dorm room, my heart ached so much from Dad and Samantha's hostility that I went as far as taking out my cutting box. I sat on the floor, clutching the box that contains a blade, antiseptic, and Band-Aids. Holding it tight. Wanting so badly to use it.

I felt Tyrant's presence all around me, and I knew it was no idle threat that he would do something terrible if he discovered that I'd cut myself. I had his phone number, and I could call him if I wanted to, but that felt dangerous as well. With an aching heart, I put the box out of sight and took out my drawing pad instead.

I drew obsessively for hours. Plants. Statues. Mazes. Tyrant asleep in his bed, as he looked right before I took Barlow and crept out of his house. Drawing calmed me down until I finally passed out on the floor and slept for ten hours straight.

Now, this essay is going nowhere fast. I need to consult a journal article, and I get up from my table and make my way through the stacks. It's Friday night, and the basement level, with its dusty books and the old microfiche newspaper collection, is totally deserted.

Or so I think.

I'm reaching for *The Journal of Italian Renaissance Studies* when a large, tattooed hand seizes my wrist. For a moment I stare at it, frozen in shock, feeling warm breath on the back of my neck. Then Tyrant spins me around and pushes me against the bookshelves.

He's standing over me in all his tattooed beauty, clothed in black with a smirk on those beautiful lips. His velvety voice twines through my senses. "I missed you, angel. Did you miss me?"

His lips brush over mine, and my eyelashes flutter. I'm hypnotized by the sight of him. The smell of him. The feel of him. He grasps the hem of my dress and starts to pull it up.

I take hold of his hands and try to push them down. "What are you doing?"

"I need to know if you've been following my rules."

He wants to look at me right here in the library to check for himself that there are no fresh cuts on my body. I look around desperately. Someone might come in. "Please don't look at me. Tyrant, don't."

He narrows his eyes. "What are you hiding from me, Vivienne? I told you my rules. You better not have broken them."

"I haven't hurt myself, I swear it. Someone might see."

"There's no one here. I won't let anyone see my girl." He slowly drags my dress up and caresses my ribs. My stomach. All my old scars. He presses a kiss to my throat with a hum of desire. "Good girl. It's been forever. I need to fuck you, angel."

I grip his arm, my eyes widening. "We're in the library."

"I fucking love libraries." He squeezes my breasts, and then his hand dives straight down into my underwear, and he groans as his fingers slip into my slit. "Always so wet for me. I've been dreaming about this pussy."

Tyrant caresses my clit until my eyelashes flutter and my knees buckle, but he catches me and holds me against him, and forces a finger inside me.

I moan in his arms. Nothing feels better than being filled up with Tyrant.

"You're just so..." He looks down and then breathes in sharply, his pupils suddenly dilating and a smile curving his lips. "Oh, angel. What a delicious surprise."

"What's a surprise?"

He draws his hand out of my underwear and his middle finger is shining with blood right up to his third knuckle. Horror ripples through me at the sight. I must have just got my period. Blood from cuts is one thing, but blood from my period? He can't see that, let alone touch it.

I gasp and try to pull away, embarrassment flooding my body. "I'll go to the restroom. I'm sorry. I didn't know."

Tyrant doesn't let me leave his iron embrace, and now he's grinning wickedly. "Go to the restroom? Take your beautiful, bleeding pussy away from me? I'm not letting you go anywhere until we get this blood all over my cock."

He can't be serious.

Tyrant brushes his lips over mine and whispers seductively,

"You're bleeding for me, angel. I need to fuck you hard and make us both a mess with your blood."

Heat blooms in my cheeks and desire clenches my core. "We can't do that. Not here."

"Yes, here."

My knees are jelly as he lowers me to the carpet and strips my underwear down my legs. My hands clench on his shirt. I should run, but I can't let go of this man. "Please don't. This is torture."

"Ah, angel," he murmurs, a mocking smile on his lips. "I love your pretty blood. I'm going to fuck you right here, and maybe you'll cry, you'll blush, you'll hate me, but I'm still going to make you come." Tyrant turns me over so that I'm on my hands and knees and then spreads me open with his fingers. "Let me look at you."

As he explores my folds and the blood that's seeping out of me and dripping down my thighs, my knees tremble, and I bury my face in my arms. What must I look like? Surely Tyrant can't find all this period blood a turn-on.

"I did wonder if you were pregnant after the last time. How interesting that would have been." Tyrant sounds intrigued by the idea.

I wondered if I was pregnant too, which was why I took Plan B when I came to my senses the following day.

"Fuck, that's so pretty," he murmurs, stroking my wetness all over me.

"Have you got a condom?" I whimper, my head rearing up as he pushes two thick fingers inside me. I can't help but moan his name. "Tyrant. Tyrant, *please*."

"Fuck you while wearing a condom? My angel only gets rawed. I bet you taste good when you're bleeding."

I gasp and my eyes fly open. I try to get away from him but he holds tight to my hips and fucks me harder with his fingers. "Tyrant. You *can't*."

"Keep screaming out like that. Bring everyone running so they can get a good look at you like this."

I hastily shut my mouth.

Tyrant draws his fingers out of me and a moment later they're replaced by his warm, slippery tongue. He licks my sex, my clit, and even pushes his tongue inside me. I squeeze my eyes shut and moan, horrified and turned on at the same time.

"Oh, fuck yes," he breathes and laps at me again.

I glance behind me. There's blood on his lower lip, and he sucks it into his mouth and swallows like I'm delicious.

"You're crazy," I whimper.

"And you're about to get fucked so hard you'll feel me for a week." He keeps a firm hold of my hip and I hear the clink of his belt and then a zipper. Something alarmingly thick—was he always this *thick?*—pushes against my tight channel and then slides roughly into me. I cry out and brace my hands against the book stacks.

Tyrant curses under his breath and thrusts deep, over and over. He seems to be enjoying the sight of our sex as much as the sensation because I can feel his fingers as he twists them on his shaft. "Fuck yes, Vivienne. You blood-red little vixen. You're getting your period all over me."

My inner muscles convulse in pleasure at his filthy words.

A moment later, he starts to fuck me in earnest, and I have to swallow down my cries. I'm so sensitive and tender down there that every thrust feels like he's impaling me right through my body.

"Oh, look at that," Tyrant says with relish as he draws out of me. I think he's talking to himself until he grasps my hair and forces me to half turn toward him. "I said *look at it.*"

Over my shoulder, his erect cock is coated in my blood. Glistening with it. Bright red all the way down his shaft.

"Have you ever seen anything more beautiful?" he asks. When he catches my eye, he adds, "What a little slut," and thrusts into me once more.

I yelp and grab hold of the shelf, but that doesn't stop my knees from burning against the carpet. "You're making this embarrassing on purpose."

Tyrant gives a nasty laugh. "We could be in my bed. Instead, you're getting carpet burn on your knees and bleeding down your thighs in the college library. Good girls who stay in my bed and obey all my rules get nice Tyrant. Bad girls who sneak off get mean Tyrant. Keep pushing me, angel, because I fucking love being mean to you."

Mean Tyrant is fucking me so hard and deep that it hurts, and yet I'm braced against the bookshelf so he can keep slamming into me. The pain feels heavenly. I crave him so much.

"Look at you arching your back for me. You love mean Tyrant too, don't you?"

"I—*ah*—need—" I manage between moans. The threat that I'm going to feel him for a week wasn't an idle one. Once the ache fades, I'll still remember every excruciating minute of being screwed in the library. "Oh, God, Tyrant, please don't stop," I whimper over and over. "Please, Tyrant, please."

As I climax, he groans and grips my hips with sticky, bloody fingers. "Your cunt fucking loves me," he says, groaning with his own orgasm. He pumps into me several more times and then draws slowly out of me.

I try to sit up, but he pushes me down again.

"Not so fast. I want to see this."

I don't know what he means until he pushes his thumbs into me and spreads me open. Nothing happens for a moment, and then warm fluid gushes out of me and runs down my thighs.

"Oh, fuck yes. Your blood and all my cum, dripping down your pretty flesh. What a well-fucked, sticky mess you are," he says with a hum of appreciation, and then spanks my ass, making me jump.

My cheeks are so hot from embarrassment and arousal that I know my face is bright red. I wonder if he's going to leave me on the floor in the stacks, a mess of blood and cum.

Tyrant finally lets me sit up, and I raise myself onto my knees, my body shuddering with pleasure and horror. That was insane. I don't think I'll ever mentally clamber back into my own body after simultaneously being sent to heaven and hell on the end of his cock.

To my surprise, he helps me to my feet, takes his black trench coat off, and wraps it around me. "There's a bathroom over here. Come on."

It's an accessible toilet with room for both of us, and he pushes me in there and shuts the door behind us. I reach for a paper towel, but he seizes my wrist.

"I'll do it."

My brow wrinkles with confusion. "First you call me a slut, and now you want to clean me up?"

"Not any slut. *My* little slut." Tyrant peels the trench coat from my body and pats the sink. "Put your hands here, messy girl."

I plant my hands on the sink. When his hand slides over my ass, I can't help but pop it out for him.

We catch each other's gaze in the mirror as he draws my dress up to my waist, and I drink in the sight of the man I've missed so much for weeks. Using damp paper towels, he wipes all the smears of blood from my inner thighs. He's careful about it, working slowly and methodically and going through a dozen or more paper towels. Every touch is strangely loving.

I watch his beautiful face through my lashes, feeling a strange tugging on my heart. "I thought you came here to torment me."

Tyrant plants a kiss to my throat. "I have to leave you with something sweet to remember me by. *Dear Diary, Tyrant is cruel and wicked, so why do I love him so much?*"

"I don't keep a diary anymore."

Tyrant smirks and throws away a bunched-up paper towel, and I realize why. I didn't say I didn't love him.

"You're writing it in your head. *Dear Diary, Tyrant loves cleaning up my pussy after he's totally wrecked it.* Wait here a moment."

I stare at myself in the mirror while he's gone. When I squeeze my thighs together, I can already feel the bruising ache he's left me with. I sink my teeth into my lower lip and smile at my reflection. Good.

Tyrant comes back with a tampon that he must have taken from my bag. I reach for it, but he holds it away from me. "I'll do it."

I look at him in astonishment. "Really? Do you know how?"

He unwraps the tampon. "I have sisters. You think I didn't mess around with these things when I was bored in the bathroom and wondering how they worked? I never actually did this before, but I can figure it out."

Squeezing my ass with one hand and pulling my sex open, He pushes the applicator into me while staring into my eyes, making me gasp. "Mm. These things are much more fun when you get to put them in the pretty girl you just fucked. *Thank you, Tyrant*," he prompts me, taking away the applicator and pushing the tampon deeper with his finger.

"Thank you, Tyrant," I whisper, gazing into his blue eyes.

He turns me around and kisses me hard, parting my lips and thrusting his tongue into my mouth, and I surrender to his kiss.

"Are you ready to say, *I love you, Tyrant, please take me home*?"

For a moment, I allow myself to indulge in that daydream. Be Tyrant's girl. Allow him to adore me night and day. Live with him. Love him.

But I'll never see Barlow again if I go home with Tyrant.

"Dad and Samantha have let me see Barlow again," I say slowly, and wince, waiting for Tyrant to say something harsh or shout at me.

He watches me for a moment, sighs, then pushes his hand into my hair and rubs the back of my neck. Then he kisses my forehead. "I know. Your baby brother is important to you."

"He's everything to me."

Tyrant goes on rubbing slow, hypnotic circles on my nape, before kissing me a final time and once again helping me into his trench coat. "Wear this home. Your dress is covered in blood."

"Thank you," I say, gazing up at him, and wondering if I should have given him a very different answer. "Are you mad I'm choosing Barlow?"

"You would think so, wouldn't you?" He kisses me while I'm still puzzling out what that means.

It doesn't sound like he thinks he's lost.

He sinks his teeth into my lower lip and then laves it with his tongue. When he pulls away, his eyes are glimmering with malice. "Remember this. You're Tyrant's girl. You follow my rules, or I will fucking punish you."

PART III: NOW

CHAPTER TWENTY-TWO

Tyrant

With a hunting rifle brandished in my right hand, I gaze around at the three unarmed victims trapped in my labyrinth.

Owen Stone. Samantha Stone. Vivienne Stone.

Husband and wife are standing side by side, her shaking and crying, him glaring at me with a mix of fear and defiance. And Stone's beautiful daughter?

Vivienne is standing apart from her father and stepmother, her face a pale mask and her nails biting into her palms. She neither speaks to me nor looks at me.

I waited months and months for this girl. *Months*. And for what? Instead of running to me when the last of her bonds with her family were broken, she ran from me. Didn't she realize that waiting for those bonds to break so I could have her was the only thing stopping me from killing them all?

I take several bullets out of my pocket and load them into the rifle, taking my time, letting them know that every bullet is for them. Mrs. Stone starts to sob harder, and I can't help the smile that spreads over my face.

"Here we are again, Vivienne. In my labyrinth, you in peril of your life while Barlow is tucked up safe and sound in my bedroom. You remember my bedroom, don't you?" I load a bullet into the chamber with an ominous sound and rest the rifle against my shoulder. "What a wonderful chance I gave you last time, and you wasted it."

Vivienne keeps her eyes averted, but she doesn't look tearful. She looks quietly furious. "Can I ask you something, Tyrant?"

"Ask away, angel," I reply, mocking her with her pet name.

"You were the one who graffitied my house. You sent the pictures of us to Dad and Samantha. Am I right?"

I watch her through narrowed eyes. "You want to make me your monster?"

"I don't have to make you into anything. For a while there, I—" Her face crumples and she takes a painful breath. "I really did think you—" She swipes angrily at her eyes. "Never mind. It doesn't matter now."

Precisely. None of that matters any longer.

"If you won't love me, Vivienne, you can fear me instead." I take a long look at the three of them. "I'm sick of the Stone family. Escape my labyrinth, or I'll kill you all. The longer you keep running, the longer you'll go on breathing."

Samantha gasps and grabs hold of her husband's wrist, but Owen Stone is glaring at me through hate-filled eyes.

"You're not really going to let us escape. You're going to hunt us down for sport." Stone turns to his daughter, fuming at her, "This is all your fault."

The words fly from my lips before I can stop myself. "Vivienne's fault? Vivienne's fucking fault? How much money is it you owe me, twenty-nine thousand, plus interest? The only person responsible for Owen Stone's death is Owen Stone himself."

For a moment I meet Vivienne's shocked gaze, and I have to force myself to look away from her.

Samantha is wringing her hands, tears dripping down her face as she whimpers, "My baby. Please don't hurt my baby."

"Hurt him? I'm going to keep him. He's my son now, not yours."

Samantha cries even harder.

"Come on. We're getting out of here." Owen Stone grasps his wife's arm and drags her off down a garden path before disappearing around a hedge, leaving his daughter behind. Vivienne watches them go without an ounce of surprise on her face that they've abandoned her.

Then she turns to me.

We gaze at each other across a narrow expanse of lawn beneath another silvery moon. Her words as I was kidnapping her from the bus station come back to me.

I've never taken anything from you. The only thing you ever bought me was one pregnancy test.

I watch her, my head on one side. Interesting that she brought that up. Because she's taken the test, or because she hasn't?

I stride forward and pull her backpack roughly from her shoulder and then step away, pointing the rifle at her. "Go. Or I'll shoot you right here and now."

She hesitates for a moment as if she wants to say something, and then she closes her mouth and hurries off in the opposite direction to Stone and his wife. Toward the house.

She's going to try and rescue Barlow again.

When I'm alone, I prop the gun against a marble bench and go through her backpack, pulling out clothing, a toothbrush, and a pair of shoes. The pregnancy test isn't here. Maybe it's in her dorm room.

I glance in the direction that Vivienne disappeared. She'll be trying to find her way through my labyrinth for hours yet. They all will. I have plenty of time to go in search of answers.

After climbing in through Vivienne's window, I perform a thorough search of her dorm room. I check her bed. Her bedside table. The trash. Every drawer. Inside all her shoes. Between the pages of textbooks. Under discarded clothes and piles of folded fabrics.

No test. I suppose she could have taken the test in the communal bathrooms if she's taken it at all.

I go to the window and gaze out onto the moonlit night, remembering how Vivienne looked when she emerged from the bus station restroom.

Deep in thought. Shocked by something. The results of a pregnancy test she'd just taken?

I stand there for several minutes, letting the cool night air wash over me. There was something significant about that moment, and I won't stop thinking about it until I've gone and investigated that restroom for myself.

Twenty minutes later, I'm on the other side of town, pulling into a parking space at the bus station. The place is deserted, and I have to break a padlock from the restroom door in order to get inside.

There are only two cubicles, and one of them has a trash can.

Lying on top of the trash is a pregnancy test, face down. I pick it up and turn it over, my blood pounding in my ears. I stare at the indicator window.

Vivienne's having my baby.

I'm going to be a father.

Vivienne's having my baby and she didn't tell me. We were face-to-face just now. We were face-to-face at this bus station. What was her plan, to skip town and do what? Have my baby in secret? Get rid of it? No, she wouldn't do that, but she was planning on hiding my child from me. *My* fucking child.

I shove the pregnancy test in my pocket and head back to my car. She can't run from me now. I have her right where I want her, pregnant and trapped in my labyrinth.

As I turn back onto the main road and race toward my house, I mutter at the dark road ahead, "You should have let me save you, Vivienne."

She wouldn't let me save her, and I take that personally.

CHAPTER TWENTY-THREE

Vivienne

I take a left turn through an archway of climbing roses and then hurry down a path, and then make a right at a statue of a woman in a toga. I've been in Tyrant's labyrinth before, but nothing looks familiar. It only takes me a few minutes to realize I'm hopelessly lost.

Desperately, I try to remember which way Tyrant took me when he was leading me from the boathouse up to his mansion, but I don't think we went through this section of his grounds at all, or if we did, I was in too much of a sex haze, or too much in love with Tyrant to look at anything but him.

The memory of his harshly beautiful face gazing back at me so tenderly that night makes my heart ache and my throat burn. He's the father of my baby, and tonight he looked at me so coldly as he declared he was going to kill me. Is it better to keep trying to escape, or throw myself at his mercy for the sake of our child?

I don't know what to do, so I keep running. There are so many left and right turns that I don't know if I've even been down these paths before. I'm looking over my shoulder after rounding a corner. When I turn to look ahead, I'm looking right at Tyrant.

He's standing across an expanse of grass, holding the hunting rifle and wearing an expression filled with fury. "Got you."

He raises the gun and points it at me. His finger is on the trigger, and as I stare down the barrel of the weapon, it resembles an endless, black tunnel.

I cover my stomach protectively and cry out, "Tyrant, don't. Not my baby."

The words are out of my mouth before I can stop myself. I have to protect the life growing inside me. I glance up fearfully because now Tyrant knows I'm carrying his child.

Tyrant lowers the gun, and there's not an ounce of surprise on his face. "Not your baby. My baby." He speaks through gritted teeth, reaches into his pocket, and throws something at my feet. The pregnancy test I left in the trash at the bus stop restroom.

"When were you going to tell me about this?" He waits, but I don't answer.

I watch him, wondering if he's going to throw the gun aside and swear to be a better man now. That he was wrong when he put the tracker in my neck, and he's going to let my family go and we can be a real family.

But Tyrant doesn't say any such thing, and he doesn't put down the gun.

"Just a few days ago I fantasized about being pregnant," I confess in a whisper. "Telling you I'm pregnant. Being with you forever. I actually thought this would be a happy moment for us."

"Can't you tell? I'm ecstatic."

A cold shiver runs down my spine. It hurts to look at him when he's so lethally furious. "What's going to happen now?"

He thinks about this for a moment. "We could have done this the pretty way. I promised you a ring. I promised you everything, including your freedom, if you only stayed by my side forever, but that wasn't good enough for you."

"Don't forget about turning a blind eye to you murdering my family."

"They're worthless, Vivienne, and you know it," he snaps back.

I start pacing up and down, pushing my fingers through my hair. I can't see any way out of this. He's never going to let me go now he knows I'm pregnant. "Will you kill me after I give birth to our child? Will you pretend this baby and Barlow are siblings and you're the father and raise them yourself?"

Tyrant gives me a sly smile. "Sounds enticing. I'm rather good with children, don't you think?"

My stomach swoops. He *is* good with children. I saw that for myself in those brief hours we were taking care of Barlow together, and thinking about it only makes me feel more wretched. We could have had something wonderful together as a real family. It hurts so much that we never will.

Every breath I drag into my lungs feels painful.

My chest feels like it's in a vise.

I can't get enough air.

"Vivienne?"

Black spots dance in front of my eyes. I reach out unsteadily to try and grab onto a tree. A hedge. Anything. I'm panicking. I'm losing it, just like I did when I saw Lucas after he tried to rape me.

Tyrant's by my side, and his hands are holding my waist. Holding me up. For a moment he almost feels like my savior. Suddenly, he seizes me by the hair and forces me to my knees. To my shock, he reaches for his belt with his free hand and unfastens it, dragging out his thickened cock.

I'm panicking, and he's got an erection?

"Open your mouth," he snarls.

"Are you…" I suck a wheezing, painful breath into my lungs. "Are you going to force me to blow you while I'm having a panic attack?"

"This isn't for me. This is for you. Open your fucking mouth."

"What are you talking ab—"

Tyrant seizes the opportunity while I'm talking to shove his cock past my lips. My eyes go wide. I brace for him to thrust aggressively, over and over, punishing me for hiding the pregnancy from him and running away.

Only he doesn't. He just stands there, holding on to my hair with his cock shoved all the way to the back of my throat.

"You need something in your mouth to make you calm. My finger. A gag. My cock. You relax when your mouth is full." He keeps a tight hold of my hair as he slowly sits down on a bench and pulls me between his legs. "Suck on me and calm the fuck down."

I glare furiously up at him, my nails digging into his thighs. I can't spit him out because he's holding me too tightly, but soon enough he'll grow soft and bored with me because I refuse to blow him.

But as the minutes tick by, Tyrant doesn't grow soft, and he doesn't seem frustrated either. His grip on my hair loosens slightly to a secure hold. My full mouth makes me feel strangely serene. Without realizing what I'm doing, my body relaxes against his thighs.

Tyrant makes a pleased noise in the back of his throat, and he murmurs, "That's better. That's how I like to see my girl."

As angry as I want to feel at being forced into submission, my body just goes on melting against my will. My cheek is resting against his thigh, and I hug his leg as he strokes my hair. He's making me use his cock as a pacifier, and it's working. I feel drowsy. I feel drugged.

"You're still helping them, Vivienne," Tyrant says softly. "You're trying to save Barlow, and when you do, you'll try to save them as well."

I shake my head. Even if I wanted to help Dad and Samantha, they don't want my help. They left me behind and they're trying to get out of the labyrinth without me.

"You won't try to save them?" Tyrant asks. "Then what is it you want?"

I wish Tyrant Mercer would give me my heart's desire.

I push his cock deeper into my mouth, and he groans as he hits the back of my throat. My hands are pressed against his belly as I pull back and slide him in deeper. This is even better than his finger or the gag. I should have been sucking his cock all along because he feels amazing in my mouth, huge and hot and thick. I keep going until he's groaning and thrusting into my mouth.

I pull away and gaze up at him in the moonlit darkness. A string of saliva connects my lower lip to the tip of his cock.

We don't speak, but a thousand words pass between us in that silence.

I grasp his thighs and pull myself up. He helps to strip me out of my jeans and sweater, and then I straddle his lap, pull my underwear aside, and sink down onto his cock.

We wrap our arms around each other and groan at the same time.

Him.

I want Tyrant.

He's my heart's desire.

Whatever happens next, I have to be his.

"Fuck, yes, angel," Tyrant says in a guttural voice as I rise up and sink down his cock again and again. "I've missed you so tight around my cock. Milk me, and I'm going to blow so deep inside you."

I moan against his mouth, and I'm almost sobbing. "I've missed you, too. I need you so much."

Tyrant wraps his arm around my waist, lifts me up, and lays me down on the grass. Pulling out, he presses tender kisses down to my belly, his lips brushing over my scars. He doesn't give a damn about my scars and he never has.

He kisses my stomach again and again. "I'm so deep inside you, angel. You're mine, forever. You and this baby." The baby growing inside me. His baby.

He sits up, takes his cock in his hand, and thrusts into me so fast and deep that I cry out long and loud.

"You know that I'm obsessed with you, don't you?" he snarls as he pounds ruthlessly into me. "Nothing has changed. I'm going to put that tracker back in your neck. You're going to say, *Thank you, Tyrant.* I still own you. Your blood. Your breath. Your pussy. Everything."

"Please, Tyrant," I beg him, holding on to his shoulders for dear life. If that's how he wants to make me his, then I'll give that to him. His tracker in the back of my neck to keep me safe. His cock in my mouth when I need to calm down. With every slam of his cock, he's pushing me closer and closer to the edge. I dig my nails in and cry out as my climax hits me. Tyrant growls and scoops me against him with both arms, thrusting deeper with each wave of his own orgasm.

Slowly, he raises himself up, and we're both breathing hard.

"Will you give me my heart's desire?" I whisper, taking his face in my hands.

"Angel, I'll give you anything."

"I never want to see Dad and Samantha again." I hesitate for a moment, and then I say it. "But I don't want them to die."

Tyrant's eyes narrow as he considers this. "I want Barlow. He's ours."

"I…" I bite my lip.

Tyrant seizes my throat, fingers digging in, and he growls, "You want him, too. Say it. Tell me you want Barlow and that you won't give him up."

I cling desperately to Tyrant's wrist. He's not squeezing hard, but he is telling me this is a hard line for him. Mercy for Dad and Samantha, but we're taking Barlow. I want my brother so much. I don't want to give him up.

There's the sound of footsteps and voices. Dad and Samantha are coming this way.

Tyrant takes off his shirt and quickly pulls it over my head, picks me up in his arms, and collects the rifle. When Dad and Samantha come around the corner, I'm sitting in Tyrant's lap. He has one arm around me, and one hand holding the gun that's braced on the ground. He glares at them through cold eyes. All his muscles are rigid as I cling to him.

Dad stops short, and revulsion washes over his face. For once, I don't duck my head in shame or tell myself that I'm disgusting and everything I want and need is wrong. I wrap my arms tighter around Tyrant and stare Dad down.

Still watching Dad with an icy glare, Tyrant plants a slow kiss against my throat, telling me silently that he's proud of me.

"I see how it is," Dad says slowly, watching Tyrant. "You've got some kind of weird obsession with my daughter. Fine, I'll make you a deal. You can have her, we'll have Barlow, and we'll all go home, fair and square. Debt paid."

"You would give your daughter up like that?" Tyrant asks.

Dad's lip curls in a sneer. "Gladly. My daughter wants us dead just so she can have Barlow."

My mouth drops open in outrage. "What have I done that would make you believe I'm so heartless? You disowned me, but I have fought for your lives."

"Don't bother trying to deny it," Dad retorts. "Your friend told me all about your plan when I ran into her at the ball."

"My friend? I don't have a friend who would make up such lies about me."

"Julia something. Julia Merrick."

I'm hit with an ice-cold wave of shock. Julia said that? Julia, one of only two friends I have in the world, has been talking to Dad about me behind my back? I never even talked to her about Tyrant. I can't think of one reason for her to betray me like that. I've never hurt her in any way. We've known each other since high school. It's not true. It can't be true.

Tyrant grips me even tighter. "Did you just say Merrick?"

Suddenly he stands up and places me on my feet, and he pushes the rifle into my hands. "Don't let them near you. Stay here. I need to go and see someone, and I'll be right back."

He stalks off into the darkness and disappears around the corner.

Dad follows him with his eyes and then turns back to me with a frown. "What's that about?"

I shake my head, mystified. "I don't know."

"Wherever he's gone, he's just going to come back and kill us," Samantha cries.

Dad steps toward me, reaching for the gun, but I aim it at him and say, with surprising calmness, "Don't come any closer, or I'll shoot you."

If he believes I want him dead, then he'll try and hurt me, and I can't let him hurt my baby. I'll kill him if he tries anything.

His expression is outraged, but he stops in his tracks. "Vivienne, I'm your father."

I don't reply. I don't belong in their lives anymore and I don't need them. I'm going to make my own family.

"So you fucked him, and now you'll do anything he'll say?" Dad says. "That man was going to hunt you down for fun. We all heard him say it."

I think about this for a moment and shake my head. "Tyrant was never going to hurt me. He wanted to force us to have this conversation. You never wanted me around, did you, Dad?"

Dad glowers at me but doesn't reply. I suppose it's a good idea not to piss off the girl holding the hunting rifle.

"And us?" Samantha quavers. "Is he going to hurt us?"

"He wants to hurt you both very much." It sticks in my throat to speak these words, but I say them anyway. "Tyrant is going to let you both go. He wanted to kill you, but I convinced him to spare your lives."

I carefully avoid any mention of Barlow.

"How can you be sure he'll keep his word?" Dad asks.

"My wish is the only thing that has convinced him to spare you, because I promise you, he hates you so much. Also…" I feel a rush of happiness as I finally say the words out loud, and with a smile on my face. "We have the most wonderful future to look forward to. I'm having his baby."

The shocked expressions on Dad's and Samantha's faces are priceless.

CHAPTER TWENTY-FOUR

Tyrant

When I return to the center of the labyrinth, Vivienne is where I left her thirty minutes ago, standing well apart from her father and stepmother and holding on to the rifle with a fierce expression on her face.

What a good girl. She didn't let those vipers get anywhere near her.

Her mouth falls open with shock as she sees who I'm dragging along by her shiny blonde hair. Julia Merrick. Alan Merrick's daughter, the city councilman who's been harassing me about marrying his daughter.

I hurl the bound, whimpering girl onto the grass at my feet. Vivienne steps forward to help her, but I hold out my hand, barring her way. "No. Stay where you are."

"But she's my friend," Vivienne says.

"This bitch is not your friend," I seethe. I lean down and rip the tape from Julia Merrick's mouth, and she gasps in pain. "Why have you been stalking Vivienne?"

Tears spill down the girl's face. She's shaking with fear, and she can barely get the words out. "I don't understand what's happening. I didn't do anything to Vivienne. Are...are you Tyrant Mercer?"

What a little actress she is.

She turns to Vivienne. "What's happening? Why do you have a gun? Please help me."

Julia appealing to my woman makes rage swirl through me, and I slap her hard across the face. She cries out and sprawls across the grass. She hurt Vivienne, and that's not going unpunished.

Vivienne turns anxious eyes on me. "Tyrant, she's already scared of you. Is it necessary to hit her?"

It's more than fucking necessary. It's the only thing that matters right now.

I take out a knife and show it to the Merrick girl. "I'll ask you again, and then I'll begin slicing up that pretty face of yours. Why have you been stalking Vivienne?"

The Merrick girl sniffles and whimpers for a moment. She meets Vivienne's eyes and then looks away again. Finally, she says in a small voice, "My father made me do it."

Vivienne lets out a cry of shock.

I stand over the young woman, seething with fury as she admits to everything. Spray painting *Tyrant's slut* on Vivienne's house after seeing me climbing out Vivienne's window and leaving the dorms. Stalking me so often that she was there the night I trapped Vivienne in my labyrinth and took the photographs of us having sex. Julia was able to climb a tree outside my walls and point a telescopic lens at us. She's a hobby photographer and used her own darkroom to develop the images and deliver them to Vivienne's family home.

"I thought you were only interested in photographing gardens," Vivienne says faintly. She's turned pale while listening to what her so-called friend has to say. "Why would you do such horrible things to me?"

I wait with narrowed eyes. I don't give a damn what Julia Merrick has to say. I crave her blood and her screams, but Vivienne deserves an answer. "You have one more second to start talking, or I start slicing."

Julia shrinks fearfully from my knife. "Because I had no choice. Dad told me it was my duty to marry Mr. Mercer. He'd done his part by approaching with the offer, and I had to close the deal. We all have to do our part to advance Dad's political career so he can become the mayor, then governor, and then eventually the president. I…I thought about approaching Mr. Mercer and flirting with him, but I was so nervous, and I didn't know what he liked. I thought if I discovered more about him it would be easier, and then when I found out that he was obsessed with my friend…" She trails off miserably.

"You had to take Vivienne out of the competition," I guess.

"I thought Vivienne would avoid you once her family told her to give you up. They hated you so much after you stole her little brother. But the photos didn't work, and I was starting to get desperate. I had no choice," Julia says, beseeching me. "I didn't want to hurt Vivienne, but…"

I feel a thud of anger as I realize what she's saying. It's worse than stalking and humiliating Vivienne. Much worse. "The three boys who attacked her in the cemetery. You told them to do it."

"Julia, you didn't," Vivienne cries.

The Merrick girl starts to sob. "I didn't want them to kill Vivienne. I thought maybe they would scare her and put her off, um, men."

I lean down and seize the front of her T-shirt, brandishing the knife in her face. "You wanted them to rape her so brutally that she'd be too traumatized to love me? You're a fucked-up little bitch."

"I had to do it," she cries, her eyes so wide with fear that the whites are showing all the way around. "Dad was at me night and day to make it happen. The only time he talked to me was to tell me to be useful to him, or else I'd lose my inheritance, my college payments, and my allowance. My future and my place in the family was at risk." She hesitates and adds in a defiant rush, "I had a good reason for what I did because family comes first. At least I didn't tell someone to rape my own child over a debt of a few thousand dollars."

All this time, Julia has focused on me, but now she glances at someone over my shoulder. Behind me, Owen Stone inhales sharply.

What. The. *Fuck*.

I slowly let go of Julia and turn around. Stone's expression is filled with guilt and alarm that he quickly tries to smother with confusion.

"Julia, what are you talking about?" Stone gives a nervous laugh.

Owen Stone, the man who resents his daughter so much that he can discard her like an old rag. Owen Stone, the man with a gambling addiction and so many debts his own wife doesn't know the state of their finances. Owen Stone, whose friend tried to rape Vivienne. Who wouldn't believe her when she told him it happened, and who hurt her so much by calling her a liar that her body and soul will bear the scars until the day she dies.

Owen Stone, who is breaking out in a cold, guilty sweat right before my eyes.

CHAPTER TWENTY-FIVE

Vivienne

I've been following the conversation between Tyrant and Julia with my heart in my mouth, too horrified by what I'm hearing to say a word. Julia looks pathetic as she sobs out every awful thing she's done behind my back for the past ten months, all the while pretending to be my friend. I've had friends turn on me before, gossip behind my back, drop me for more interesting, wealthier, prettier people. I never imagined that someone would hate me so much that they would send three people to do one of the cruelest things you can do to a person short of killing them.

All that was shocking enough, but hearing her last words turn my mind white with shock.

At least I didn't tell someone to rape my own child over a debt of a few thousand dollars.

I never told Julia about nearly being raped by Lucas Jones. I never told anyone except for Dad and Samantha, and Tyrant found it out for himself. For what Julia is saying to be true, it would mean that Dad borrowed money from his friend, and when he couldn't pay him back, he told Lucas to do whatever he liked to me as payment.

I turn to look at Dad, shaking my head, not wanting to believe what Julia is saying. Hoping that I'll see outrage on his face and that he'll speak vehement words of denial.

Dad is looking at Tyrant in fear, and he's turned pale and started to sweat. The rifle drops from my nerveless fingers and thuds onto the grass at my feet.

"Dad," I say in a broken voice. "No. Please, no. Say it's not true."

"He can't," Tyrant says through gritted teeth. "Can you, Stone?"

The center of the labyrinth is totally silent. A chilly wind whips across the grass, making all the fine hairs on my arms stand on end.

I turn to Julia for answers. "How could you possibly know anything about what happened to me when I was fifteen?"

My so-called friend can't meet my eyes. She's sitting on the grass with her hands tied behind her back, and she stares at the ground. "I was at your house one night hiding in the bushes, trying to discover whether the photographs that I'd left on the doormat had done the trick and you weren't seeing Tyrant anymore. Your dad was drinking beer on the porch with someone. A man. I don't know who. They were talking about Mr. Stone's debt to Mr. Mercer. The friend said Mr. Stone couldn't even offer you to Tyrant because you would scream and struggle too much, just like you did with him. Mr. Stone replied that it wouldn't work anyway because Mr. Mercer had already slept with you."

A sickened feeling twists my guts. I picture Dad and Lucas casually drinking beer while discussing how difficult I am to assault.

Tyrant addresses Julia with eyes narrowed in hate. "You knew someone had tried to rape Vivienne, and you told those three boys to do the same thing because you knew it was the most traumatizing thing that could happen to her."

Julia sniffles. "I thought it was the only way that I could help my father."

There's a moment of disgusted silence, and then Dad bursts out, "At least this girl understands family loyalty. Vivienne had nothing before she came to live with us. We gave her everything, so she should have let Lucas do whatever he needed to do to her and then just moved on with her life."

Whatever he needed to do. I shake my head in disbelief at Dad's cruel words.

An unexpected voice speaks from my other side. It's Samantha, and she's looking at Dad with almost as much horror as I feel. "Owen, say it's not true. You didn't tell Lucas to do that to your own daughter, did you?"

Dad gazes at her in surprise and then annoyance. "Don't pretend to be on Vivienne's side. You've told me so many times how Vivienne gets on your nerves. This way she could have been useful to us."

"We have a child," Samantha cries. "How do I know you won't offer him to someone to pay off a debt? We always owe people money because you can't put your family first and get help. I tried to overlook it for the sake of our marriage, but if you're going to treat your children so callously then I can't do this anymore."

"Can't do what anymore?" Dad asks angrily.

Samantha takes a deep breath. She's shaken, but she squares her shoulders. "Our marriage. I don't want you anywhere near Barlow. I'm divorcing you, and I'll make sure you never see him unsupervised ever again."

Dad glares at Samantha for a long moment. His jaw is ticking. A vein is throbbing in his temple. Suddenly, he lunges for the rifle that's laying at my feet. I gasp and kick it toward Tyrant before Dad can reach it. Tyrant picks the gun up.

Taking the opportunity while we're all distracted, Samantha turns and flees behind a hedge and we can hear her running through the labyrinth.

Dad takes off after her, murder in his bloodshot eyes. "Come back here, you ungrateful bitch. You won't take my son from me."

I give chase. I can't let Dad out of my sight. He might escape, and I haven't had time for any revenge. I need him to hurt after what he's done to me.

Tyrant calls after me. "Vivienne, you—" He breaks off, growling, "Oh, no you don't, you little bitch. You can't get away from me so easily."

Julia must have tried to make a bid for freedom as well. I keep pursuing the other two. Tyrant can handle Julia, and Dad and Samantha can't be allowed to escape.

There are several rapid turns, and I lose them amid the narrow hedges and stone statues. Turning on the spot, I listen for footsteps over the sound of my own harsh breathing. I hear a cry and run in that direction, but I keep getting lost and going the same way over and over again. I don't think I'll ever be able to solve Tyrant's labyrinth.

Finally, I round the corner to see Dad on top of Samantha. Dad slowly lets go of her throat and stands up. Samantha's eyes are wide and fixed. Tears have leaked over her cheeks and temples as she fought for her last breath.

She's dead.

As much as she hated me, I feel a trickle of sadness for my stepmother. "What kind of maniac are you?"

Dad rounds on me with a flushed face and reddened eyes. "You fucked that man and plotted to steal my son, and you call me a maniac? You're as crazy as your bitch of a mother was, Vivienne."

"My mother was sick and neglectful, but she was never cruel," I cry. "It should have been you who died on a dirty floor, not her." Bile rises up the back of my throat hearing him talk about Mom. She was about as far from Mother of the Year as you could get, but in her lucid moments, she cried and told me I deserved better, and that I was a good daughter. That she loved me. She was hopelessly lost to her addiction, and I was too young to know how to help her, but she still loved me.

Dad, though? He's twisted. He's beyond help. I wish I'd never wasted one second trying to win his approval. There's hatred in my eyes as I look at him. He's finished and he knows it. He's never going to get out of here alive.

"I'll kill you as well," Dad snarls. "You don't deserve to be happy with that piece of shit. You don't deserve to be happy at all."

I don't flinch or try to flee when Dad reaches for me and wraps both hands around my throat. I take a long look at my father's face, committing to memory every single detail of this moment in case I'm foolish enough to feel guilty about it later. His fingers tighten and it's hard to breathe. Spots begin dancing at the edges of my vision.

"*Vivienne.*" Tyrant sounds panicked. He's come around the corner and seen me with my father's hands wrapped around my throat, and there's a murderous roar as he races toward us, but it's not necessary. I'm done begging for Dad's life, and I don't need Tyrant to kill him for me either.

I reach into my sleeve, rip off the knife that's taped to my forearm, and I drive it into the side of my father's neck.

His eyes widen. He makes a choking sound. I yank the knife out and blood sprays all over a statue of a satyr playing the pan pipes.

Dad's grip on my throat loosens. He steps back from me and clamps a hand over the spurting wound and then looks at his palm, unable to believe what he's seeing. "You stabbed me?"

I lift Tyrant's shirt and show my father all the scars that cover my ribs and stomach. "Do you see these?"

"You fucking *stabbed* me?" Color is rapidly bleeding from his complexion. His eyelashes flutter, and I think he's going to faint from blood loss any second. "Help me, Vivienne. You can't let me die like this."

"You want me to help you, even though you never helped me?" I speak loudly and clearly so he can understand me in his last moments. "These scars? They're my love for Tyrant. My love for Barlow. Their love for me. You're not standing in my way any longer and telling me what I do and don't deserve. I deserve *everything*. And you deserve to die."

Dad stares at me with wide, glazed eyes. Then he crumples to the ground, his knees hitting hard before toppling forward and lying there motionless as blood soaks the grass.

CHAPTER TWENTY-SIX

Vivienne

A tall, strong figure sweeps in and wraps his arms around me. "Angel, are you all right?"

Tyrant touches my bloody hands. Feels me all over for injuries. Strokes and then kisses the red marks on my throat. I look at the bloodied knife in my hand and throw it aside. Dad's dead, and so is Samantha. Lucas is already dead, and Julia will be punished.

Am I all right?

Yes, for the first time in my life, I am. All the invisible ropes holding back my happiness have been torn away. I take Tyrant's face in my sticky, bloody hands. "You were right, Tyrant. You knew they were terrible people from the beginning, but I still protected them."

Tyrant glares at me, his eyes blazing. "Say that again."

"Say what?" Then I realize what he means. "You were right, Tyrant."

"Yes, I was fucking right," he seethes. "Owen Stone couldn't get his shit together for his wife and his newborn son, and you hurt for years because of him. I learned everything I needed to know about that asshole the first night I met him. I should have put a bullet in him then." He breathes hard through his nose, looking furious. Then his anger recedes. "But I'm happy you killed him instead. Stuck him in the throat with the knife you hurt yourself with because of him. That's my kind of justice."

"Thank you," I whisper, wrapping my arms around him. "I'm sorry it took me so long to realize the truth."

Tyrant is silent for a long time. Finally he says, "You're fiercely protective of people, angel. That's what I love about you. But I do love hearing you say I was right."

"I protected the wrong people. I don't think I believed I deserved any better than the way they were treating me. Maybe there were signs that Julia was my enemy as well, and I just didn't see them."

He takes my face in his hands and narrows his eyes at me. "And now?"

"I'm glad Dad's dead. It felt good to kill him after everything he'd done. I wanted him to know why, so I showed him my scars."

"That's my brave girl," Tyrant murmurs, and kisses me. Then he seizes my hand and walks me through his labyrinth. "Come with me. There's one more thing for us to deal with before we can have some peace."

We return to the center of the labyrinth where Tyrant left Julia tied to a bench. He uses his knife to cut through her bonds and then stands back.

She slowly gets to her feet, staring at our joined hands as she says glumly, "I guess I've got no chance with you then."

"Obviously," Tyrant tells her in a steely voice, tightening his grip on me. "And you never did. The choice was never between Vivienne and another woman. The choice was Vivienne or no one."

"Where are Mr. and Mrs. Stone?" Julia asks, glancing around.

"Dad killed Samantha," I tell her. "I killed Dad."

"And I thought my family was messed up," Julia mutters, wiping away her tears. "I told you the truth about everything I did and why. I know there's not much chance of this considering how angry you must be with me, but please let me go."

Julia did terrible things and then admitted to them without even trying to conceal her wrongdoings. It doesn't make sense to me. "Why did you spill the truth so quickly? You didn't even try to protect your father."

"Because she's a coward," Tyrant seethes. "She's brave when she's hiding in the shadows and sneaking behind your back, but the moment you drag her into the light, she crumples like the spineless little bitch she is."

Julia turns her face away from Tyrant. "Fine. I'm a coward. But did it occur to you that I didn't enjoy doing the things I did to Vivienne? It's been a year of sneaking around and scheming, and I wanted it to be over more than anyone."

"Oh, poor you," Tyrant mutters.

I glance at the man I love, and then back at Julia. "Tyrant wants to kill you, and he wants to kill your father as well. You nearly destroyed me, so I can't say I have much sympathy for you." I watch her for a moment, wondering how I'll feel if I watch her die. I don't think I care what happens to her either way. "I'll offer you a chance you probably don't deserve, and if you mess it up, I won't care if Tyrant guns you down in the street. Take your family and leave Henson by midnight tonight. I don't ever want to see you again. If you're still here after that, then it's your stupid fault for what happens to you next."

Hope and relief lighten Julia's face, and she steps toward me. "Vivienne, thank you."

Julia tries to embrace me, but Tyrant blocks her way, baring his teeth at her. "Back the fuck off."

She hesitates and actually has the temerity to look annoyed with him.

"I thought you were my friend," I burst out. "I would have never hurt you just because my father wanted something from you. I would have died first."

Julia rolls her eyes the tiniest amount, and mutters, "Of course you would have."

How did I not see it? Julia Merrick is a selfish bitch.

Tyrant makes a call on his phone, asking one of his security men to escort Julia from the labyrinth. When he arrives, my former friend takes one last, envious glance at us, taking in the tight, protective hold Tyrant has on me while I'm standing as close to him as possible.

"What are you going to do now?" she asks me.

I stroke Tyrant's sleeve while he glowers at her. "I'm going to stay here with Tyrant, and I'm going to have his baby. And I promise you, I'm going to be very, very happy."

We turn away and leave her behind. No one else matters

anymore. No one but the two of us, Barlow, and our baby. Hand in hand, we walk up into the house together, along the twisting, turning pathways and through gates and stone arches.

I try to memorize the way we're going and commit various features of the garden to my mind, but soon I feel turned around and confused. "You're going to have to teach me all the labyrinth's secrets. I feel lost already."

Tyrant arches a wicked brow at me. "All of them? But then I won't be able to chase you down for fun. How about I teach you just enough to make things interesting?"

The way he's smiling at me makes heat ripple up my body. I like his idea of interesting. I take one last look over the garden. The maze where I fell for Tyrant. The place where I finally learned the truth about everything. "Is it really over?"

"It's never over for us. It's only just beginning."

I turn to him, and I say the words that he's wanted to hear, and I've longed to say. "I wish Tyrant Mercer would steal my heart forever."

He takes my jaw in his hand. "You're going to give me this precious, gold-plated heart to take care of always?" He presses a large, warm hand against my belly. "You and our baby, and Barlow too?"

Happy tears spring into my eyes. I have Tyrant, we have my brother, and we have this baby. I had nothing for so long, and now my life is full of love. We're a family.

"We're all yours forever. All of us," I tell him, and he slants his mouth over mine in an eager kiss.

I kiss him back, my beautiful, fierce man.

We find Angela in Tyrant's room by the window, watching

over Barlow as he sleeps, and she gets to her feet with a delighted smile as she sees us. "It's the pretty little miss who was here before. Welcome back."

Tyrant gazes down at me, still holding tight to my hand. "That's right, it's Miss Stone. Soon to be Mrs. Mercer and the mother of this little one." He places his hand over my stomach.

Angela smiles in delight. "You mean it's happening? You're going to be a father? I knew the two of you would make a beautiful family. We're going to need to prepare so many things for a baby in the house. And this baby? Are we keeping this baby as well?" She gazes down at Barlow, who's started to wake up at the sounds of our voices.

"Oh, yes. We're keeping this baby. He's ours."

Delight rushes through me as it finally hits me. Barlow, my beloved baby brother, will never be taken from me again. I go to him, pick him up, and cuddle him against my chest before putting him back down. Samantha was right to fear Dad using Barlow like he tried to use me. I'm so relieved he's safe here with us.

Angela gives Barlow a fond look and heads for the door. "I'll be in the kitchen first thing in the morning if you need anything for the baby. Don't tax yourself, Miss Stone. You must take care of yourself now that you're expecting." She gives Tyrant a stern look. "Be gentle with your fiancée. No more of those chasing games in your garden while Miss Stone is pregnant."

When she leaves us alone, Tyrant turns to me with a gleam in his eyes.

"No chasing? What if you walk quickly? I hear exercise is good for pregnant women."

I angle my chin up so my dangerous man can claim my lips. "I've heard the same thing too."

Tyrant kisses me thoroughly, laughing softly between kisses. "I can't believe I finally have you. You and him." With a smile, he turns to Barlow and lifts him out of his bassinet. "Can you say daddy?" He points to himself and says slowly, "Daddy. Da-dee."

Barlow is gazing up at Tyrant with big blue eyes. My lover's sinister features and tattoos have always fascinated my baby brother. Suddenly Barlow breaks into a delighted grin and exclaims, "Da!"

Tyrant grins even wider. "That's right. I'm your daddy. Who's a clever boy?"

I can't help but smile as I watch them. "I suppose it's fine to be teaching Barlow to call you daddy? It won't confuse him?"

Tyrant gives me a sly look. "Why shouldn't he call me daddy? This is my baby boy." He plants a possessive hand on my belly. "This is my baby." He leans in and kisses me. "And this is my woman."

My heart flutters. We all belong to Tyrant. "We should tell Barlow the truth eventually. He could grow up and someone could say something just to hurt him."

Tyrant muses on this as he rocks Barlow back and forth in his arms. "I want both our children to know I'm their father and you're their mother, so how about this? Eventually, we can tell Barlow his birth parents died in a terrible accident, but before they died, they begged his sister and her husband to raise him as our own."

I gently play with one of Barlow's curls. A story like that is probably kinder than the truth, and we'll never not give Barlow all the love and protection he deserves. I nestle into Tyrant's side, wrapping my arm around his waist and holding Barlow's little baby hand with the other. "That sounds perfect."

Tyrant lays Barlow carefully back into the bassinet and then turns to me, taking my face in his hands.

"Look at you, my blood-soaked angel," he murmurs between kisses. "You're the one who's perfect. The way you killed that piece of shit?" His teeth sink into his lower lip. "My beautiful, murderous, pregnant woman. I've never seen anything sexier."

Tyrant takes off his pants, pushes his shirt from my shoulders, and drags me against him. I moan at the feel of his body pressing against mine. He scoops me up in his arms and carries me over to the bed before lavishing my body with his kisses and tongue.

As he sucks slowly on my clit with my thighs wrapped around his shoulders, I breathe hard and ask, "You were so patient with me. Why did you wait so many months when you could have just taken me?"

"Because you were protecting Barlow, loving Barlow, needing Barlow, and I loved to see you like that. I was so hungry for it, and I knew if I was clever and patient, I could steal you both. Angel, the way you protect him makes my dick hard."

Tyrant sits up, captures my hand, and wraps it around his thickened shaft. There's a surge of wetness between my legs, so I pull him closer and push the broad head of his cock down my inner lips. With one thrust and a ragged cry from me, he's buried all the way inside me. Tyrant is my knife, and I am his sheathe. He cuts deep, and I am free.

My lover moves in a steady rhythm, his palm covering my lower belly. Cradling our baby. Feeling his cock moving in and out of me. I'm transfixed by his beautiful face, lit silver by moonlight that turns his blue eyes quicksilver bright.

He murmurs to me coaxingly as he fists my hair. "You're taking me so well. Look how perfect you are filled with my cock."

I whimper at the sound of his voice.

"That's it. You're moaning so beautifully for me."

His voice is hypnotic and makes my climax rise so fast and fierce that he draws a ragged cry from my lips. He ups the speed of his thrusts, pounding me greedily until his own orgasm breaks over him and he bursts inside of me.

My body is heavy with pleasure and exhaustion as he pulls slowly out of me and draws his fingers through my sex, smiling to himself as he swirls his cum over my pussy.

"I still can't believe you're pregnant," he murmurs with a smile. "And I only had to threaten half the pharmacists in Henson not to give you contraception. Such a good girl for taking my seed so well." He kisses my stomach just above my pubic bone.

I smile and play with his hair. "Oh, yes. I'm such a good girl for running from you and defying you for months and months. Digging the tracker out of my own neck and not telling you I'm pregnant."

"Well, you know I love the chase." Tyrant gets out of bed and heads for the bathroom. He comes back a moment later with a wet washcloth, a tube of antiseptic, and a Band-Aid. "You hurt yourself when you took that tracker out of your neck, angel. Let me clean you up."

I roll onto my belly and move my hair aside, letting Tyrant clean and bandage me up.

We've been through so much together in such a short time. I think of cutesy couples beaming at each other and saying things like, *When it's right, you just know.* For us, it's more like, *When it's so deliciously fucked up, you just know.*

"You'd already asked me to stay, and I'd agreed, and you still put a tracker in me."

"I knew you'd run. You were too sweet and innocent still, and I needed to be able to keep you safe until you were mine."

"And now?" I murmur, my heavy eyelids closed as exhaustion washes over me.

He kisses my temple softly. "Sleep, angel. You're so beautiful when you're asleep, and I want to watch you."

Only Tyrant could say something so creepy and make it sound like a love song.

I close my eyes, and drift off, warm and safe in his arms.

There's a sensation of something being pushed onto my finger. I hear a spit and a groan, and something plush and blunt rubbing wetness around my pussy.

"Fuck, yes, angel," someone says in a voice heavy with lust.

My eyes fly open with a gasp, and I grab hold of muscular shoulders. The most beautiful man I've ever seen is thrusting his rock-hard cock into me. Splitting me open with a delicious burn. His tattoos are moving across his muscular chest and stomach with every drag and thrust of his cock. His eyes are heavy lidded and he's gazing at me like I'm the most beautiful thing he has ever seen. My tangled hair. My blood-smeared body. Even my dozens of thin, shiny scars.

Is this a dream? Why am I having sex with Tyrant?

Before I can get my bearings, I'm distracted by the sight of something large and glistening on my ring finger, and the shock of it causes everything to come flooding back. I'm with Tyrant. I'm in his bed, and I'm pregnant.

"Tyrant! What's on my finger?"

"We're engaged." He brushes my lips with his and keeps moving his hips in a steady, core-clenching rhythm.

I gaze up at him from beneath my lashes. "You're supposed to be romantic and go down on one knee, not ambush me in the middle of the night. What if I say no?"

"With my cock this deep inside you, my baby in your belly, and with you trapped within my labyrinth? Just try it."

The threat in his voice has my sex clenching even tighter on him.

He pulls out, turns me over onto my stomach, and thrusts into me again, the sharpness of this new angle making me cry out. "If you do try to run, I'll find you and drag you back here." He lifts something glinting from the bedside table and holds it in his hand.

It's a hypodermic with a thick needle.

I gasp in shock and try to sit up "What are you—"

Tyrant captures my wrists in one hand and pins them behind my back, forcing me back down. "You're going to be my wife, and my wife doesn't have a choice. The ring is for everyone else to know you're mine and for you to know you belong to me. This is for me.

These are my wedding vows. Hold still."

Tyrant pushes the needle beneath the skin in the back of my neck, an inch above the spot where he put the last one, and it blazes with pain. It hurts so much that I have no idea how I slept through it last time.

With the needle still in my neck, Tyrant pulls back with his hips and thrusts deeper into me, and he groans in pleasure. "You feel that?"

"Yes," I whimper in response.

Tyrant grinds his cock into me and says in a heavy, lust-filled voice, "Yes, you fucking do." He loves that I can feel the tracker being forced into my flesh.

He draws the needle out with a harsh breath of satisfaction, then puts it back on the bedside table. "If that tracker ever goes dark or you take it out, I will punish my wife until she begs for mercy. Do you understand me?"

"Yes, Tyrant," I moan, a heavy, pleasurable feeling flooding my body. Every inch of me belongs to him.

He gives a dark chuckle as his hands land on either side of my head. "You just keep doing everything I say, and I'll be your devoted husband who lives only to make you happy. I'm your servant. I'm yours to command."

As he thrusts deeper and deeper while I'm trapped beneath him, it feels very much the other way around. I moan into the pillow, arching my back so he can fuck me deeper.

"Everything I do is for you," he pants in my ear. "I live for you. I die for you. I'll never let you go, and I'll never give up all my secrets. By the time you figure them out for yourself, it will be too late. The monster in the labyrinth will have his claws too deep in your heart."

Tyrant goes on like this, threatening me and praising me, promising me the world but only if he's holding me tight in his arms the entire time.

"Who's Tyrant's good girl?"

It's the easiest question I've ever answered. "Me. Always me."

He fucks me harder, making my pulse race faster and pleasure burst through my body. "That's right, my sweet angel. Now show me how much you love me and come for Tyrant."

I cry out and dig my nails into the mattress as I climax. I fear him. I love him. I belong to him. Forever.

CHAPTER TWENTY-SEVEN

Tyrant

"To the bride and groom," Ace says, holding aloft his wine glass.

"Soon to be husband and wife," I say to my brother, reaching for Vivienne's hand with a smile and raising my own glass for the toast. We're getting married in the morning, and the bridal party has gathered around the dining table in my home. My best man, Ace, along with Vivienne and her bridesmaids, Carly and Camilla.

Vivienne and my youngest sister have become close these past few months. Over dinner one night, Vivienne told Camilla all about witnessing the incident with the men who ruined her sixteenth birthday, and then me beating them up.

"Did you fall in love with him right then?" Camilla asked Vivienne, and Vivienne admitted with a shy smile that she did. Camilla gave me a fond look and said, "That moment made me love my brother even more."

Since then, they've shared many cakes, shopping, and work sessions, Vivienne studying, while Camilla balances my books. They spread their books, laptops, receipts, and sewing patterns out on this dining table and keep each other company. Often Carly joins them, and I'll hear bouts of chatter and giggling as they take turns playing with Barlow when I'm elsewhere in the house.

Vivienne lifts a wine glass full of lemonade and clinks it against everyone else's, before taking a sip with a smile on her lips. She's wearing a pale, shimmering bustier dress that reveals her four-month baby bump. I can't get enough of seeing her with that adorable, sexy bump showing. I hope her wedding dress fits close to her body. I don't know because she hasn't let me catch a glimpse of her wearing it. She says it's bad luck.

Carly finishes her mouthful of wine and asks my bride, "Did you hear the news about Julia Merrick and her family?"

I laugh under my breath as I help myself to a platter of garlic shrimp before passing it to my sister. Camilla gives me a curious glance as she spoons shrimp onto her plate.

"What happened?" Vivienne asks her.

With the gleam in her eyes of someone about to tell a really good dinner party story, Carly glances around the table to make sure she has everyone's attention, which she does. "Well. My goodness. Everything has happened to them. First, Mr. Merrick's wife walked out on him. It seems he'd been having an affair with his assistant and someone emailed Mrs. Merrick screenshots of their text conversations and dirty selfies they'd shared with each other."

Vivienne's eyebrows shoot up her forehead, but Carly isn't finished. I settle back in my chair with a smirk on my lips to listen.

"Then the IRS came for Mr. Merrick and arrested him for cheating on his taxes, and the feds are investigating him as well for links to criminal gangs around the state. That was bad enough, but then Julia's brother Damien was beaten up by a former friend who discovered Damien had assaulted his sister. The sister had taken proof to the cops, but the cops in Henson did nothing. Someone finally convinced her to speak up to her family about it. It was all too much for Julia, who went on a rant online about how her brother and father had done nothing wrong and they were all being persecuted for no reason. Her post was filled with so much hate and name-calling that her new university expelled her. Then she got drunk and ran a red light. Now she's in the hospital with a broken pelvis."

And two broken legs. The car accident had nothing to do with me, but I think it's my favorite part.

Vivienne turns to me, both eyebrows raised. "That's so much bad luck to befall one family."

I play with the stem of my wine glass. "I don't know. You could say they did it to themselves. They made their own luck."

"I never liked Damien," Carly says with a shudder. "He was so creepy, especially around drunk girls at parties. He would always be trying to separate them from their friends."

"That sounds like that's the end of Mr. Merrick's political aspirations," Ace observes. "I never did like him. So slimy."

He offers me the salad bowl, and I accept it. "That's enough about the Merricks or you'll ruin my appetite. Who wants to hear about our honeymoon plans?"

Everyone does, and Vivienne describes the beach house in Hawaii that we've rented for two weeks.

After dinner and when everyone's gone home, after telling us to get a good sleep before the big day tomorrow, I sit on the bed, watching Vivienne take off her earrings in front of the dressing table. She's taken off her dress and is wearing a satin slip.

"Tyrant..." she says slowly, in a way that tells me she's about to say something I won't like.

"What is it?" I reply, tensing up, but my voice is carefully even.

"I put flowers on Samantha's grave today."

I slowly relax. Is that all? "Did you, angel?"

"I was feeling sad for her, and the way she died. She wasn't good to me, but she loved Barlow like I love Barlow. I wanted to say goodbye."

Goodbye seems like an excellent sentiment to me. "Whatever you need to put the past behind you," I tell her, trailing my fingers across the backs of her shoulders.

Vivienne is silent for a moment, and then she asks, "You wrecked Julia's family, didn't you?"

I meet her gaze in the mirror. They got off lightly. I wanted to kill them, and I still might. It depends on how angry their memories make me and if I believe they're suffering enough to go on breathing. "They destroyed themselves. I just nudged things in the right direction. Are you going to tell me I was wrong to do that?"

A smile tugs at her lips. "No. I'm not. I'm going to say thank you, Tyrant. I'm relieved that they aren't living happily ever after somewhere else. You were right."

I get to my feet, cross the room, and growl as I pull her closer. "Fuck, it makes me hard hearing you say that."

"You were right, Tyrant."

"Mm-mm," I hum appreciatively, kissing her throat. "What else do I love to hear?"

She reaches back and strokes the nape of my neck with her fingers. "I'm Tyrant's good girl. I'm Tyrant's slut. Please, please fuck me hard."

I lift her up in my arms and carry her toward the bed. "Anything for my woman."

The church is filled with light and flowers as I wait impatiently at the altar, my hands clasped together. The pews are filled with family, friends, and my closest associates and their wives and children. I wish there were more people here from the bride's side, but her family is all dead, and she's short by one of her two friends since Julia and her family left town.

Camilla and Vivienne have grown closer and closer to one another. They're almost the same age, and they have a great deal in common. She's making some of my people her people as well. These days, my housekeeper Angela and my driver Liam are more on her side than mine. Last week, Angela scolded me when Vivienne accidentally bumped her elbow against the doorframe. When I pointed out I wasn't at home, she told me I should have been there.

I kissed my woman's bruise with a smile, telling her that I would rip out the doorframe if it was what she wanted. Angela thought seriously about whether we should do it for an hour.

My brother Ace is my best man, and he's standing by my side. He must notice how tightly I'm clasping my hands as he remarks, "I've never seen you nervous before. Afraid she's not coming?"

"No. I'm impatient. I know she's here." My bride has a tracker in her neck, and I set my phone in my pocket to buzz the moment she's within fifty feet of me. It buzzed ten minutes ago. Where *is* she?

At the other end of the church, the double doors open, but only wide enough for Camilla to slip through and hurry down the aisle toward me in her soft violet bridesmaid dress. Everyone in the church turns around to look at her expectantly, but then they all go back to their murmured conversations when they realize it's not the bride.

Camilla comes up to me and whispers, "Everything's fine. Vivienne's making last-minute adjustments to her dress in one of the side rooms. She's anxious for everything to be perfect for you."

I glare along the church aisle at the big double doors. Anxious? My woman is pregnant. She can't be anxious about anything. I push past my sister and stride down the aisle, my footsteps echoing on the tiles. A murmur of consternation travels around the church, but the guests are not my concern; Vivienne is.

I push through the double doors, spy a door leading off to one side, and yank it open.

Vivienne whirls around with a gasp. Her skirt spreads out around her and her bodice shimmers and sparkles. There's a small bump where her stomach is, her dark hair is pinned up with curls framing her face, and a long white veil cascades down her back.

My breath catches in my throat. Vivienne has always been beautiful, even while I was resenting her for being so perfect. Even while sobbing her heart out. Wearing a masquerade mask. Filled with fear. Covered in blood. Especially while covered in blood. But now, seeing her dressed up so beautifully and knowing that it's for me?

Vivienne clenches her hands on her skirt and her voice is anguished. "Oh, no, Tyrant, it's bad luck for you to see me before the wedding." Her eyes are huge and worried, and there's a line between her brows.

I take a quick glance over her but she looks immaculate to me. "What is the problem?"

Vivienne's eyes widen and she can't seem to get any words out. "I…"

I stride forward and clasp the side of her neck and stroke her jaw with my thumb while glaring down at her. "You're the most beautiful woman I've ever seen."

A small smile appears on her lips. "Why are you saying these words while looking so ferocious?"

I glance behind me and see that Carly, Camilla, and the priest as well are standing in the doorway watching us. I need to be alone with my bride. "Everyone, get out."

Camilla pulls the other two away and closes the door behind them.

I turn back to my bride with narrowed eyes. "Are you fussing with your dress and working yourself up into a bundle of nerves while carrying my baby?"

"I thought a crystal was missing just here—" She reaches for a fold of fabric, but I seize her hand and place it on her belly, covering it with my own.

"You look so fucking beautiful I'm getting hard."

A scandalized blush erupts on her cheeks. "Tyrant, we're in church." A moment later, she can't seem to help her curiosity as she reaches for my pants and feels my cock. Her curiosity turns to surprise and delight as she traces the hard length of me.

I know how to soothe my bride's nerves. I reach for my belt and undo my pants. "On your knees, angel. Get that pretty mouth full of my cock."

She sinks to the ground, her skirt spreading around her, and takes my cock in her mouth. Slowly, her eyes close as she sucks. Not back and forth, just holding me in her mouth and moving her tongue against me.

I sink down onto a chair and pull her between my knees. "That's just beautiful, angel. You're so fucking pretty with your eyes closed and your lips wrapped around me."

Vivienne moans softly and relaxes her body, completely lost in the sensation of her full mouth, her safety between my legs. There's nothing for her to think about or worry about right now. I stroke Vivienne's hair and her cheek. I've got her.

She stays like that for ten minutes, suckling me, squeezing my thighs, floating in warmth and peace. My balls start to ache. People out in the church are probably getting restless. I don't give a fuck. When you've seen your woman about to hack at herself with a knife because she's in so much pain, moments like this are even more precious.

Finally she stirs, and her sucking becomes purposeful. Horny. I'm usually delighted for her to blow me when she's finished warming my cock, but today I stand up and pull her to her feet.

Then I grab handfuls of her dress and begin to drag it up.

Suddenly, Vivienne glances around for a clock, but there isn't one. "Tyrant, how long have we been in here? We're getting married now."

"They can all wait." Beneath her wedding dress, she's wearing a white lace G-string and suspenders. "Holy fuck," I murmur in a low voice, dragging my finger up the seam of her sex over the fabric.

"We're in church," she moans again.

"I said *holy* fuck, didn't I? Put your hands against the wall." I turn her around and she does as she's told, and I pull her dress all the way up to uncover her ass and tug her panties aside. Her lips are glistening with wetness.

"You're so swollen and slippery, angel."

"You know that warming your cock in my mouth does that to me."

Vivienne reaches behind herself to help me with my pants, and her hand dives in to grasp my dick the moment I have my zipper undone. She massages me up and down, moaning softly. My pregnant bride in her beautiful white dress. Hungry for me.

"Oh, I know it." I grasp the base of my cock, line it up at her entrance, and thrust inside her.

"Tyrant," she cries out loudly and braces her hand against the wall as I thrust. "Tyrant, oh my God, Tyrant. Please, please, please."

"Everyone out there can hear the bride being railed senseless," I say into her ear with a wicked smile.

Vivienne gasps in horror and her cries turn to barely a

smothered whimper.

I can tell from the way she's breathing and moaning that it won't be long until she climaxes. She manages to hold it in for about a dozen thrusts and then she forgets herself again as her orgasm tears through her. Feeling her shatter around me tips me over the edge, and I wrap both arms around her stomach and drop my head onto her shoulder, holding tight to my woman as I burst inside her.

Slowly, I lift my head. "Is it bad luck to fuck the bride before the ceremony or just to see the bride?"

Vivienne smiles woozily and pulls her G-string back into place. "Seeing as I'm pregnant already, I don't suppose it makes a difference either way. We're in nobody's good graces after the things we've done."

I turn her toward me and take her face in my hands. "You're in my good graces, angel. Always. How are you feeling? Do you want to hug my leg and suck on my dick for a while longer?" That usually helps her when she's feeling anxious. I'm obsessed with how cute she looks when she's using me as a pacifier.

Vivienne smiles and shakes her head, and there's not a trace of worry in her eyes. "I'm fine now, thank you."

I smile and plant a kiss on the end of her nose, and then cover her face with her lace veil. "Wonderful. Let's go and get married."

Drawing her arm through mine, I escort her toward the door. The priest has returned to the front of the church, but Camilla and Carla are waiting outside for us. Camilla shakes her head at me, exasperated, and Carla has a scandalized smile on her lips as she passes Vivienne her bouquet.

The music begins, and all the heads turn in the church as the bridesmaids begin their slow walk down the aisle.

Vivienne is basking in the music and all the smiles as we follow slowly behind them. Suddenly she gets the giggles, and whispers to me, "Wait. You're supposed to be up there so I can walk toward you."

I smile down at her, delighted to see her in such a sweet and giddy mood. I know how nervous she was about today and having so many people looking at her. "I'll walk you up there. I don't want you to be by yourself, and I'll be jealous if anyone else does it."

As we slowly approach the enormous gold cross above the altar, she rises on her toes and whispers to me, "Your cum is on my thighs."

I smile even wider. "Exactly where I want it when I marry you."

When we reach the priest at the front of the church, I give him a polite nod, and then turn to Vivienne and draw her veil back.

Her cheeks are flushed. Her bump is pressing into my stomach. Her eyes are the brightest I've ever seen. I can't believe I get to spend the rest of my life with Vivienne. She touches my cheek and then turns and searches the front rows until she sees Barlow. Her brother—now our adopted son—is on Angela's lap, and he waves a little toddler hand to Vivienne when she waves to him.

My bride turns back to me with the most breathtakingly beautiful and happy smile.

"Who's Tyrant's beautiful woman?" I whisper against her lips.

Vivienne smiles again and wraps her arms around my neck. "Me."

I don't remember what happens for the rest of the ceremony. I've already said my vows and so has she.

EPILOGUE

Vivienne

The maternity ward at the hospital feels almost like a hotel, and we have our own private room with a double bed. Not the world's most comfortable double bed, as it's a hospital bed, but still, there's room for Tyrant to sleep here with me and that's what matters.

It's just past seven in the morning, and our son Huck is fifteen hours old. He's lying on the changing table while Tyrant has his forearms braced on either side of him. Tyrant is gazing at Huck with rapt attention. Every little thing the baby does, he's drinking in. I don't think my husband has moved since the nurse finished weighing and changing him ten minutes ago.

"He's just so perfect. I didn't realize he'd be so perfect. Look at his fingers, Vivienne. His *eyelashes*. They're so small. How is he even possible?"

Tyrant has barely slept all night. He's wearing sweats and nothing else, and the sight of my dangerous man with his bare chest covered in tattoos, enraptured by the sight of our baby, makes me smile. I'm propped up against the pillows, and as exhausted as I am after labor and birth, I don't feel the least bit sleepy.

Tyrant looks up, catches me watching him, and smiles at me. Picking our son up in his arms, he carries him over and slides into bed with me. With one arm around me and one around our son, he holds us both close.

"You're amazing, angel. I can't believe you were able to do this. You're so strong and beautiful. You're incredible." He presses a kiss to my mouth. "How are you feeling?"

There's a small line between his brows as he gazes down at me, and I know what he's asking about. The medical staff all saw the scarring on my belly as I was giving birth. Tyrant knows how hard it was for me to reveal them to my obstetrician at the beginning of my pregnancy, but it got easier every time. Slowly, the scars stretched and changed as my belly grew bigger and bigger. As they changed, it became easier to stop thinking of them as "my scars" and instead see the evidence of our baby growing inside me.

"I was too caught up in everything that was happening that I didn't even think about it," I tell him truthfully. It's because of Tyrant's love and support, my new friends and new home, my studies, plus regular appointments with a therapist, that the girl who was so lonely and afraid is becoming a distant memory. I'm healing. I'm growing. We all are. All four of us.

"Look at him. He's perfect," I whisper, gazing at our baby. "I can't believe this is our life now. You, me, Barlow, and Huck."

"Speaking of Barlow, Angela will be here with him any minute."

"Wonderful. I can't wait for him to meet Huck."

While we wait, we cuddle our sleeping baby and discuss the future. Tyrant's work and plans for Henson. My studies, which I'll be returning to in four months. Tyrant's promise to get me pregnant again as soon as possible.

"We need a girl if you're going to sew all those adorable little dresses I've seen you sketching," he points out with a smile.

It's true. I have been drawing little girls' clothes. And little boys' clothes. Fantastical, make-believe clothes. Costumes for dress-up days, parties, and stage plays. Dressing up is some of the most carefree time I ever spend, and children love it as well.

"A girl would be lovely…" I start to say, and then break off with a laugh as I see the determined gleam in Tyrant's eyes. "You'll be trying your hardest as soon as we're able. I can tell."

"You know I will," he murmurs and brushes his lips over mine.

There's a knock on the door. Tyrant gets up and places Huck in his bassinet before opening the door for Angela, who's carrying Barlow in her arms.

Tyrant takes our toddler in his arms and raises him up into the air. "Little man, we've missed you. Come and give Mommy a kiss."

I hold out my arms for Barlow and he cuddles into me. I've missed him so much.

Our housekeeper has a smile on her face as she approaches the sleeping baby. "Mrs. Mercer, he's so beautiful. You are so clever. Well done." She beams at me and gives me a kiss on the brow. "I will return in a few hours for Barlow. We are making everything perfect for you at home."

"Thank you, Angela. We're so grateful," I tell her with a smile as she heads out of the room.

Once we're alone, Tyrant asks Barlow, "Would you like to meet your brother?"

"Yes, Daddy!" Barlow says eagerly, and Tyrant picks him up and carries him over to the sleeping baby.

I watch my husband, my son, and my baby, thinking of all the wishes I poured into my diary when I was fifteen. All my breathless dreams and fantasies I had about Tyrant. About being happy and protected.

I watch Tyrant and Barlow gaze together at our new baby, and there's a smile on my lips. Sometimes it pays to wish for happiness with everything you have.

"Tyrant?" I call, and my husband glances up at me. "I love you."

A smile breaks over his face and he reaches out a forefinger to stroke my cheek. "Angel, I love you, too."

Acknowledgments

As I mentioned in my author's note, this book was inspired by my lifelong love of Jareth the Goblin King from the movie *Labyrinth*, but the bolt from the blue came from a caption my beautiful cover model Jord Liddell wrote on one of one of his Instagram posts. *Am I not merciful?* It reminded me so much of the Goblin King that I immediately gasped and immediately began to scribble down a rough premise for a dark love story between a dangerous and violent baby stealer and a hurting but determined heroine.

Seventy thousand words later, here we are with *Fear Me, Love Me*. Thank you, Jord, for the inspiration and being my wonderful cover model, and thank you to his partner Rhiannon Carr for being so lovely and supportive and facilitating the process.

I needed an extra name to go with a very extra character. Tyrant is named after an unstoppable and unkillable enemy who stalks the player's character in *Resident Evil 2*. His last name, Mercer, is taken from the sharp-tongued, treacherous leader of the Thieves Guild, Mercer Frey, from the game *The Elder Scrolls V: Skyrim*.

Thank you to the Breeder Readers group, which is my online happy place. You've given me so much love and support since the men ran a train on Chiara in *Third Comes Vengeance*. I've written all that love into this book.

Thank you to my beta readers Aly, Darlene, Edresa, Evva, Liz Booker, and Xenia for your support, encouragement, and excitement. Unhinged men and red flags for life.

Thank you to my amazing proofreader (I spelled it right this time LOL) Rumi Khan, and as always thank you to my editor Heather Fox. You've definitely inspired some of this baby fluff with all your baby happenings!

Books by Lilith Vincent

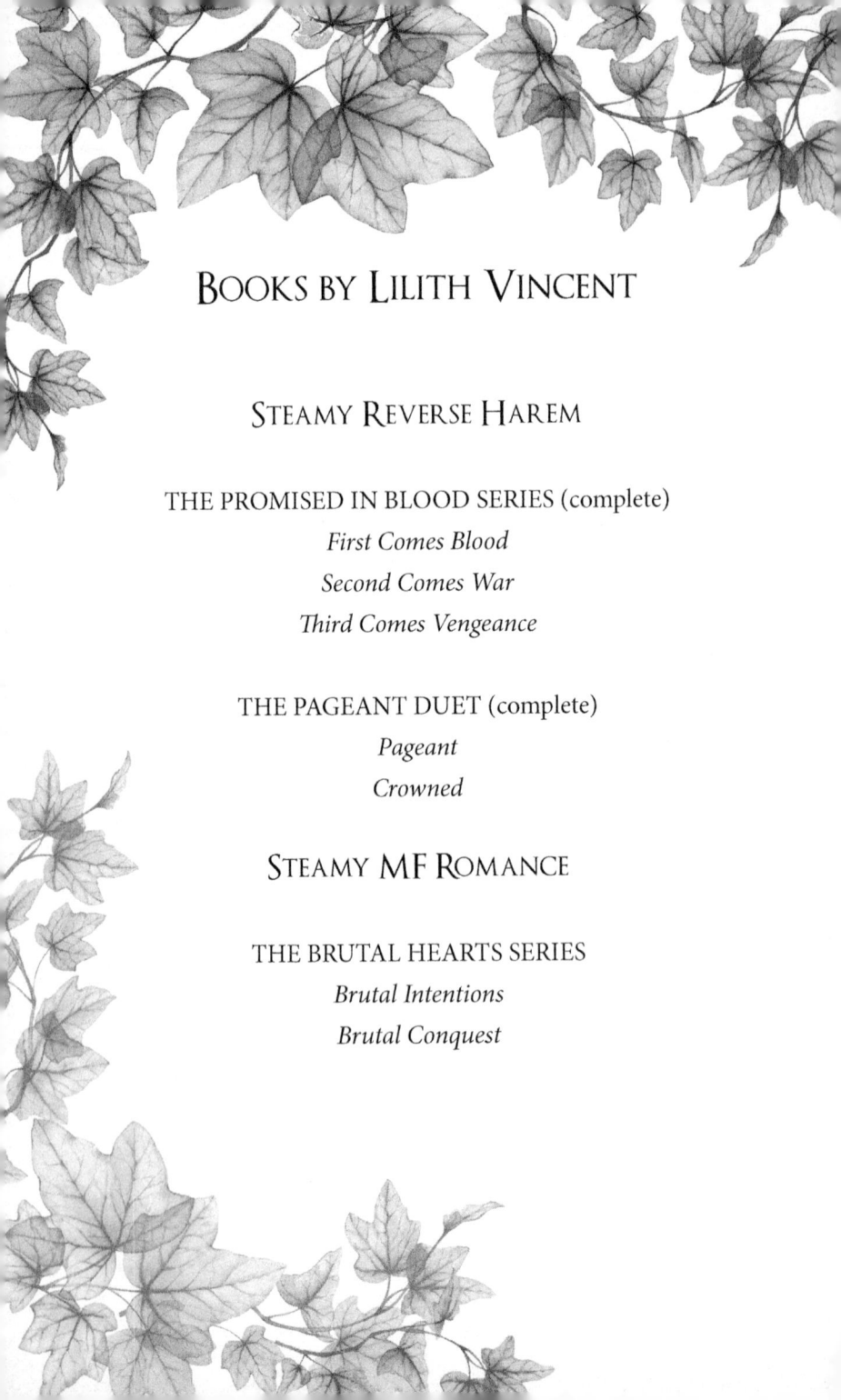

Steamy Reverse Harem

THE PROMISED IN BLOOD SERIES (complete)
First Comes Blood
Second Comes War
Third Comes Vengeance

THE PAGEANT DUET (complete)
Pageant
Crowned

Steamy MF Romance

THE BRUTAL HEARTS SERIES
Brutal Intentions
Brutal Conquest

About the Author

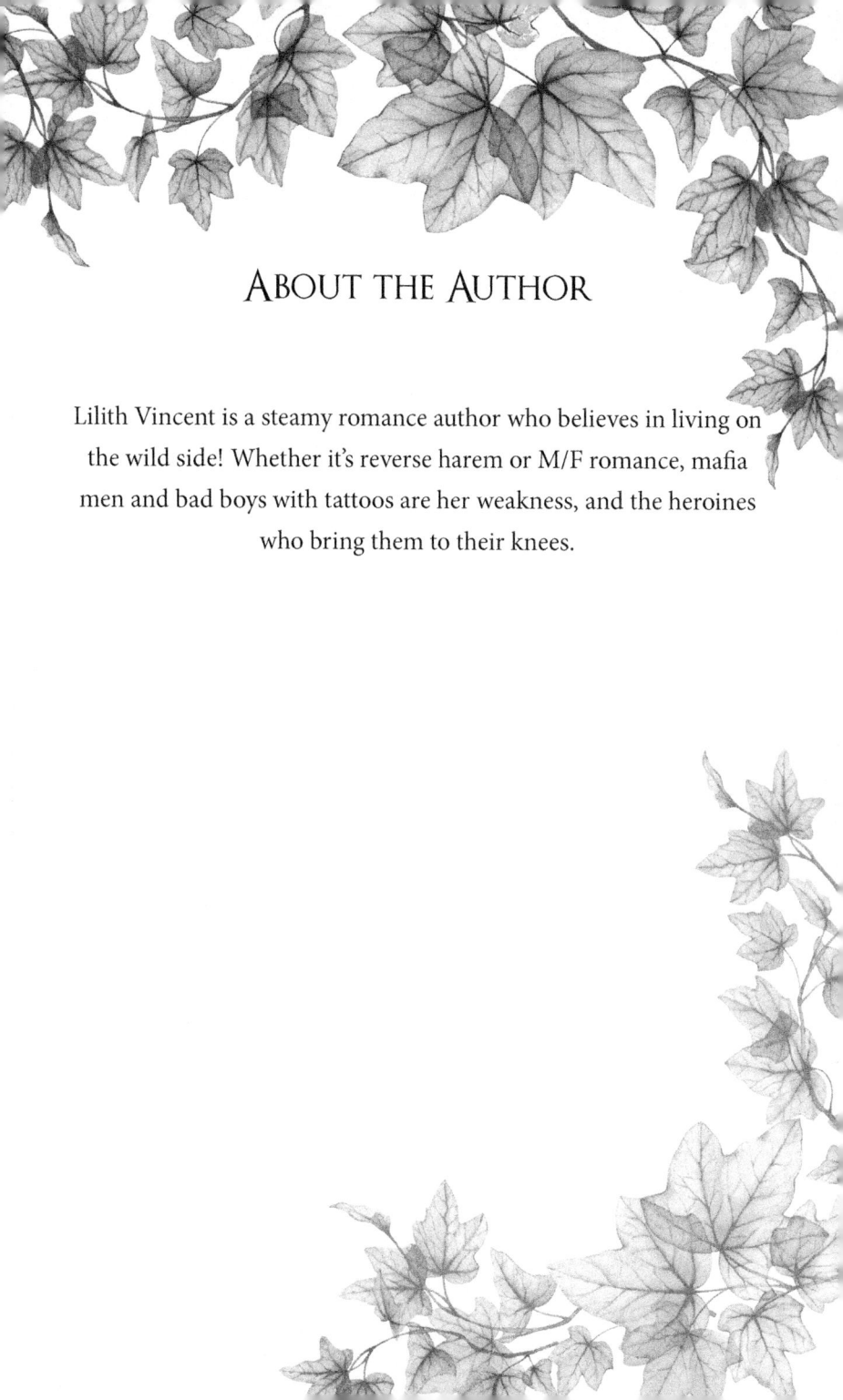

Lilith Vincent is a steamy romance author who believes in living on the wild side! Whether it's reverse harem or M/F romance, mafia men and bad boys with tattoos are her weakness, and the heroines who bring them to their knees.